The Man
Who Wanted
to Know
Everything

Also by D. A. Mishani

A Possibility of Violence
The Missing File

HARPER

NEW YORK • LONDON • TORONTO • SYDNEY

The Man Who Wanted to Know Everything

A Novel

D. A. Mishani

Translated from *Hebrew* by Todd Hasak-Lowy

HARPER

THE MAN WHO WANTED TO KNOW EVERYTHING. Copyright © 2016 by Dror Mishani. All rights reserved. Printed in the United States of America. No part of this book may be used or reproduced in any manner whatsoever without written permission except in the case of brief quotations embodied in critical articles and reviews. For information, address HarperCollins Publishers, 195 Broadway, New York, NY 10007.

HarperCollins books may be purchased for educational, business, or sales promotional use. For information, please email the Special Markets Department at SPsales@harpercollins.com.

Originally published as *Ha-ish sheratsah leda'at hakol* in Israel in 2015 by Achuzat Bayit.

Translation copyright 2016 by Todd Hasak-Lowy.

First Harper Perennial paperback published 2016.

Designed by Jamie Lynn Kerner

Library of Congress Cataloging-in-Publication Data
Names: Mishani, Dror, author. | Hasak-Lowy, Todd, 1969- translator.
Title: The man who wanted to know everything : a novel / D. A. Mishani ; translated from Hebrew by Todd Hasak-Lowy.
Other titles: Ish she-ratsah la-da'at ha-kol. English
Description: First edition. | New York, NY : Harper Paperbacks, 2016.
 | Series: Avraham Avraham series ; 3 | Originally published as Ha-ish sheratsah leda'at hakol in Israel in 2015 by Achuzat Bayit.
Identifiers: LCCN 2016008616 (print) | LCCN 2016026495 (ebook) | ISBN 9780062447906 (softcover) | ISBN 9780062447913 (eBook)
Subjects: LCSH: Police—Israel—Fiction. | Women—Violence against—Israel—Fiction. | Murder—Investigation—Fiction. | Israel—Fiction. | Psychological fiction. | Domestic fiction. | Jewish fiction. | BISAC: FICTION / Mystery & Detective / Police Procedural. | GSAFD: Suspense fiction. | Mystery fiction.
Classification: LCC PJ5055.34.I825 I8413 2016 (print) | LCC PJ5055.34.I825 (ebook) | DDC 892.43/7—dc23
LC record available at https://lccn.loc.gov/2016008616

ISBN 978–0–06–244790–6

16 17 18 19 20 RRD 10 9 8 7 6 5 4 3 2 1

In memory of my father,

MORDECHAI MISHANI
(10.4.1945–9.4.2013)

When half way through the journey of our life

I found that I was in a gloomy wood,

because the path which led aright was lost.

And ah, how hard it is to say just what

this wild and rough and stubborn woodland was,

the very thought of which renews my fear!

So bitter 't is, that death is little worse;

but of the good to treat which there I found,

I'll speak of what I else discovered there.

Dante Alighieri, *Inferno*

The Man
Who Wanted
to Know
Everything

Prologue

At the beginning of December 2014 a Boeing 737 landed at Ben Gurion Airport with a young woman inside, her hair short and her eyes large and brown. Police superintendent Avraham Avraham watched her from inside his hiding place while she passed through the glass doors and entered the arrival hall, rolling before her a cart with three suitcases. Until the last moment he didn't believe she would come and was certain he'd be returning home alone. He looked at her from a distance for another moment before leaving his hiding place, and his eyes met her eyes, which searched for him among the crowd of greeters.

They had no great plans then for the future except for living together a few months. To discover each other again and only afterward to think about what's next. And they did indeed discover each other, slowly and cautiously, in the hidden glances of people used to watching. He discovered that Marianka likes to shower early in the morning—and for a long time. When she comes out she leaves behind a small lake on the bathroom floor, with wet footprints leading to the bedroom. She discovered that Avraham sneaks into the kitchen after dinner, without anyone seeing, in order to continue eating alone from behind the closed door. After their contents were scattered around the apartment, Avraham tried to store the suitcases on top of the wardrobe in the bedroom, but since there wasn't enough space one suitcase remained beside their bed for the entire winter.

Marianka asked to see his new office, and he took her there one Friday, in the morning, when the station was nearly empty. In contrast to his room on the first floor, the office of the commander of the Investigations and Intelligence Units was spacious and looked out from the third floor onto Fichman Street, along which residential towers sprouted from the sand. He could look through the window at the gray morning skies or the cool evenings covering the city where he was born. For the first time he was also able to light a cigarette in his office, only then, of all times, he had quit smoking.

The winter was unpredictable, and when Avraham noticed how changes in the weather affected Marianka's moods he began reading the forecast with trepidation each morning. When the temperature dropped and rain fell, she was happy. When the sky was clear and the air mild, almost warm, she told him about the snow in Brussels and was unable to hide from him the longing in her face and voice. This was actually the only thing that overshadowed his joy. During times of inactivity he stood before the window in his office and waited for the rain for her.

At the end of February, when the newscasts announced that the winter's last storm was approaching, they decided to take a day off to welcome it together. And they did just this, only a few hours after the start of the storm the murder that changed their plans occurred.

PART ONE
The Victim

1

She saw the gun that night after she went up to persuade Kobi to come to bed, or to at least not sit outside in the cold. The time was one in the morning and the gun was lying on the table in the small utility room on the roof, but she didn't assign any importance to it because she was too hurt and exhausted and since she was afraid of so many other things. Besides, the gun wasn't a reason to be afraid, just the opposite. It was a source for her sense of security.

A few days later she recalled that night and understood. Everything could have happened differently had she watched Kobi more during those hours.

Yesterday morning, while they were still in bed, it was impossible to know how their last anniversary together would end.

Daniella and Noy woke up before them, scattered fourteen balloons on the bedroom floor and jumped on their bed. When the girls went to get dressed and just the two of them remained in bed, Mali drew close to him. She touched him from behind, and whispered in his ear, "Happy anniversary," and was surprised when she felt his shoulders and back respond to the touch of her hands. His neck was warm from sleep and his cheeks still unshaven. The storm's first rain could be heard through the window, and the lights in the apartment were turned on because the sky was dark. In the kitchen a festive breakfast the girls had prepared waited for them: orange juice they squeezed themselves and croissants they'd bought the day before and warmed up. They were not allowed to boil water by themselves, so Mali made the coffee.

She saw that Kobi was tense, but she didn't say anything about the interview in front of the girls when they sat down at the table. She offered to iron his dark pants and white shirt, but he said that he'd iron them himself before leaving, at noon. She didn't say any more about this, not even when they were again alone in the bedroom, so that the disappointment wouldn't be too great if he didn't get the job, but when they said good-bye she kissed him on the lips and even whispered in his ear, "Good luck today."

She took the girls to school and had meetings until eleven. In most cases only the husbands showed up, and even when the wives came they almost never said a word, but Mali tried to speak to them as well, like she always did, explaining to them, too, the differences between kinds of mortgages and the various payment possibilities. One of the men, whose wife's hair was covered with a kerchief, her face silent and pretty, stared right at her. He had a beard, and his jacket, which he didn't remove, gave off a smell of mothballs and old, damp fabric. His wife rocked the blue stroller back and forth so that their baby wouldn't wake up. When he burst out crying she undid two buttons on her black dress and nursed him in front of the two of them without shame.

Between eleven and twelve she hadn't planned any meetings, so she asked the branch manager for permission and went to buy Kobi a gift, even though they had agreed not to buy anything for each other. She debated walking to the city center but because of the storm she drove to the mall instead. The streets were flooded, and most of the traffic lights were out. And perhaps because of the unrelenting rain she decided to buy him an umbrella, to replace the one he'd lost a few days earlier, and not a punching bag or a new button-down shirt for his interviews. At Zara the umbrellas were too expensive, but at For Men on the third floor she saw a black umbrella with an elegant, wood-like handle. The young salesgirl, whose fingernails were long and sharp and covered with shiny black nail polish, agreed to lower the price. She was so young, maybe in high school still. Her hair was black and she wore black lipstick and had a piercing in her nose. When Mali entered she was reading a book, which she set facedown on the counter as Mali approached the register.

Mali stared at her, maybe for too long, and when the salesgirl asked her, "Is something wrong?" Mali just said, "No, I'm sorry. Did you remove the sticker with the price?"

Mali finished her last meeting at two, exactly when Kobi's interview was supposed to start.

She imagined him sitting across from the interviewer, trying to mask his emotions. As always, he probably had no idea what to do with his hands. Spread them out on his knees and then rested them on the table, next to the pages of his résumé, and then again on his knees, in order to hide his fingers moving under the table. She didn't call him before the interview nor from the car on her way to pick up the girls. And since his car wasn't in the parking lot under their building she was sure he hadn't yet returned, but in the elevator that took them to the seventh floor she could smell his aftershave. And the door wasn't locked like it was supposed to be.

She went into the bedroom and heard the water running. Their dog, Harry, was lying on the floor in a puddle of urine and didn't lift his head. And Kobi's keys had been tossed next to him, along with the small satchel he took with him to meetings.

That wasn't a good sign.

It was three o'clock and Mali was sure he wouldn't be home.

The girls turned on the television in the living room and Mali made them something to eat. The water in the bathroom was still running by the time the pasta had softened so she knocked on the door and asked Kobi if he wanted to eat with them and from the shower he answered no. They started without him because the girls were hungry, and while they were eating they heard him leave the bathroom and close the door to the bedroom.

"Is everything okay?" she asked, certain he was awake, even though he lay on the bed with his eyes closed.

She was familiar with these mood swings of his, and without even giving it much thought had been preparing herself since this morning that it would happen today, too. Had he been asked why he switched jobs so many times in recent years and instead of telling the truth had he evaded the question? She pleaded with him to divulge that it was her fault but knew that he wouldn't do this.

Kobi didn't open his eyes, even though she stood there for a minute or two. The large picture from her second pregnancy hung above the bed then, like a bitter reminder, or a memorial.

Mali asked, "You don't want to tell me how it went?"

That afternoon a barrage of hail slammed against the windows, after which silence fell over the apartment. Mali helped Noy with her math homework while Daniella continued watching TV.

Kobi came out of the bedroom at five with his big bag for boxing classes, said he was taking her car, and asked where her keys were. She asked him what happened to his car and if he didn't already go to boxing class yesterday, but she didn't get an answer. When she reminded him they were going out that evening, he didn't say a word, either, and when she asked, "Why'd you shower before boxing?" he looked at her as if she had said something awful.

She was tense all afternoon and evening and checked that she had locked the door behind him at least twice.

Looked out through the blinds in the living room in order to see if he had returned.

When she placed the wrapped umbrella on their bed, for him to find it there, she again saw herself in the large photograph and still didn't know if she'd tell him about the pregnancy tonight, as she had planned to. She had hesitated before agreeing to be photographed then, but Kobi urged her to and said that if they didn't take the picture she'd regret it, because this was going to be the last time she'd be pregnant. Over the years she learned not to hate the giant picture, in black and white, which showed her long, dark body and the swollen belly Kobi loved to caress, even in public, and which she, too, touched sometimes during the pregnancy, when she was alone. She could be seen from the side in the picture, her body turning a bit toward him, who stands behind her, so that the difference in height between them wouldn't be so apparent. The two of them naked, and his arms simultaneously hiding and exposing her breasts. She didn't like the idea that guests would see her like this, perhaps she was ashamed her father would see, but Kobi was actually quite excited about it. After what happened in Eilat she wanted them to take the picture down, but Kobi asked that they keep it up to remind the two of them of better days, and there were moments when she thought he was right, because when she looked at the giant photograph it brought her back to herself.

The rain started up again before dinner and its drumming on the windows and the roof intensified her restlessness. But the girls were quiet, as if they noticed that she was in need of their help. Most of the time they kept themselves busy in the living room and their bedrooms. Only at six thirty did Daniella say that she was hungry, and Noy reminded her that Mali had promised they'd try on costumes for Purim.

She took down the box of costumes from the bedroom closet and Noy tried on Elsa's dress from the *Frozen* movie they bought her last year, but it was too small and Daniella refused to try it on and said that she's not going to dress up this year. Mali insisted that she try it on because the dress had cost a fortune and she hoped that this year she'd be able to buy only one costume instead of two, but when she held it up in front of Daniella's small body opposite the mirror she met her own eyes and immediately averted her gaze.

There was no reason for all this to come back now, apart from, perhaps, her fear of Kobi's mood. And the pregnancy.

His boxing classes lasted between an hour to an hour and a half, so she thought he'd arrive for dinner. At a quarter after seven she called him so he could buy some pita bread and hummus on his way home, but his phone was turned off. She tried him a few more times, and in the end they ate without him and the girls went to bed at eight thirty. When the neighbor's daughter came up to babysit, Mali told her that they had given up on the idea of going out because she has a fever. She called Kobi again and this time his phone was on but he didn't answer. And when she went up to the roof to see if it might be possible to hang out the laundry, heavy rain clouds stood in the sky and the wind shook the water tanks, so she decided not to hang things for now and then spoke on the phone with her sister, Gila. When Gila asked her if they were going out to celebrate, she explained that they hadn't managed to find a babysitter for the girls.

Kobi returned around eleven, without an explanation or apology.

Just a year before, on the day of their thirteenth anniversary, everything was so different.

They left Daniella and Noy with her parents for the first time since Eilat and went to stay at a bed-and-breakfast in the Golan Heights for two nights. Kobi began working for a company that provided security at construction sites near the border and his moods were excellent. They planned to hike, like they used to before the girls were born, to spend a whole day walking along one of the rivers and another day at the Hula Nature Reserve, but the weather was awful, so they barely left the bed-and-breakfast. Instead, they watched movies on DVD and slept together for the first time in several long weeks. They talked for hours in front of the fireplace. In the evening they went out on the deck, wrapped in blankets, and Kobi spoke enthusiastically about taking a trip to his father's farm in Australia that summer and maybe even buying an apartment because they finally had two salaries again. When they called the girls to say good night, it seemed to Mali that they were on their way to becoming a normal couple.

But all that was during the previous winter, and since then life again changed for the worse.

Kobi was fired because his supervisor at the security company, who was ten years younger than him, had it out for him. He was sure he'd find other work, but after a few weeks she felt him sinking, avoiding her and the girls and his friends, and barely leaving the house. Then he began going to boxing classes, two or three times a week. He would return with his face beaten and bruises on his arms and stomach, and would immediately shower and go to sleep. The sign of distress she recognized back when they'd first met appeared again as well: when it seemed to him that no one was paying any attention he'd stretch his neck back and inhale deeply, as if he were unable to breathe.

She thought he'd go to bed without a word when he returned from boxing that night, too, but he surprised her.

He turned on the television and sat down on the sofa in the living room. Mali said, "We were supposed to go out tonight," and sat down next to him. A reality show of the sort that Kobi despised was playing, but he insisted they not turn it off.

"Kobi, are you okay? You haven't talked to me since you came back from the interview."

He continued staring at the screen but said to her, "I'm sorry. I can't talk right now."

"You can't tell me how it went?"

He didn't want to. He only said, "I didn't get the job," and when she asked him, "How do you know? They told you on the spot?" he nodded his head. And she didn't even know where the interview had taken place or with which company. After he got fired he decided not to interview for any more security positions and she supported him. But in recent weeks he stopped looking at all, so she was happy when he said he had an interview and didn't even ask him where it was. And perhaps she really didn't look at him enough that night, because if she had she would have seen in his face more than despair.

Harry lay at his feet, his body still reeking of urine. "I didn't wash him because I was afraid he'd get cold on the roof," she said while Kobi continued staring at the screen.

"When are you going to take him to the vet? You can't let him keep suffering like this."

"Maybe tomorrow."

"The girls can't look at him, you know? They don't go near him. Like he's already dead."

Was there some other way to reach him that Mali hadn't found? She could have told him about the pregnancy as she had planned, but she didn't want to talk about it like this.

"I spoke to Aviva today. She said her brother might have something for you. Do you remember him? He started importing electric bikes."

Kobi said, "I'm not looking for work anymore," and Mali fell silent.

Did the late-night newscast on TV start then? She remembered the news very well. Homes and streets were flooded and there were power outages across the country. Kobi got up from the sofa and sat down on the leather stool near the screen, as if her presence next to him was disturbing, and she, too, got up and left. When she returned to the living room he was watching a newscast on a different channel. On the TV screen two medical personnel assisted by a policeman could be seen rolling a stretcher with a sheet-covered body on it.

"Where is it?" she asked him.

He inhaled as if it was difficult to breathe, because he hadn't noticed her approaching from behind. The sheet-covered body was put inside an ambulance next to which stood two policemen wrapped in raincoats.

"Was that here? In Holon?" she asked, and he said, "Yes, on the other side of town."

"And did they say who that is?"

The report was nearing its end and she didn't manage to hear if the murderer had been caught or if the cause of death was known, but she could tell that a woman lay under the white sheet. "Can you turn that off? It scares me and I want us to talk," she said quietly, and despite everything touched him on the shoulder. She didn't give up that night, because in moments like this, one couldn't give up. She went to their bedroom and returned with the umbrella, which was still lying on the bed. She said to him, "Didn't you see what I bought you?"

But the umbrella didn't make him happy. Perhaps even the opposite. When he removed the wrapping paper he looked at it uneasily. "To replace the one you lost," she said. "And it's not as expensive as it looks."

He put the umbrella on the floor without thanking her, and it was this of all things that put her over the edge. "Are you seriously set on celebrating our anniversary like this?" she asked, and when he got up she almost screamed at him, "Kobi, do you hear me at all? Do you hear that I'm talking to you? It's Mali from class. The war started." He turned to her and his eyes lit up and it was then that she must have understood that something terrible had happened.

The two of them were around sixteen years old when they met. The year was 1991. January. Ten years before they got married.

This was their first conversation, or at least the first they remembered, and sometimes, mainly when they fought, she would use it in order to pull him out of his silence.

Mali's father woke her at two in the morning and told her that George Bush was bombing Baghdad, and she got dressed quickly and called Kobi and said, "Kobi? It's Mali from class. The war started," and he answered her in a sleepy voice and with the foreign accent he still had back then, "Now? In the middle of the night?"

During the last few years she tried to imagine herself and him at that age without looking at old pictures but couldn't. Kobi was skinnier then, and his body was soft, like the body of a boy. His chest and back were so smooth that she could caress him for hours. Mali knew nothing about him other than that he came from a city called Perth without his parents and lived with his mother's relatives in Holon. He was an excellent basketball player and was exempted from English, because he spoke much better than the teacher and corrected her mistakes to the amusement of the students until she asked that he not come to class. There were rumors that his mother killed herself in Australia but afterward she learned that this was entirely untrue. Most of the boys in their grade feared this boy who came from Australia with jeans and Nikes and clear blue eyes that no one else had back then, so they made up stories about him. On the first day of school, when he introduced himself in homeroom, he said that he immigrated to Israel in order to volunteer for an elite unit.

And it was completely by chance that they met each other. A matter of fate or luck, like so many things that would happen afterward.

She didn't think he could be interested in her because no one else was interested then. Her body was too long and thin, she didn't get great grades, and she wasn't audacious or daring, either. She had been the school champion in sprinting and long-distance running for three years, but this wasn't something that drew the attention of the boys. But her last name was Ben-Asher, and *Bengtson, Kobi* was the next name on the class contact list, and so she was supposed to call him in the event of a war breaking out. Three hours after the phone call, at five thirty in the morning, she and her father came by in the old Subaru pickup to give him a ride to the hospital. He waited for them downstairs, a Discman in his hand and white headphones on his ears.

She was embarrassed by the truck, whose upholstery gave off the smell of sewage pipes, and maybe by her father, too, who didn't know English but nevertheless tried to talk with Kobi on the way.

"What will you do there?" her father asked, and she explained to him that they'd spray water out of thick hoses onto those injured by the chemical weapons that Saddam Hussein would launch in the direction of Tel Aviv. And before he dropped them off across from the hospital he asked Kobi to keep her safe.

That was their first meeting, and who could have guessed then that years later they all would stand together under the chuppah?

A week after this, Kobi came to their house and she was beside herself with excitement and embarrassment. Her father was late returning from synagogue and while they were waiting for him her mother also tried speaking with Kobi in broken English. Gila was already fleeing from dinner on Friday nights, and this was a relief because Mali had no doubt that if they were to meet, Kobi would fall in love with her twin sister, who a year earlier left school and was already making money at work. Afterward a siren went off, which of course happened when they were finally alone in her room, and they were forced to close themselves up with everyone else in the sealed room, which was her parents' cramped bedroom. She was filled with shame because her father's underwear was lying all over the floor.

The first time they slept together was also on a Friday night, a few months later.

Her parents took a trip to visit relatives in Tiberias, and she invited Kobi to sleep over, even though her father didn't allow it. Mali didn't make a sound while they were doing it because she knew that Gila was listening to them through the wall, and she was indeed waiting for her by the door when Mali came out to wash her legs, still stunned by what had happened.

Mali continued waiting for him in their bedroom, but Kobi didn't come. And since Eilat he never let her go to sleep alone, not even when they fought. She lay in their bed and for a moment was able to see the boy with the headphones on his ears who waited for her and her father in the dark, his hands in his pockets. And perhaps that's why, at one in the morning, she tried one last time.

She went up to the roof and found him sitting on the white plastic chair in total darkness. This was her chance to tell him about the pregnancy, but she didn't. Something smothered and wild about his look and his sitting there in the cold frightened her. She caressed his head and his chest over the black polo shirt he was wearing. She whispered to him, "Don't leave me alone in bed, Kobi. Please," and also gave him every sign that if he came to bed they'd have sex. There was a deep cut on his neck that night, but he always returned from boxing with injuries.

When she passed through the utility room on the way downstairs she saw the gun, which hadn't been there that afternoon. She tried to fall asleep and placed her hands on her stomach, but then the face of the girl who sold her the umbrella at the mall suddenly appeared inside her, and was immediately replaced by the covered body they saw before on TV. She opened her eyes with panic. The next image was the one she tried so hard to forget: the heavy hand coming toward her out of the darkness and crushing her throat.

2

Avraham identified the body immediately but didn't say so since he thought it best for as few people as possible to know, and also because of the silence. There were two patrolmen and some medical personnel standing in the kitchen and waiting for instructions. One female officer stood by the entrance. And everyone who walked or spoke did so on the tips of their toes and in a whisper, as if to not wake the woman who lay on the rug in the living room.

One of the patrolmen pointed at her when Avraham entered, but he had already noticed her. She lay on her back, and only her right eye was open. On the rug under her were images of colorful birds. And perhaps he didn't tell anyone that he knew who she was during those first hours because of the shock he felt in the presence of her body. Ever since he had been appointed commander of the district's investigations and intelligence branches, Avraham knew that his first murder case would come, and yet when it began he wasn't certain he was ready.

The evening prior to this it was announced on the news that
the storm would start in the morning hours, and when
Avraham woke up, heavy rain could already be heard.
He called the station and informed the investigations
coordinator, Lital Levy, that he was taking a day off.
Anyway, he was supposed to participate in an unnecessary training session on cybercrime at national headquarters. He made black coffee and brought the mugs to
bed and he and Marianka stayed under the blanket in
bed all morning, watching four episodes of *The Bridge*
on his laptop.

Avraham's eyes again closed.

His father entered the room, placed his hand on his
forehead and declared that he could stay in bed instead
of going to school. When the door slammed behind his
parents, warm pleasure spread over his body because he
understood that he was staying home alone. Should he
get up right away? Grab another moment under the blanket? They wouldn't be returning until the evening and he
would have time to wander around the apartment like it
was all his. Make himself a giant breakfast.

Marianka shook him gently when she heard from his
breathing that he was asleep, and every time he opened
his eyes the detectives on the screen discovered another
body. He asked, "What, they already have another
murder?" and Marianka stroked his forehead. He had
no chance of figuring out who the murderer was before
that strange Danish detective Sonya Cross did, not that
he cared.

That afternoon they took the car and drove to Tel Aviv. Avraham wrapped himself up in his ugly blue army parka that he last wore during the district's organized trip to Mount Hermon in winter 2007, and Marianka wore the wool jacket she brought with her from Brussels. They parked in an almost empty lot by the beach and took advantage of a lull in the rain to sit on a wet bench facing the sea, which crashed on the rocks in front of them. No one else was on the boardwalk other than an Arab couple with a baby. And Avraham's phone didn't ring.

Most of the police in the district were busy clearing the roads clogged up with rain or evacuating flooded buildings or dealing with traffic accidents. This is what he, too, did on days like this during his first years with the police. Now he was commander of Investigations and Intelligence, thanks to solving an assault case that occurred not far from their spot on the boardwalk and to those two boys he saved from death. There wasn't a chance he'd be required to stand at some intersection in the pouring rain and direct traffic in place of the light that had collapsed.

When the rain started up again they took cover in the Dolphinarium and afterward had rice-and-bean soup in the market. And Marianka didn't speak longingly of the winters in her hometown in Slovenia, or in Brussels. When Avraham's phone rang for the first time, a little after four thirty, he didn't answer, and only when it rang for the third time did he realize it may be urgent. And maybe because he hadn't expected what he'd hear, he didn't remember what exact words Lital Levy used to inform him of what happened. Did she tell him there had been a murder? Or only that a woman's body had been found in her home? Lital didn't mention the victim's name on the phone, because if she had mentioned it, Avraham would have remembered immediately and wouldn't have been dumbfounded when he discovered her face at the scene.

"Who's there?" he asked, and Levy said, "No one. Just the patrolmen who closed off the scene. And Forensics is on their way but everything's jammed up and it'll take them some time. Can you go?"

"It'll take me a half hour. If Ma'alul or Shrapstein come back, send one of them as well."

Only when they finished the call did he realize that she didn't give him the address, and he called her back but the line was already busy.

Marianka suggested that he drop her off near the scene and that from there she'd take a cab, but he insisted on taking her home. They drove quickly and in silence. When they reached downtown everything still looked real and unreal at the same time, like it always does during a storm. Trees had fallen on the sidewalks and the streets were dotted with pools of water in which the evening lights flickered, as if Holon had transformed into Amsterdam or Venice. Avraham suddenly recalled that the first Maigret novel he read took place from beginning to end in a rainstorm and that the clothes and shoes of the large French inspector were completely soaked throughout. Was that a murder case? And would he know how to investigate a person's death? He couldn't remember how that fictional case had ended, but he did remember that he read the book when he was nineteen, one Saturday, when he remained at the base while taking an interrogation course in the army.

On Sokolov Street people walked bent over forward as they struggled with the wind, and he drove in a car with a steamed-up windshield, as if he were cutting through a cloud of fog. For a moment it seemed to him that he was still lying in bed and watching himself in a television series.

What already disturbed him then was that the murder occurred in one of the calmest neighborhoods of Holon, where there were burglaries and stolen vehicles but almost no violent crimes. And worst of all was that Lital Levy didn't mention anyone who had been arrested at the time of the incident or any suspect who had escaped.

Two empty patrol cars and an ambulance were parked in front of 38 Krause Street, and curious onlookers were gathered on the sidewalk behind police tape. Renovations were under way in the building on the corner of the street, and in front of the building next to it sat a Dumpster for the disposal of building refuse. The entrance to the building was closed, and Avraham stood in front of it waiting for them to let him in and afterward simply pushed on the doorknob. He had time to prepare himself for what he was going to see, since the building had no elevator and the apartment was on the top floor.

The woman lying on the rug was named Leah Yeger. She looked just over sixty. Her right eye, the open one, was green but there was nothing to be seen by looking at it.

Avraham searched the pocket of his coat for his note-pad, because he needed to write down his first impressions, but the notepad wasn't there and in its place he found a receipt for two cups of black coffee and a pretzel that he had bought at a snack bar back on Mount Hermon in 2007. That didn't matter, because he remembered without writing and he didn't miss a thing. He asked that everyone leave the apartment except for one patrolman and the paramedic who determined the time of death. His shoes were covered in plastic bags and there were gloves on his hands. And no one was allowed to approach the living room until the forensics technicians arrived.

In the meantime he saw everything. He saw the hand marks on her neck and also the red ends of her ears and the swollen tongue, hanging sideways out of her mouth. She laid on the rug, among blue, red, and yellow birds, some of which held their beaks open as if they were trying to call for help. His eyes slipped away from the body and were drawn to the half-filled mug of coffee and the tray of biscuits on the table in the kitchen. And to the car keys that were in a bowl on the sideboard. The television was on with no sound.

Avraham took off his coat and placed it folded up on the floor just outside the entrance.

There was no doubt that the living room was the scene of the murder: a picture with a drawing of two women sitting in a yellow field had fallen off the wall, presumably during the struggle with the murderer, and next to it, on the rug, was a broken lamp. The patrolman who remained in the apartment, an officer whose face Avraham recognized but whose name he didn't know, said, "Luckily there wasn't a fire," and Avraham suddenly remembered that he hadn't asked him who found Yeger. And only then did he discover that her daughter was still in the bedroom.

"She's here now? By herself?" he asked.

"Not by herself. There's an officer and a paramedic with her."

Once, at times like this, he would have gone down to the street and smoked a cigarette in order to think and buy some time and perhaps call Ilana Lis, his old boss and former commander of investigations. But at the beginning of winter he quit smoking, because Marianka begged him to and because his fortieth birthday was approaching. Only occasionally did he still try lighting the pipe Marianka bought him in Brussels, but now the pipe was at the office. And he could not call Ilana Lis. So he returned to the kitchen and found a sheet of paper and a pen and nevertheless wrote down a few words the paramedic said about what was already clear to Avraham because he saw it himself: Yeger apparently *died from strangulation. After a struggle.* The temperature of her body indicated that until approximately two or three hours earlier she had still been alive.

Her hands were closed. When they'd open them at the Institute of Pathology perhaps they'd find something between her fingers, he hoped, other than the slit marks left by her fingernails in her palms, when she clutched them, and perhaps a few slices of skin that she peeled off her own neck when she tried to free herself from the hands choking her. This was, then, his biggest hope.

And though he hadn't yet expressed it to himself in words this way, he did already feel that something was off about the scene. *Too clean perhaps? As if someone straightened up the scene after the murder? Or maybe before?* And he also felt that something else had been taken from the flat, other than her purse and keys.

At around six he called Eliyahu Ma'alul in order to verify when he'd arrive, and when he said that they were delayed on their way back from the training session in Jerusalem because of an accident between two buses, Avraham no longer had any choice and went into the bedroom to conduct the first round of questioning with the daughter. She sat on the bed, and Avraham brought a chair into the room and sat across from her, very close because the room was small. The paramedic was asked to leave, but the female patrol officer, who called the daughter Orit, remained and held her hand throughout their conversation.

He began and said, "I offer my condolences," and then he introduced himself and added, "Please tell me how this happened," and immediately regretted his flawed phrasing, even though she understood what he meant.

"She was supposed to pick up my daughter from day care," she said. "This is her set day because I don't have anything planned for her in the afternoon."

"When was she supposed she pick up your daughter?"

"Day care ends at three thirty. But she didn't get her. She didn't come."

Her eyes, like the eyes of her mother, were green. The next day he realized she was only thirty-three and divorced but at the time of the interview he thought she was forty.

"How did you know she didn't come?" Avraham asked, and she said, "They called from day care that my daughter was still there. I also called her cell and the house but she didn't answer. I thought maybe she was stuck in the rain."

"And when did you speak with your mother before then?"

"At around one."

"And she didn't say she wasn't coming? Do you know if she was here in the apartment when you spoke?"

Orit Yeger nodded her head. And then added, "I think so."

"Was someone with her when she spoke with you?"

"Who could have been with her?"

"I don't know."

"No. I don't think anyone was."

"And did she sound okay? Like she normally does?"

"Yes. If I thought something wasn't okay I would have . . ."

She stopped and Avraham didn't go on right away so that she wouldn't burst into tears.

"So when did you come to check what happened?" he asked after a while.

"I was at day care and afterward came here because I had to go back to work and I wanted to leave my daughter here. We heard the TV from inside."

"Do you work in the area?"

"In a clothing store in the center."

"And where is the day care located?"

"Not very far."

He explained to her that he was asking these questions because he was trying to figure out exactly when the body was found.

"I arrived at four fifteen. When I called the police."

"And do you recall if the door was open or closed?"

"Closed. But I have a key."

Now she burst into tears because in her imagination she saw the moment when the door opened. And it was actually because of this that this time Avraham didn't wait for her to stop crying and immediately asked her, "When you opened the door, did you happen to notice if it was locked?"

She hesitated before saying to him, "I don't remember anything. I think I turned the key."

"And you're certain there was no one in the apartment other than your mother?"

She collapsed onto the officer sitting next to her and didn't answer his question. He should have just continued the investigation later, at the station, but he didn't restrain himself and asked, "Where is your daughter now?"

She said, "She saw everything. She asked me, 'Why is Grandma on the floor?' but she understood. I pushed her out and shut the door, but she saw."

The time was 7:10 p.m. and there were two television crews down below the building. And Avraham was still the only detective at the scene. All the rooms other than the living room were undisturbed and there were no signs of burglary or a search for something. Despite this he asked Orit Yeger if there was a safe in the apartment or if her mother kept large amounts of money with her, and the daughter said not that she knew of. Only her purse could not be found anywhere: not in the bedroom and not in one of the cupboards in the kitchen, where she kept it when at home. As Avraham assumed, the keys to the apartment had been taken, because they weren't in the lock or in the bowl in the living room, next to the keys to the car. Before this, during the conversation in the bedroom, he had already written to himself on the sheet of paper: *Murderer locked the door behind him?* He extended the walk-through and asked her questions, some of which he had already asked earlier, only because he didn't want to leave her alone. And suddenly he remembered that Leah Yeger had a son as well, so he asked, "You're not an only child, correct?" and she nodded and asked him, "Has anyone informed my brother?"

Only once Ma'alul arrived, his uniform as wet as if he had walked from Jerusalem, Avraham was able to collect the neighbors' testimonies. Most of the tenants were of no help to him because they weren't home in the afternoon and mainly wanted to know if it was safe to remain in the building. In one of the apartments he met two young parents who were packing baby clothes and diapers into a large bag because the wife insisted that they go sleep at her mother's. Their twins were in the apartment throughout the day with the nanny, and they gave him her phone number. In fact, only one neighbor shared any information of value with him. He lived on the second floor, under Yeger's apartment, and said that around two, while he was resting in his bedroom, he heard a noise from the apartment above. "Something fell," he said, "or was dragged." There were shouts as well but he wasn't sure who shouted because his hearing isn't very sharp. It lasted two or three minutes, of this the neighbor was certain.

Avraham asked him, "What lasted?" and the neighbor said, "The noise. There were sounds of a struggle coming from up there." Yeger was a quiet neighbor and she usually rested in the afternoon hours, like the neighbor himself. So he opened the door and walked up half a flight of stairs, only then it got quiet and he decided not to knock on the door. But his afternoon nap had already been disturbed, so he didn't go back to bed, and a few minutes later he heard footsteps and through the peephole saw a policeman going down the stairs. He thought that someone had called him because of the noise and that the policeman had checked into the matter, so he didn't call the police himself.

While gathering testimony from the neighbor there was a call from Benny Saban, the district commander, and Avraham apologized to the old man and went to speak with him outside. Saban, too, was in the training session at the national headquarters and was supposed to drop by the crime scene on his way back, but his wife had bought theater tickets and the heavy traffic forced him to continue straight home. He asked Avraham, "So what do you have to tell me?"

And Avraham said, "Not a thing for now."

"But what does it look like? Domestic violence? A burglary?"

Apparently it wasn't a matter of domestic violence because Yeger was a widow, and according to her daughter, she didn't have ties to any other men. And was there any chance that this was a break-in gone bad, in the middle of the day, when all that was taken from the apartment was a purse and maybe a set of keys, and in the rest of the rooms perfect order prevailed?

"In short, Avi, do we need to involve Central Unit or should the investigation remain with us?"

That was the first time he told anyone. He had to report it to Saban, and this also was a reason to keep the case in the district and not to drag it over to the central investigation unit. He said to Saban, "The case has to stay with us because she's one of our rape victims," and Saban either didn't understand or didn't hear.

"What did you say?" he asked.

"The woman who was murdered here. Her name is Yeger. She had already been assaulted in the past. And we dealt with the case."

For a moment there was silence on the phone.

"You said she was raped?"

"Yes."

"And we caught the rapist?"

The rapist was arrested on the day that Yeger filed her complaint, and had already been charged and convicted.

"And now it was a rape again? Who did it to her now?"

Did Saban think that the case had already been solved?

"I don't know," Avraham said, "but according to the findings at the scene I don't think she was sexually assaulted this time. We found her dressed. But we'll wait for the examination and see."

Before hanging up, Avraham told Saban that apparently there had been a policeman in the building a short time after the murder, but Saban only asked if it was nevertheless worth it for him to come to the scene and Avraham told him that they'd manage. He immediately returned to the neighbor's apartment.

On his sheet of paper, which was becoming more and more filled up with short sentences in his rounded, childish handwriting, he had written, *Aharon Pranji, neighbor from the apartment below: heard a noise around 2:00 p.m., something falling or furniture being dragged, sounds of a struggle.* A long blue line connected the last sentence to the word *struggle* that appeared at the top of the paper, in the things he had listed earlier from the mouth of the paramedic. Under the last sentence he wrote: *Was a policeman there minutes after the murder?*

"Explain this point to me one more time please," Avraham said. "A few minutes after you heard the noises, even though you didn't call the police, you saw a policeman in the stairwell?"

"Yes. Like I told you. Ten or fifteen minutes after."

"Do you know if someone called and requested the police?"

In the questioning he conducted so far no neighbor said that he called the police.

"That's what I assumed. That someone else called the police. And that the policeman checked and saw that everything was okay. That's why I didn't call."

"The man who went down the stairs was wearing a uniform, you're sure of this?"

"Yes."

"And that's not someone who lives in the building?"

"No policeman lives here. I've lived here forty-five years now."

"Do you remember if any other people came down the stairs before or after him?"

The neighbor couldn't know this. He hadn't looked through the peephole the entire time. He also admitted that he fell asleep a bit afterward and woke up when he heard Leah Yeger's daughter screaming. But he did watch the policeman through a window when he left the building and saw that the policeman did not get into a car.

In the kitchen where they sat there was a smell of cooked chicken. Pranji offered him warm tea and Avraham declined, but then he suddenly felt thirsty and asked for a glass of water. The last line that he wrote before leaving was: *A policeman on foot didn't get into a car. Need to clarify: maybe he left the other apartment on the top floor?*

Like always, Avraham was relieved by Ma'alul's presence. He returned to the scene and told Ma'alul that Saban called and that he wouldn't be coming tonight and Eliyahu looked at him with his deep-set eyes, which reminded Avraham of his father's eyes, and smiled. He asked Avraham if there was anything new in the neighbors' testimonies and Avraham said, "We might know the time of the murder. The neighbor from the apartment below says that he heard sounds of a struggle from here around two. And it's also possible that there was an earlier call to the police. Before the daughter arrived. The neighbor saw a policeman coming down the stairs a few minutes after two."

Without saying so explicitly, both of them considered the same disastrous possibility at that moment: was a patrolman sent to the building at the request of the police, who then politely knocked on Yeger's door, and when he didn't get a response simply left? Of course there was another possibility as well, but for now they didn't even want to think about it. "That policeman needs to be found," Ma'alul said. "I'll find out who it was with the police and at the station. And you should go home now. You're by yourself here for a few hours now, aren't you?"

Did something in Avraham's eyes give away how he felt? He reached for his pocket but there were no cigarettes there.

When Ma'alul asked him, "Was the body here when you had arrived?" he just nodded and saw again the open green eye and was filled with regret for not touching Yeger's forehead when he entered the apartment, as if he had done things differently she would still be alive. He tried avoiding Ma'alul's gaze and asked him where her daughter was, and Ma'alul told him that she left.

"Alone? Without an escort?"

"What escort, Avi? Her ex-husband came to take her and I okayed it. There's no reason for her to be here, right?"

Her brother, on the other hand, had been informed of his mother's death and was on his way to the scene. Avraham wanted to wait for him but Ma'alul told him, "Get out of here already. Everything will be all right. He lives in the north and won't be here for an hour. I'll speak with him. And you'll rest. In any case there's nothing else to do here, and tomorrow you have a long day ahead of you."

This was true, but all the same Avraham lingered at the scene for a few minutes, as if he were having difficulty saying good-bye or feared that if he left he'd miss something that he wouldn't be able to see again. But that evening he didn't discover anything there that he had failed to discover at first glance. In the other apartment on that floor a sixteen-year-old boy, wearing a red sweatshirt, opened the door for him. His parents weren't home but neither of them was a policeman, and it wasn't possible that a policeman had paid them a visit that afternoon because his parents were at work and he was at school. And only when Shrapstein arrived did Avraham call him and Ma'alul to the kitchen, tell the two of them that Yeger had previously been a rape victim, and see Ma'alul's dark face turn pale. Like Saban, Ma'alul asked if the rapist had been caught and Avraham said that he had and that he was still serving his time in prison. Then he asked them to come to an early staff meeting the following morning and when he got into his car he realized he forgot his coat at the scene.

He didn't turn on the car and sat in it without doing a thing. The street was empty, even though the wind had died down and the rain now fell in a light drizzle. Ma'alul called to ask if the blue army coat at the scene was his and then promised to take it with him and bring it back to Avraham the next day.

Suddenly it was clear to him that he was not watching himself on a television show but rather was in the city where he was born and had lived almost his entire life, on Krause Street, below a building whose number was 38 and on whose third floor a woman he knew had been murdered. At the beginning of his first murder case.

When he entered the station to pick up copies of the documents from Yeger's rape case he asked David Ezra, the desk sergeant, if the policeman called to 38 Krause Street that afternoon had been located. Ezra told him, "Not yet, Avi. Not yet. Eliyahu asked me to check and I'm trying to figure it out for you, but c'mon, give me some time. Do you know what went on here today with this storm?"

Avraham rushed to place the folder in their study without Marianka seeing it, but on the way from the station he still managed to glance at them.

Leah Yeger was raped in 2012. The detective who received her complaint, escorted her to room 4 at Wolfson Medical Center, and dealt with the case was Esty Vahaba. This was an easy case because Yeger knew the rapist and turned to the police a few hours after she was assaulted. He was charged and sentenced to only four and half years in prison, due to his age and other mitigating circumstances, but he couldn't have harmed her today because he was still serving his sentence in prison.

Someone else killed Leah Yeger. Someone else violently attacked her and then took her purse and the keys to her apartment and locked the door behind him.

Had he surprised her when he knocked on the door of her apartment or did she know he was coming and was waiting for him? And was he still in the apartment when the policeman—Avraham hadn't thought about this possibility before now and it alarmed him. He didn't say a word to Marianka about the rape when she asked him to tell her what happened. Only that a sixty-year-old woman was found dead in her home.

"Her husband did it?" she asked, and he shook his head.

"Her husband's dead."

"So you don't know who killed her?"

"No."

"And you're in charge of the case?"

"Yes."

"How are you feeling?"

He felt terrible.

The morning they spent together first in bed and afterward at the seashore was far off now, as if it had happened months ago. He took off his clothes and put on sweatpants and a T-shirt and got into bed without eating dinner or even watching the reports about the murder on the late-night news. Marianka lay next to him, in the dark, but fell asleep long after him. Of all the things he saw at the scene, it was the colorful birds that wouldn't let go of him.

"Do you have a lead?" Marianka asked him before he fell asleep, and for some reason Avraham immediately said, "Yes," without knowing what lead he was referring to.

3

The second sign was given to Mali the next day in a phone call with Harry, but she didn't understand this one as she should have, either. She was hurt by Kobi ignoring her on their anniversary and especially by the fact that he let her sleep alone for the first time, and of all days on the one when she had felt the fear of the heavy hand.

When Harry called she was waiting for Gila in a café. A man with glasses who wore a white sweater and a scarf sat two tables away from her and looked at her over a newspaper. She was sure that it was Kobi calling when she searched for her phone in the pocket of her coat that rested on the seat opposite her, because ever since she left the house she had been waiting for a call from him. An international number appeared on the screen, and she knew immediately that it was Harry, and debated whether to answer him. She feared that with him of all people she wouldn't be able to control herself and that the anger would erupt.

She tried not to think about what happened yesterday, but since the morning hours her fury with Kobi had grown more and more intense. Had he stayed alone on the roof all night? When she woke up, a bit after six, he wasn't next to her. She had a feeling he wasn't home, and when she passed through the apartment she discovered she was right. On the roof, next to the white plastic chair, she saw his empty coffee mug. "The Best Dad in the World." She didn't look for the gun, but it's possible that it was no longer on the table in the utility room when she passed through it on her way downstairs. The door to the entrance again wasn't locked.

She didn't know if she should look for him. And she didn't call him, because he didn't answer her even once yesterday. Before waking the girls she had a shower, and when she was getting dressed in the bedroom she heard the door to the apartment opening. A moment before this, when she stood facing the large mirror and watched herself while buttoning her shirt, she again felt that she was looking at another woman, like yesterday, and she closed the closet door. Kobi was in the kitchen. He stood before the table reading the paper.

For a moment she had hope: perhaps during the night he decided it was premature to give up and was searching for work in the want ads? There couldn't have been another reason, since Kobi never before went down to buy a paper in the morning. When she stopped behind him and said good morning, without touching him, she saw that he was reading an article about the murder that occurred in Holon. And that her "good morning" frightened him. He folded up the newspaper and left the kitchen with it after giving her a dry good-morning greeting in return. She didn't read newspapers at home, either, but on the table in the kitchen there remained an issue of *Israel Today* and she opened it. In the first few pages there were only articles about the storm damage and pictures of flooded streets and snow in the Golan mountains. The article about the murder appeared on page sixteen, and in the center of it there was a picture of an old woman. Her name was Leah Yeger, and it seemed to Mali that she had encountered the name before, but she didn't recognize the face that peered out at her from the newspaper.

The woman was sixty years old and was murdered in her apartment on Krause Street in the afternoon hours. *Her daughter found the body when she came to visit.* And a gag order had been placed on the remaining details of the investigation.

Mali prepared coffee just for herself and bowls of Corn Flakes for the girls. Kobi pretended to be sleeping, and when she entered the bedroom again she behaved as if he wasn't there or as if the two of them were ghosts. The girls didn't ask about him, as if the fact that there were days when they had no father went without saying. Before they left she nevertheless said aloud, "You remember that I'm working this afternoon and that you're picking up today?" without checking that he was awake.

Afterward there were the errands.

This was her free morning, and she was forced to begin it at the post office. She waited more than twenty minutes in line before paying their property tax and the water and electric bills, which like always during the winter months had grown despite efforts to cut back. In front of her in line was a clerk from a law firm who was sending dozens of certified letters. The storm had weakened, but from time to time rain continued to fall. Before ten, when the stores at the mall opened, she went to Electronics in order to check prices on a dryer, but again had second thoughts at the last moment, because soon warmer days would be coming and it would be possible to manage without it. The nausea didn't go away, and Mali hoped that it was tied to the pregnancy and not to the fear. She put off the call to the doctor.

Even on regular days most of the errands fell on her, but in periods like this the load was unbearable. Kobi didn't take the girls to day care or to school and didn't pick them up, even though he was at home most of the time. He grew quiet and disappeared, and even when he spoke it wasn't in order to offer her help. The clothes piled up in the laundry basket, the dishes in the sink, the refrigerator was emptied out a couple of days after she returned from shopping. And the apartment transformed from a place of refuge to a hostile environment. Kobi almost never went out, except for boxing, and his silent presence at home paralyzed everyone: her, the girls. Everyone moved more slowly, spoke quietly. Even the dog was dying without making a sound.

"Mali, is that you? I can barely hear you."

When she heard Harry Bengtson's voice she immediately felt that she was liable to burst out in tears, and she choked them back as she straightened herself in the chair and took out a bag of brown sugar from the copper dish. She said to him in English, "I hear you, Harry. Do you hear me? I'm not at home, I am in a café." The waitress placed a mug with a latte before her and asked by moving her lips if she wanted something to eat, and Mali signaled no with her head. She assumed that Harry called in order to wish them a belated mazel tov on the anniversary, but this was a strange assumption since he hadn't done that before and it was possible that he didn't know when it fell. It seemed to her that he was a bit drunk, as he had been more than once when calling. "Is everything okay with Jacob?" he asked her in English. "I'm trying to get hold of him but can't. His damn phone is always turned off. Why the hell does he have a phone if he has it off all the time?"

Harry was the only one that still insisted on using Kobi's full name, the sound of it catching her a little off guard each time. His voice was coarse and deep and hadn't changed at all over the years. The first time they met she hadn't understood a single word he'd said.

"Yes, he's okay," Mali answered him in English. "It could be the battery died. Did you try calling him at home?" She didn't know the last time Kobi had spoken with his father or what he had told him, and she imagined that he hadn't told him a thing. Not about the firings and not about the loans and definitely not about the failed job interview. A few years ago she discovered that most of the things Kobi told his father about their lives were complete lies, even though Harry could have helped them if he had known the truth. Kobi decided not to say a word about Eilat to him, either, and she had no reason to object to this. She heard him ask, "Do you know why he tried calling me yesterday? I didn't hear the phone and he left me a strange message. He said something about . . . Were you with him when he called me, Mali? Are you there?" When she answered him she lowered her voice because the man with the glasses continued to stare at her without hiding behind the newspaper. She said, "I'm here, Harry. I'm in a café. And I wasn't with him when he called. He didn't say what he wanted?" She did think it strange that Kobi called his father yesterday. They spoke on the phone three or four times a year, no more. Even when they went to visit him for the first time, Kobi didn't let him know that he was bringing Mali with him.

Harry was silent, as if he didn't hear her, and because she was scared that he'd hang up before managing to tell her what Kobi said, she raised her voice when she asked him again, "Harry? He didn't tell you what he wants?" And he said, "Mali, I'm still here."

The spontaneous trip to Australia changed their lives.

Kobi and Mali had broken up while they were in the army, since it was hard keeping in touch long-distance and because Mali wanted to try out new relationships. In the first months of the relationship between them, at school, she was in love with Kobi, but his isolation already scared her back then. Gila received a draft exemption, worked in Tel Aviv, and switched boyfriends every two weeks. And the fact that Mali was stationed at an intelligence base in Shomron, full of men, created nonstop friction between her and Kobi. They mainly spent the weekend breaks arguing. He interrogated her about her relationships with the commanding officers and about the people she shared a room with. When he called the base and she wasn't in the office, he got furious even once she explained to him that she had gone out for a run. She hesitated for weeks before telling him that she wanted to break up—and she knew why. Kobi simply refused to accept the breakup. He continued to call and write long letters. One Shabbat when she remained at the base he even went to visit her parents and asked them to persuade her to give him another chance. But then he suddenly broke off contact, and for years they didn't see each other, not even by chance. Mali heard stories about him from friends they had in common and sometimes he called on her birthday or the holidays, and they held a polite conversation, without revealing to each other what was really happening to them in their lives, in order not to cause any pain. And she was strict about not calling him, even when she wanted to, so as not to give him any hope.

When they met one morning, by chance, in line at a health clinic—she had gone there because she had the flu, and he had some tests that were supposed to be done two days earlier—she didn't think that they'd start going out again, because she had just been through a painful breakup with a guy who she met during her studies at a business college and who everyone thought she would marry. Kobi suggested that they meet up that evening for a drink and she agreed, and two days later they went to a movie. She was already a bank teller and still lived in her parents' apartment, and Kobi rented a studio apartment close by. She told him openly how she discovered that her ex-boyfriend was cheating on her, but didn't mention his name even once. Kobi said he was about to start working for Mossad after being accepted into a training course for agents, and that he first planned to travel to his father in Australia for a few weeks, and suddenly asked her if she wanted to join him.

How many times had she thought about that moment since then?

She wasn't sure that was a good idea, but because of the breakup and since she hadn't gone on the gap-year trip that everyone went on after the army, in the end she told him yes. Yet it wasn't only those reasons but something in him as well—or perhaps in them actually. When they sat next to each other in the dark of the movie theater and his leg accidently touched her thigh, she recalled his soft, smooth body and the careful movements of his hands on hers. She decided she would be spontaneous, at least once in her life, and her parents supported her decision, perhaps because they feared she would wind up alone. Even her father didn't oppose her traveling with Kobi and asked only if she'd be sleeping with him in the same room.

What she knew about his father before they met was that he was a professor of botany, and thus she was surprised when she saw him. He was sixty years old then, maybe sixty-one. A large tan man with a white beard and a red bandanna wrapped around his head who waited shirtless for them in the house's yard, watering the plants and feeding his two giant black dogs, Cerebus and Aortos. With no suit and no glasses. Only his clear eyes were Kobi's eyes exactly.

On their first day there he drank half a bottle of whiskey, after finishing a bottle of red wine during the meal, and despite this wasn't drunk when he took them around the farm, which was located in the heart of a valley called Valley of the Giants, and a forest with the tallest trees she had ever seen in her life. Afterward, when they sat in the yard and Kobi went in to shower, Harry admitted that he didn't know that Jacob would come with a girlfriend and asked her how long they'd been going out. She told him that they met in high school and broke up and met again just a few weeks earlier, by chance. When Harry asked her, "Did you two come to tell me you're getting married?" she laughed because this hadn't occurred to her until that very moment. She said to him, "For now no," and Harry's face was serious when he said, "Fantastic. So do you think something might happen between us or am I too old for you?"

All this was so different from her parents' house and from the life she knew up to then, and in fact afterward as well. And not only because of the large house and the barks of the dogs at night and the dense forests she went out to run in each morning, but also since Harry Bengtson was different from her father, who was short in stature and quiet and wouldn't think of saying things like that to someone. Harry staring directly at her was embarrassing, but she tried to smile, and Harry himself smiled and said, "I'm kidding. I wouldn't do a thing like that to him, even though I love dark-complected women. I've caused Jacob enough harm. And it appears to me that he feels good around you."

Kobi returned, and Harry became silent and then rose from his seat and wrapped his arms around his son's shoulders. "How long haven't I seen you, boy?" he asked, and it seemed to her that Kobi blushed and flinched while at the same time a smile of joy lit up his face as he was embraced by his father.

Mali didn't stop looking at the two of them during the four weeks they spent in Australia. In his father's presence Kobi was shy and restrained, and Mali imagined that this is exactly how he was as a five- or eight- or ten-year-old boy, before he became a teen and decided to go to Israel by himself. Next to his father his shyness stuck out, as well as his gentleness. The hesitation struck when he stretched out his hand to caress her one evening, when just the two of them were on the hammock in the yard, as if after years he were asking permission to touch her. She moved her head closer to his hand because she was waiting for him to touch her. Something in Kobi's body, in contrast to the bodies of other men who had touched her, was always close by and right and simple. And she saw that he had changed since high school, that he had lost self-confidence and walked like someone who was afraid to fall, but she thought that this would actually help him to not get hurt. They barely spoke about his father, but it seemed to her that Kobi admired Harry at the same time that something in his father scared him. During the week,

Harry stayed in a small apartment by the university, and Mali and Kobi rented a car and traveled, so they didn't spend much time with him, but from the conversations she did have with Harry it became clear to her that he knew almost nothing about his son. Kobi hadn't told him what he dared to tell her when they met again: that his dream of getting accepted into an elite unit vanished when he fell during testing and that he hadn't been accepted into an officers' course and that after being released he began studying business management "in order to make the first million before the age of twenty-five," but he was kicked out of school because he was accused, unjustly, of cheating on one of the tests.

They spoke about his mother only once, when Mali saw her picture hanging up in his childhood room for the first time. Kobi told her that she had spoken Hebrew with him since he was a baby, mainly so she wouldn't forget the language herself. She had been a poet and had hoped to teach literature at one of the colleges in Perth but never found work before dying of cancer that wasn't diagnosed in time. Mali recalled the stories that were told about Kobi when he had arrived in Holon, about how his mother had gone crazy and killed herself after his father hospitalized her in a mental institution. She asked Kobi if he left Australia because his mother died, and he said no, that he left because he couldn't stand the women who replaced her in his father's bed. "But I also wanted to be a commando, remember? And I heard that the most beautiful women in the world are in Israel."

Inexplicably, it was actually when they returned from

Australia that it became clear to her that at some point they'd get married.

And since then they had seen Harry Bengtson three times in all.

Two years after the visit to the farm he appeared at their wedding, even though he announced that there was no chance he'd come. He brought with him an Aboriginal woman, about their age, by the name of Lawanda, who was stocky and tall and didn't speak a word the entire time she was in Israel. Three years after this he called one evening and said that he would be arriving the next week in order to see the granddaughter who had been born to him. And the last time, four years ago, when they traveled with the girls and spent the summer with him. And she did know that since Harry had a heart attack Kobi had been calling him more, but she didn't know that he called him yesterday. Nor what message he left with him.

Her sister, Gila, still hadn't arrived at the café yet, and the man with the glasses wasn't at his table, but his scarf was on the chair he had been sitting in. Mali again said to Harry, "I'm not at home right now, but did you try calling him there? I think he's at home," and Harry coughed and asked, "Are you sure he's okay? Because on the phone he didn't sound so good to me."

Mali said, "I don't know what you mean, Harry. What did he say on the message?" And then for the first time she heard about Kobi's plan to leave.

"He said something about coming for a visit. Next week or even before then. Do you know anything about this, Mali? And why not have all of you come?"

She didn't answer immediately. Tried to remember if Kobi had spoken about a trip to Australia. They couldn't travel together because she hadn't asked for a vacation from work and the girls didn't have a break from school until Passover, either, and in any case they didn't have money for the plane tickets. And ever since Eilat Kobi hadn't left her alone in the apartment for even one night. She said, "I don't think we can come, Harry. Maybe he meant that we'll come in the summer?" But Harry responded, "He said next week. Do you think he'll come? And he cried on the message, Mali. Do you know why he was crying?"

The crying that she had been choking back since yesterday morning stood in her throat, but she succeeded in controlling it. She rested the phone for a moment on her knees so that Harry wouldn't hear. Afterward she said, "Harry, I can't hear you. I'll go back home and call you from there, okay?" And he said, "But don't forget to call, Mali. I'm worried about him." This was the first time she'd heard Harry speak about him like that.

She hadn't intended on returning home before work or trying to speak with Kobi, but after the conversation with Harry she couldn't do otherwise. She shortened the meeting with Gila as much as she could without Gila noticing that something had happened, and even while Gila spoke she thought only about what Harry had said. And she couldn't say anything to her about the pregnancy, either.

She had nothing to be ashamed of, but nevertheless she suddenly filled up with shame over their lives and over

what she would say about them to her sister if she dared
to reveal anything. She just wanted to return home and
ask Kobi if he really intended to leave her alone with the
girls and travel to Australia, and she wanted to hit him, if
she were able, or to sit him down across from her and not
let him go anywhere until he told her what had come over
him. She knew he wouldn't call, since she was always the
one forced to appease him, since Kobi simply didn't know
how to stop fighting. This was his problem at the places
he worked as well. Small sources of tension, which other
people knew to undo or ignore, Kobi turned into bitter
wars. And if it seemed to him that someone hurt him, he
was unable to forgive them.

Gila placed a new bag on the table, and before even
ordering coffee told her about the man who kept her from
sleeping last night. He was six years younger, a lawyer,
and they met when she showed him an apartment in a new
luxury project in Tel Aviv, by the sea. Afterward she asked
Mali, like always, as if intending to anger her, "How are
you all with money? Has he already found work?" And
when Mali answered not yet, Gila said, "Can you tell me
what he's waiting for?"

These sentences didn't actually distance her from Kobi
but rather brought them closer together. Maybe because
despite everything she understood what had come over
him and how humiliating the interviews were for him and
how much scorn he had to absorb, and she also knew that
she had a part in this. When she told Gila she had to run,
she already wanted to go home not only so she could ask
him about Australia but also so she could hug him without

saying a word and tell him about the nausea and about the fact that the fear was returning and that yesterday, before she fell asleep, she felt the heavy hand that comes from the darkness, but when she got home all that was forgotten.

The door again wasn't locked.

Kobi stood in the living room among clothes and objects that he had removed from the cabinet and the closet by the entrance. The doors to the girls' rooms, which she had arranged that morning, were open, and there, too, she saw toys thrown about and clothes and books on the beds and on the floor. And his look scared her, just like the previous night, when he had turned around to face her. Harry came out from the bedroom and looked at her and then came up to her with slow steps and lay down on the floor. Kobi said quietly, "I can't find the umbrella. Do you know where it is?"

He wore the black polo shirt he had worn the day before, and his hands shook. "It's there, under the sofa," she said to him. "You left it there after I gave it to you yesterday. And are you going to straighten up this whole mess?" Kobi looked in the direction she pointed and said, "Not that. The old umbrella."

She looked at him in fear, without understanding. He moved the cupboard in the living room and the armchairs from their places and rolled up the rug. The stool was overturned and far from its place near the television, as if he had sent it flying with a kick. "You said that you lost it and that you don't remember where, no?" She tried to control her voice. "That's why I bought you a new umbrella."

And anyway the rain had already stopped.

Kobi's eyes continued to search for the umbrella as he mumbled, as if to himself, "I don't remember where I forgot it. You sure you didn't see it anywhere?" She stood there another moment and then went down in the elevator and got in the car and did not try to stop the crying, and even if she had tried to stop it, she wouldn't have succeeded.

4

His sleep was short but when Avraham woke up at five fifteen he was ready. The shock that seized him for a moment at the crime scene at the sight of the body had disappeared, and its place had been taken by a desire to be at the station working. His cell phone hadn't received any new messages, but he nevertheless hoped that when he arrived at his office, findings from the forensics lab would be waiting for him, perhaps because of a dream that he dreamed at night, in which Ilana Lis informed him over the phone that the fingerprints the murderer left on the plate in the kitchen had been identified—and then the call was disconnected before she told Avraham his name.

Marianka got up with him, even though she didn't have to. While they ate breakfast Avraham studied the newspapers and the lines passed sadly before his eyes as he expected: "Body of Sixty-Year-Old Woman Found in Holon," "Yeger murdered in her home," and, of course, "police still don't have any leads." Leah Yeger's murder joined four acts of murder that had taken place since the start of winter and still hadn't been solved, and a wave of investigations that had been opened against senior members of the police, all under suspicion of sexually harassing female officers. The joke at the station was that the only thing less pleasant these days than being a female cop in the Israeli police was being a male one. In all the papers Yeger's face could be seen in the passport photo provided by the family, while only at him did a different face peer out, one beaten and lifeless.

Avraham prepared rolls with cream cheese and thin slices of tomatoes and made black coffee for the two of them. When Marianka asked him what was written in the paper, he spun them around to her on the table as if she could read them. While drinking the first cup of coffee the need for a cigarette was still intense, and he took another roll for himself instead. In recent weeks he had gained ten pounds, not because he'd quit smoking but rather due to the fact that since Marianka arrived he ate two dinners each evening—the one they ate together and the one he ate alone after that, when he snuck into the kitchen without her seeing. Afterward they sat at the table for a few more minutes in uncharacteristic silence, as if the silence had crawled to their apartment from the scene where the body was found.

The meeting of the special investigation team that had been scheduled for that morning began at seven thirty exactly, and this was the only thing on the first day of the investigation that happened as planned and as he had hoped.

Avraham arrived early and thought Ma'alul would be late like always, but Eliyahu entered the conference room first, his dark bald head and the hair around his temples wet as if he were coming out of the shower. Other than them, Commander Eyal Shrapstein, Investigations Coordinator Lital Levy, and Sergeant Esty Vahaba, who was in charge of Leah Yeger's rape case and who was being temporarily added to the team, participated in the meeting. District Commander Benny Saban was supposed to arrive at some point but had been detained at Tel Aviv district headquarters.

When the members of the team entered the room, Avraham tried to forget that this was the first time he was running a special investigation team meeting about a murder case. In the past he had taken part in investigations opened for deaths occurring in unnatural circumstances, but Ilana Lis usually stood at the head of them. She, too, would always arrive early and wait in the conference room for everyone. Like him, she sat at the head of the table back then, rectangular glasses resting on the end of her nose and her eyes on the pages spread out before her. Waiting patiently for everyone to get coffee for themselves and grab their seats. During those same briefings, Avraham sat in the spot where Eliyahu Ma'alul was now sitting. Always with a blue pen in hand and an open notebook. Waiting for Ilana to begin speaking. But Ilana was now on sick leave, in and out of cancer treatments at the hospital, and Avraham was by himself, commander of the Investigations and Intelligence Units, and the responsibility fell on his shoulders only.

"As you know," he opened the meeting, "yesterday, at four fifteen, the body of Leah Yeger, resident of Holon, sixty years old, was found at 38 Krause Street. She was found by her daughter. At present we don't know much about what happened to her, but I hope that this will change when findings from the forensics lab arrive. I want us to visit her apartment again, with one of her family members, or with a few of them, but at present it appears that only a set of keys and a handbag were taken from the victim. They were not found anywhere at the scene. On the other hand, there are no signs of a break-in and her car wasn't stolen; the keys were discovered in plain sight at the scene. We have no eyewitnesses to the murder, but it appears we have a witness who heard, a neighbor who lives on the second floor. Around two the witness heard sounds of a struggle from the apartment above him, and his testimony correlates with the time of death as determined by the paramedic. The testimony also matches the autopsy, according to which Leah Yeger was murdered after a struggle, by strangulation, after being struck on her head. And as I said, there's a high likelihood that we'll have good DNA findings and it appears we will be receiving them today. According to a conversation I had this morning with the lab, there are findings from under the nails and between the fingers of the victim that can be used to produce DNA of the person with whom she struggled. In any event, the state of the scene and the circumstances of death indicate an unplanned murder, perhaps the result of an argument that deteriorated into violence. An additional detail, which I ask you to keep secret even within the station, so that it doesn't accidently leak out, is that Leah Yeger was victim of a rape we investigated. In the meantime we have a gag order on this. Yesterday she was not sexually assaulted."

He looked at Esty Vahaba when he said these things. She dealt with the rape investigation, and Avraham's glance explained her presence in the room. When she sat next to Ma'alul she looked to Avraham like his daughter, and perhaps therefore he felt an immediate closeness to her, as if they were siblings. Like he and Eliyahu, Vahaba was short and her eyes were dark and very serious. Her facial expression nearly didn't change even when Avraham turned to her, and if being there disconcerted her, she hid this well. The only thing Avraham knew about her was that she wasn't married, that she lived with her parents and supported them, and that the two of them were deaf.

Avraham paused for a moment when he lifted his head from the papers and examined the faces of those present in the room, as Ilana always did. Shrapstein wasn't listening to him, or so it seemed. His eyes were stuck on his cell phone. The day before as well, when Shrapstein arrived at the scene before evening, he did everything he could to avoid a conversation with Avraham and spoke to Ma'alul most of the time. Avraham saw him for a moment before he went home, walking around with his hands in his pockets and examining the window and door hinges, as if he were debating whether to buy the apartment. It was clear to everyone that Shrapstein had not gotten over Benny Saban's decision to appoint Avraham and not him commander of the Investigations and Intelligence Units.

A short time after the appointment he requested a transfer to the Fraud Investigation Unit or some other national unit, but in the meantime he was being forced to continue working in full cooperation with Avraham. It was impossible, however, to force him to hide his resentment.

"During this initial stage of our investigation," Avraham continued, "and until findings from the lab are received, and if we are lucky and they point to the identity of the attacker, I think we have at least two scenarios that we need to develop. The first is a break-in gone bad, or in any case, a random act of violence. The second is a connection between the murder and the rape."

Ma'alul interrupted his speech and said, "Avi, I would like to say something in this context. May I?"

Avraham signaled with his hand that he could speak. Shrapstein continued looking at his cell phone.

"Last night," said Ma'alul, "after you left the scene, Yeger's son arrived. I questioned him on the spot, and he conveyed to me information that seems to me to be of some importance. According to his testimony, and Esty can elaborate on this in a moment, the family members of the person convicted in her rape have not come to terms with the results of the trial. They harassed the victim before the trial and demanded that she drop the charge, and after the conviction the situation worsened and they threatened that they would harm her in revenge. Following the reading of the verdict there was even a skirmish between the families in the court parking lot."

Avraham looked at him dumbfounded, and Eliyahu identified the question in his eyes and smiled as he added,

"Wait, wait, Avi, that's not the end. And I didn't update you because it was late and I assumed you were sleeping. The man who was convicted is called David Danon, and his son who threatened the victim is called Ami. He's the owner of a construction company and resides in Rishon. I contacted him immediately and he denied that they threatened Yeger, but it was clear they had an account to settle with her; I have no doubt about this. He claims there was no rape and that the sexual relations between Yeger and his father were consensual. From his perspective, his father shouldn't be sitting in jail for even a day. In any case, he has an alibi for yesterday, and the alibi has been checked and confirmed. He was in a business meeting with clients. He's willing to take a polygraph and will be arriving at the station this afternoon."

Most of the details about Leah Yeger's rape that Esty Vahaba later delivered were known to Avraham from reading copies of the documents he took home the previous night, and he tried to listen to her and not think about the betrayal of Ma'alul, who for a few hours hid from him a possible direction for the investigation.

David Danon, who was convicted of the rape, was Leah Yeger's husband's business partner. They jointly owned a taxi and operated it themselves or through hired drivers. After Yeger's husband died of a heart attack, Danon asked to purchase her piece of the partnership, but Yeger refused because this was her main source of income. A few months after she became a widow, they met in her apartment in order to talk about the business, and it was then that she was assaulted. She filed a complaint that same night and was taken for medical tests at Wolfson Medical Center, and the findings were unambiguous. Despite this, Danon argued that the sexual relations were consensual and that this wasn't the first time they had had sex. According to his argument, there was a romantic connection between them that began when Yeger's husband was still alive. He was arrested that same night and brought before a judge the next day. The case was relatively simple, and Danon was convicted, primarily on the basis of the medical test and Yeger's testimony, and sentenced to four and a half years in prison. His family, as Ma'alul had said, refused to accept the conviction. Vahaba said that they even hired a private investigation company in order to gather incriminating evidence about Yeger.

Avraham's gaze passed from Ma'alul's face to Leah Yeger's face in the picture that he asked Lital Levy to hang on the board, next to the photographs from the scene. A picture that was taken when she was still alive. He didn't participate in the rape investigation, but he did meet Yeger at the station and was familiar with the incident from discussions at division meetings, and he wondered if the picture was taken before the rape or after. Yeger looked directly at the camera, and her facial expression in the photograph was serious, with a shadow of a smile. The facial expression of someone who grew up in the days when photographs were something you prepared yourself for, he thought. When she was photographed was her husband still alive? Did everything start to go wrong the moment he died? First her husband's heart attack and a short time after that she's assaulted by his partner. And accused by the rapist of having consensual intercourse with him before her husband died. And now the murder. Yeger herself apparently opened the door for a person she knew, and was then attacked and strangled. And if her husband were still alive, none of this would have happened. David Danon wouldn't have dared to attack her, and the man who entered her apartment yesterday perhaps wouldn't have found her alone. But what are the chances that she would have set up a meeting with or opened the door for one of Danon's family members?

Vahaba's diction was quiet and matter-of-fact, and when she finished reviewing the rape file Avraham said to her, "Thank you, Esty. You'll work on this angle with Eliyahu. Call the rapist's family members in for questioning as well as the private investigators who they hired. And if there's DNA from the scene today we'll be able to know easily if it belongs to a relative of his, without even asking for samples from them, because his DNA is in the database, right? Other than that, order her call log from at least the last month and check if she received any calls from them, okay?"

He asked Shrapstein to receive Leah Yeger's son and daughter and gather additional testimony from them, and at the same time work on the hypothesis that she was murdered during a break-in or burglary. He faced everyone but referred mainly to Shrapstein when he said, "I don't know if you noticed, but renovations are under way in two buildings on the street. This means that there are workers in the area and this must be checked as well. Check who the workers are and if they have criminal or terroristic backgrounds and if someone from among them has been absent since yesterday. Other than this, we have to find her handbag. And before you leave, go over the pictures from the scene, okay? Perhaps you'll see something you didn't see before."

This was an investigation procedure that he'd learned from Ilana Lis, and it seemed to him that only Shrapstein noticed it. To examine photographs from the scene a day or two later with fresh eyes. To present them to police who aren't participating in the investigation and hadn't before looked at the scene. Maybe someone will notice a detail that no one saw before. Shrapstein and Lital Levy got up to leave when Avraham said, "Just one more word," and Lital Levy sat back down in her seat. "We received testimony that we haven't managed to verify so far regarding a police officer who was in the building a short time after the murder," he added. "We're making sure that the testimony is correct, and if so, who the officer is and if he arrived at the building as a result of someone contacting the call center. I request that you don't speak about this testimony, either, with anyone before we understand what's going on."

He thought the meeting would end with this, but Shrapstein suddenly asked him, "How old is your witness, do you know?" and Avraham didn't understand his question at first. He didn't remember the exact age of the neighbor from the second floor or his name, and the pages on which he wrote his notes at the scene remained on the table in his office. "He told this story to me, too, yester-day," Shrapstein continued. "He grabbed me on the stairs when I got there. He's seventy-plus. And had just woken up when the whole thing happened."

Vahaba also didn't understand what Shrapstein was trying to say and asked him, "So what?" but Shrapstein turned directly to Avraham as he continued. "Did you maybe clarify with him if he usually wears glasses?" he asked. "And did he manage to put them on before he saw the policeman through the hole in the door for less than half a second?"

Vahaba and Lital Levy looked at Avraham, but he didn't answer. He didn't ask the neighbor a thing about glasses. And didn't remember if the witness was wearing glasses when he questioned him yesterday.

Saban was detained at the Tel Aviv district headquarters and his meeting with Avraham postponed until the afternoon.

Avraham returned to his office and for a few min-utes merely stared at the construction site visible from his window and the cars passing by on Fichman Street and waited for the phone to ring. He studied the photos from the rape file again and examined David Danon's face, and since the phone didn't ring he himself called the forensics lab at the national police headquarters but they still didn't have news about the samples taken from the body and from various items in the apartment. He asked why the delay, and the clerk said to him, "Are you serious? Do you think this is the only case we're working on here?"

Other files were sitting on his desk as well, at various stages of progress, but he couldn't open any other file. He tried to recall if the neighbor from the second floor wore glasses during their conversation. The investigation was being conducted without him at the lab in Jerusalem and in interrogation rooms on the two floors below, and he did nothing concrete and wondered if this is how a division commander should direct a murder investigation, or in fact, if Ilana Lis would direct it this way. The first stage in solving a case is selecting the investigators correctly, she always told him, but he wanted to question Leah Yeger's daughter again himself and speak with her son, whom he still hadn't seen, and sit in the interrogation room opposite the rapist's relatives. Mainly he wanted to return to the murder scene, even though on that day he still didn't know what to look for. And in the meantime he restrained himself and didn't call Ilana. When the chemotherapy treatments began she informed him that she was not willing to have anyone other than her family members accompany her through the process, and when Avraham tried to understand why, she said to him, "Because I don't want anyone seeing or even hearing me in the state I'm going to be in. Not even you."

The wooden pipe that Marianka had bought him in Brussels was in a drawer, and he took it out and held it unlit in his mouth. After he decided to quit smoking he tried to use it a few times when he was alone in the office, but it went out over and over and he finally gave up, but every so often would bite it between his teeth in order to relax. Afterward he went down to the cafeteria and bought himself a cheese sandwich and ate it in his office while reading the brief reports that Shrapstein had sent from questioning Leah Yeger's son and daughter, and which he found in his in-box when he returned.

The son claimed that he hadn't been in contact with his mother for a few months, and thus couldn't say a thing about her life, if she had relations and if she was involved in disputes of any sort. *According to the witness,* Shrapstein wrote, *he had no conflicts with his mother, including conflicts over the inheritance or some other financial matter.* He was thirty-six years old and was employed as a superintendent of a high school in the north. *Yesterday afternoon he was serving army reserve duty and he there received the message about his mother.* When Shrapstein asked him when was the last time he spoke or met with his mother, the son claimed he hadn't spoke to her in months and didn't remember the exact date on which they spoke. Afterward he was asked if in his opinion someone wanted to harm his mother, and he said there's no doubt that it's *one of the rapist's relatives.* The daughter, by contrast, had a close connection with her mother. They met a few times a week and spoke on the phone at least once a day. Despite this, she also didn't know if her mother was involved in a dispute of any sort and claimed that to the best of her knowledge no one wanted to harm her.

Avraham read the reports twice and then tried to speak with Shrapstein on the phone, without success. What bothered him about the reports was the gap between the fact that the son hadn't spoken with his mother for a long time and his conviction that he knows who attacked her.

And there was an additional thing, which Avraham wrote to himself in pen at the bottom of the report in order to remember to ask Shrapstein: *How is it that her son wasn't in contact with her despite the rape she went through?*

Ma'alul had tried to call him twice since the morning meeting, but in the end they met in the cafeteria, accidentally. Avraham went down to eat lunch a little before two, even though he wasn't hungry, and Ma'alul entered the room a few minutes after and sat down next to him. Ma'alul ordered for himself a large cheese pastry with an egg, and even before taking a bite of it asked Avraham if he could taste the cooked chicken and potatoes that made him nauseous and that he left on his plate. He asked Avraham, "Did Shrapstein see her kids already?" And Avraham nodded. And only when Ma'alul continued as if nothing had happened and asked him, "And did you meet with Saban? Is he interested in the case at all?" Avraham said to him what he already wanted to tell him during the meeting.

"You should have updated me yesterday about the rapist's son. It's a shame you waited until the meeting this morning."

Ma'alul set the fork in his hand down. He said, "Why? It was late and I knew we were going to meet first thing this morning," and Avraham said to him, "Because I needed to know that yesterday and not discover it at the meeting like everyone else."

Eliyahu returned the plate with the chicken to Avra-

ham and wiped his mouth with a napkin. It seemed to
Avraham that he had been hurt by his words when he said
quietly, "Avi, what happened to you? I understand that
there's a lot of pressure on you, but you do know you're
not working alone, right? That you have people to rely on?
You know very well that I can't immediately report everything that happens and I definitely don't think I need to
report everything like this *to you*. Did I try to hide something from you?"

His deep-set eyes searched for Avraham's gaze and
didn't find it. Avraham remembered the dream in which
Ilana hid the name of the murderer from him and thought
that perhaps because of this he wanted to call her so badly,
when Ma'alul continued and said, "Please conduct this investigation with peace of mind and with the team, Avi.
And do me a favor, let's not start dealing in bullshit, okay?
This isn't the first case for any of us, and it isn't the first
time we're working together, either. So let's work freely
like we know how."

But this was his first murder case! Perhaps there's no
difference between an investigation like this and any other
investigation? Nevertheless there was a difference, because
in most of the cases he investigated the victims could speak,
and even if they didn't know everything or hid details, he
relied on the fact that he'd succeed in reading between the
lines and the lies, and he couldn't ask Leah Yeger a thing,
despite the open eye and gaping mouth that was frozen as
if in the middle of a breath or an effort to tell him something.

Ma'alul waited for his answer and Avraham pushed

the plate in his direction and tried to appease him when he asked, "When did you work until?" And was stunned when Ma'alul responded that he was at the scene until two in the morning and didn't return home but rather went to sleep at the station in order not to be late to the meeting. "And it was actually nice," he said. "Do you know how long it's been since I slept here? I felt thirty years younger."

It was strange, how each of them responded to the case differently. Ma'alul was right when he said that Avraham was dealing in bullshit. Throughout the day he waited for a call from the lab that didn't come, for a meeting with Benny Saban that was postponed again and again.

When his meeting with Saban finally started, a bit after four, Avraham was still under the influence of the conversation with Ma'alul. Saban blinked at him from behind his wide desk when he said, "You understand that it will be a disaster if we don't solve this case quickly?" And Avraham nodded. "Did you see *Yediot* and *Haaretz* today? They're coming down hard on the police commissioner because of the assassinations we haven't solved and the inquiries into the police officers' sexual harassment cases. You understand that this is an investigation that he'll take personally, right, Avi?"

"He" was the police commissioner. Avraham said to Saban quietly, "We'll sol–" when Saban interrupted his words, adding, "And the worst is that damn rape, Avi. That this woman was raped and now she's been murdered. Do you think there's a connection between the incidents?"

He still had nothing to share with Saban, but he said that there were good findings at the scene and then he told

him about the threats from the rapist's family. If it be-
comes clear that this is the angle, then there's a chance to
solve it quickly: David Danon's DNA was in the police database, and if a relative of his assaulted Leah Yeger they'd
know it within twenty-four hours at the most. Also if Leah
Yeger was assaulted by one of her family members. Saban
asked if these were the main angles of the investigation,
and Avraham answered that for now yes, but he doesn't
exclude the possibility that she was murdered during a
burglary gone wrong. Since the afternoon, Shrapstein had
been going over burglary cases in the area and was trying
to obtain a list of laborers who worked at construction
sites in the area, and intelligence agents in the district were
searching addicts and dealers in stolen property for the
contents of Yeger's bag, primarily the credit cards and cell
phone. If the burglar is a known criminal, it's reasonable
to assume that his identifying marks are in the police database, too.

"Do you think that it could be her son?" Saban suddenly asked, and Avraham said, "Don't know." Something
in the things the son said to Shrapstein bothered him, but
because he hadn't met him himself he couldn't say what.
And he again thought about the fact that the son was the
one who confidently directed them to the rapist's family
members.

Without a doubt Leah Yeger wouldn't have hesitated
to open the door for her son.

Avraham didn't say a thing about this aloud, but Saban
said to him, "So let's exhaust these angles for now. That's
what's most available to us, no? And let's extend the gag

order until we have a suspect in hand. I don't want any detail of the investigation to leak out and especially not the fact that she was raped and that afterward there were threats made against her. Do you realize how we'd look?"

Avraham stood to leave his office when Saban recalled what he had told him yesterday during the phone call at the scene, and asked him, "And what about the policeman who was there? Do you know yet?" And Avraham responded not yet.

"You haven't managed to locate him yet?"

"According to the log there wasn't a prior message to the call center, and no police officer was sent to the building before the message at four thirty. The eye witness might be mistaken."

"And if he wasn't mistaken?"

If he wasn't mistaken, then Leah Yeger's murderer might not be a relative of David Danon or her son but a policeman instead. And another possibility is that during the murder, or a short time after it, someone contacted the call center and a beat cop was sent to the scene of the incident, and someone is now trying to hide this and even erased the call from the log.

Saban was astounded by this possibility even more than by the possibility that Leah Yeger was murdered by a cop. "Why would someone do a thing like that?" he asked, and Avraham said, "If someone contacted the call center and a policeman arrived at the scene and knocked on the door and then turned around and left without doing a thing while the murderer was inside the apartment and while Yeger was maybe alive, he has good reason to hide it."

Saban didn't want to think about this at all. He closed
his eyes for a moment and then rose and closed the door
to his room.

"Let's hope that this isn't what happened, Avi. Or
that your witness is mistaken," he said quietly when he
returned to sit in his chair. Afterward he asked Avraham
to place his cell phone on the table to ensure that he wasn't
recording the conversation. "This entire conversation is off
the record, Avi. From my perspective it didn't take place,
not this part of it, is that clear? You did not inform me
that a policeman may have been there and I knew nothing
about it, do you understand?"

It took Avraham time to understand what Saban was
telling him, because during the time he spoke Avraham
was thinking about something else. He saw in his imagination the beat cop going up to the apartment and knocking
on the door, and on the other side he could picture Leah
Yeger struggling with a man who had attacked her and
trying to call for help. A man who was perhaps her son.
"If a policeman was there during the time she was murdered, the entire district is in deep trouble," Saban continued. "And even if that's true, no one's saying that we
have to concentrate on that now, correct? For now that's a
marginal detail in the investigation, and our task is to find
the murderer and not the policeman who perhaps screwed
up. Are you with me, Avi? Do you agree with me?"

Only in the evening, when Avraham returned home and re-
constructed the conversation with Marianka, did he un-

derstand that Saban had hinted to him that if indeed prior contact was made to the call center and the log had been erased, that it was better for both of them not to look into the matter. It was possible to accuse the neighbor of making a mistake, and as for the existence of the policeman who came down the stairs and disappeared, if there was such a person, there was no other evidence.

"Do you really think this is what he asked of you?" Marianka asked, and Avraham said, "Yes."

"And what did you answer him?"

"That for now we have other angles to investigate anyway. But that I'll investigate this case as I know how."

"And what did he say?"

"Nothing. What could he say?"

When they sat down at the table in the kitchen to eat dinner, he wanted to talk about her, about her day at work, but Marianka insisted on talking with him about the case, and he tried to tell her and again omitted the rape from his story. They ate pasta with tomato sauce and drank red wine, and Avraham told her about the findings that were supposed to arrive from the lab in Jerusalem and about the keys and wallet that weren't found, about the questioning of the laborers working in the area and about Shrapstein's conversation with Leah Yeger's son, but he didn't tell her about David Danon and his family's threats.

During the time he spoke was there a glimmer of longing or sadness in her eyes over the fact that she gave up her position with the Brussels police, or did it just seem so to him? He wanted to spare her the sadness and therefore said that he didn't have photographs from the scene in his possession when she asked to see them. She touched his hand when she said, "You look worried, but it sounds to me that up to now you did everything you should have, no?" And he said, "Could be."

"And you haven't started smoking again, right?"

All this was so different from the apartment he would return to at the end of a workday before Marianka arrived.

A radiator worked in the living room, and when he opened the door he entered lit and heated rooms, and for the first time in a while he had someone to talk to. So why was it that every time he stuck the key in the keyhole he was sure she wouldn't be there? And why, even though she was, did he act as if he were alone? Marianka suggested that they continue watching episodes of *The Bridge*, but the last thing he wanted to see were detectives who know everything. He washed the dishes, and when he heard her turn on the television in the living room he closed the kitchen door and made himself an extra sandwich. Afterward he went into the living room and sat down next to her, and a bit before he surrendered to the heat coming off the radiator and fell asleep on the couch, in his clothes, he did ask her how her day was at work, and she started to tell him, but his eyes were beginning to close.

Her question, "Do you remember that this weekend my parents are coming to visit us?" he could no longer hear.

5

That afternoon, while she was at work, Mali succeeded in
hiding her tension and functioned as always. She stayed at
the bank until six thirty, and on the way back went to her
parents' to pick up the girls. They had just eaten dinner and
her mother placed an extra plate on the table and served
her rice and bean soup. This was the dinner they ate in her
childhood, in the winter, when her father returned from
work, at five thirty or six, and perhaps because of it Mali
wanted to remain there. Perhaps it was also the pregnancy
that caused her to want someone to take care of her so she
could stop taking care of everyone for a moment. When
she left the apartment at noon it was in disarray and Kobi
was wandering around the living room looking for his umbrella, and she would have to straighten all that up when
they got back.

Her mother, like always, didn't notice. She talked
about her winter migraines and the water stain the rain
made on the ceiling. Only her father looked at Mali while
she ate. From time to time he placed his hand on Daniella's

light hair, and when she finished eating he helped her wipe her mouth with a napkin. And even though Mali asked her mother to do homework with Noy, she discovered that the books hadn't been opened and that Noy hadn't prepared for a math test, and this of all things caused her to feel that she was losing control and that her family was disintegrating.

Kobi hadn't called since she left him in the apartment. And Mali hadn't stopped thinking about the conversation with Harry and about Kobi's plan to leave her with the girls and travel to Australia. Would something have changed if she had dared to speak to her father that evening? But what could she have said in front of the girls? That this time the collapse is too frightening? That Kobi is falling and that they're falling together with him?

Afterward, in the apartment, she found a letter on the dining room table, written on the back of an electric bill envelope. And even though it was two lines long and didn't say much it gave rise to a bit of hope in her, because in it Kobi finally spoke. *I'll be back in the morning. Sorry about everything. Tomorrow I'll explain to you what happened.*

The apartment wasn't in disarray as she thought it would be when they returned to it, and Mali saw that Kobi tried straightening it up, especially the girls' rooms. But Daniella, who never missed a thing, asked her, "Why did someone make a mess for me?" And Mali said, "I tried to arrange the closets but I wasn't able to finish before work." In their bedroom there were clothes and bedding scattered on the floor, but her clothes, which Kobi had removed from the closet, had been placed on the bed as if he had started to fold them and then gave up. The umbrella that she'd bought wasn't discarded on the floor in the living room. He stood it up next to their bed as if he wanted Mali to see. Their luggage was in its place in the utility room on the roof, and when she saw it she was almost certain that Kobi hadn't started packing for a trip when she surprised him around noon.

She tried to get Daniella to bed without a shower but it took her time to fall asleep, and while Mali sat on her bed and caressed her thin arm they talked about Purim, and this conversation Mali wouldn't ever forget. Daniella asked if she had to dress up and Mali said that she didn't and then asked, "But why don't you want to? Because we didn't buy you a new costume? All your friends at day care will be dressing up," and Daniella turned over in her bed and said to her, "Not because of that. Because I'm scared," and a few days later, when Mali recalled her answer, it gave her the chills. That evening, of all times, no calming sounds came from outside: not the neighbors' conversations and not the distant noise of buses running on the boulevard. Mali tried to smile when she asked, "Of what, my sweetie? Of costumes?" And Daniella was silent and after some time said, "Of princesses, mom."

Afterward Mali helped Noy with her homework in the living room, despite the late hour, and the math exercises relieved her because they caused her to think about other things. Maybe they weren't yet disintegrating? Was that just another temporary fall? They'd had difficult periods since Eilat, and actually there were some like that even before then. They never spoke about a separation, but two years ago Mali did suggest to Kobi that they go to therapy, only this wasn't a practical suggestion because there were things the two of them couldn't say.

When Noy asked to go to sleep, Mali ceased trying to extend the evening. She brought her to bed and when Noy asked her "Where's Dad?" she said that he'd return in a bit because she was certain of this, despite the letter that he left. And until around midnight she was still hoping. She continued straightening up the house and tried Kobi one time on his phone and then went up to the roof as if there was a chance that he was hiding from her there. Harry lay in the utility room and next to him was a small puddle of vomit, and she filled the bowl with water and opened the door for him in order to air it out, but he didn't want to leave.

Only at midnight did she remove the key from the key-hole before changing clothes in the lit bedroom.

This was a basic rule that Kobi was forbidden to break: it didn't matter what was happening between them, he wouldn't let her sleep alone. She lay in bed and tried thinking about the conversation with Daniella and about the pregnancy that she still hadn't told anyone about, just not about the heavy hand. The fear was with her in the room despite the illuminated lights and the phone. She felt it there and didn't close her eyes. She opened a window despite the cold wind, but the street was still silent and the fear didn't leave. And her mistake was that she wanted to call Gila, because when she looked at the clock she saw that the time was almost one thirty. *The same time.* And then Mali could no longer control the fear, and it returned and placed its hand on her throat.

That was her first trip alone since the girls were born, and she wasn't sure she wanted to go. Kobi encouraged her, because all branch managers were supposed to participate and on Thursday and Friday morning professional development sessions were being held for mortgage advisers and there'd even be an informal discussion with the board members. An opportunity not to be missed, he said. And he and the girls would have a good time at home.

On Thursday morning she and her coworkers took off from Tel Aviv airfield and before ten got their rooms at the Royal Club Hotel on the beach. She was lucky because she got room 723, with a balcony looking out on the sea.

The first day was long and ended with a dinner in the hotel's dining room, after which she went out with her close friend Aviva and a few friends from other branches to a pub on the beach called Zorro. After this, when she was asked about it, she didn't remember if there was a man at the pub who was staring at her. During the lectures that day and also the next morning she sat in one of the last rows in the conference hall, next to Eran Amrami from the Jerusalem branch, who worked with her at the Holon branch until two years ago. At the end of the second day, before Shabbat began, a celebratory meal was held in the events hall. Prizes were awarded to the outstanding employees, and speeches were given by board members. Those who kept Shabbat went up to their rooms, and everyone else continued to the dance party in the hotel's discotheque, which was open to outside visitors. They received vouchers for drinks at the bar, and Mali drank two glasses of white wine. When she was asked at the police station if she felt that someone was looking at her during the party, she didn't know what to answer. Most of the people at the discotheque were bank employees, some of whom she knew well and some of whom almost not at all, but there were others as well, tourists perhaps, though on that weekend at the beginning of March the hotel was not at full capacity. And there were also waiters and maids and janitors, men and women, but she didn't remember anyone in particular, and everyone was interrogated. During the police investigation it became clear that a Swiss tourist, a forty-three-year-old man, was staying at the hotel, who left suddenly in the early hours of the morning, and the police asked her to look at the pictures of him that were taken from security videos, but she couldn't say if that was him because the cameras were old and the pictures blurry. There were no cameras in the hotel hallways, in order to maintain the guests' privacy, but the lobby and parking lot were under camera surveillance, and Mali spent hours looking at tapes, with no results. At the entrance to the hotel there was of course a security guard, but because the restaurants and the discotheque were open to visitors it was impossible to truly know who was coming and going, but based on text messages, and also from Aviva's testimony, Mali went up to her room before one in the morning.

Was he already in the room? Did he enter it when she was at the discotheque and lied in wait for her in the bathroom? Or maybe on the small balcony, hiding behind the heavy purple curtain? She didn't check if the door to the balcony was locked before she lay down to sleep, and the female detective from the Eilat police who gathered her testimony thought that this was because she was drunk, but back then she simply wasn't a person who checked if doors were locked.

Perhaps you said to someone something inviting that you didn't intend to say? You met someone at the club and it may be that you don't remember? How can you be sure that you went up to the room alone or that you didn't arrange with someone to meet him in the room if you drank?

But she wasn't drunk, not to the point of forgetting, and this was evident from the text messages that she sent to Kobi before laying down to sleep: *I wasn't outstanding this year. No employee-of-the-year award and no bonus. Are you already sleeping?* Kobi sent her a message immediately: *There's no such thing, to me you're always outstanding. We miss you. I'm watching a movie in bed.* She turned on the television in order to see what he was watching.

Did you go to the bathroom before you fell asleep? And you didn't wash your face? You went to bed without removing your makeup? The policewoman asked her so many questions. And the next day there were indeed remnants of makeup on her face.

On the television an episode of *Friends* was being

broadcast that she'd seen countless times, and she watched it as she got into bed, in warm pajama pants and a long-sleeve shirt and not in the clothes that she wore to the party. And a short time after this she fell asleep, apparently, because the next thing she remembered was the hand.

It came from out of the darkness and crushed her throat.

Did she wake up a moment before she felt the weight of his hand on her neck and then the second hand on her mouth, only because it cut the air off, or because of its smell? The smell she remembered. A smell of beer and a smell of a body she didn't know and a smell of sweaty cotton and a smell of soap. Mali recounted it to the detective, but she lost her patience and said that the smell wouldn't help, that they needed a description of his facial features or physical build, but she couldn't supply the detective with this due to the dark and because the assailant wore a ski mask over his face. He wore jeans, of this Mali was certain, and it seemed to her that his left shoulder was lower, or drooping, as if he had a curvature in his back. Through his weight she felt that he was thin and narrow.

The other questions they asked her Mali didn't understand, either. Not the questions about her family and about her relationship with Kobi and why he wasn't with her in the hotel, and not the question about whether the rapist was violent. At the hospital they clearly saw signs of the ties around her elbows and ankles, and there was also the small cut he made on her neck, at the beginning, with a knife that seemed to her to have been a regular knife, for cutting vegetables, maybe not in order to truly injure her but rather so she'd understand that she was in life-threatening danger. When the policewoman insisted on asking again if he was violent throughout the time of the rape, Mali didn't know what to say to her. He didn't remove the knife from her neck for even a second, but there were moments in which he wasn't violent, or at least not only violent, perhaps mainly the moments in which she closed her eyes. The time at which everything occurred was known as well because right at the beginning she heard another ding from her cell phone, another text, which she only afterward saw was sent by Kobi: *The movie's over. Are you asleep?*

It was sent at 1:44 and she remembered that immediately after she heard the ding she again tried to plea with the assailant that he stop, but she didn't succeed because of the cloth that he wrapped around her mouth, but nevertheless she didn't stop trying to say to him, "Stop. Please stop. I'm begging you. I have two little girls. I have two little girls. I have two little girls."

Was he able to understand her at all? For some reason she thought about her father and Gila and especially about the girls, not about Kobi. "I have two little girls" was a sentence she grasped on to like a drowning person to a life preserver. She imagined her father looking at her and imagined herself running quickly when everything was over, running like she once ran, in high school, for miles without stopping. And there was also a moment when she did see Kobi in the room, and he was smiling at her as if he were trying to calm her. But when she wanted to call to him for help, he disappeared.

In the end the assailant removed the ropes that he had tied around her hands and legs as well as the scarf that covered her mouth. He again placed his hand over her mouth as he said to her through the ski mask, in English, "I'm coming back. If you try to scream I'll murder you," and she heard him enter the bathroom and the faucet coming on. She couldn't see a thing from the bed because the door to the bathroom was in the hallway, right next to the entrance to the room, and because of the darkness. So she waited. The television was still on, because she remembered that she heard a commercial. The policewoman didn't understand why Mali didn't scream at that moment or flee from the room, and Mali tried to explain to her that she didn't know he was no longer there. She didn't hear the door to the room closing because of the television and the running water, and only after a long time, perhaps an hour, did she dare to get up.

The bathroom was empty, and the faucet was on.

Her impulse was to call Kobi. Her phone was still next to the bed. But she first took off her pajamas and put on the clothes she wore that evening and went out into the illuminated hallway, and unlike what she thought, she didn't run but instead walked slowly along the length of the hallway and went down a floor in the elevator, where she saw for the first time in the mirror her face and the cut bleeding on her neck.

It wasn't her.

And the time was almost three when she knocked on Aviva's door, room 606.

The next morning Kobi was already there and she remembered him standing in the doorway at the hospital. She didn't cry even one time before she saw him, but when he hugged her, without saying a word, the crying burst forth, wild and uncontrollable, and Kobi held her in his arms until the policewoman and doctor entered the room and asked him to leave. He refused and demanded to stay with her even when the policewoman insisted, and only when Mali asked him to go did he agree.

Mali got up from her bed because it was clear she wouldn't be able to fall asleep. And walking relaxed her somehow. Her hands and legs weren't tied together. And the living room was lit. She peeked through the blinds at the street with no traffic. Only parked cars. The cell phone was clenched in her fist. Suddenly she thought about his car. She hadn't seen it since yesterday, and where could Kobi have gone without it? Her anger at Kobi came and went, but it was mixed up with a desire for him to return so that she wouldn't be alone. She checked that the door was locked before entering the girls' rooms. The windows in their rooms were shuttered, and from the stairwell, too, only silence came.

Would it have been different if her attacker had been caught? During the first weeks, Mali didn't want to know a thing about the investigation. She didn't recognize herself, like during that first instant facing the mirror in the elevator. She didn't understand who the woman was who couldn't overcome the panic attacks that froze her in unexpected moments or couldn't choke back the uncontrollable outbursts of crying. And in moments of silence she thought only about the girls, about what they were seeing.

Kobi was wonderful then, better even than she could have imagined. She was still on leave and they were eating lunch together at home when he informed her that he quit his work. It wasn't a perfect job; he never thought before this that he would be a security guard at clubs and construction sites, but the pay was reasonable and the work in shifts left him two and sometimes three open mornings a week on which he could continue looking for another job, or maybe even return to school. When she asked him not to rush to leave, he revealed to her that he had demanded not to do any more evening shifts but that the man in charge of his region wasn't willing to hear it. They fell into a fight that almost ended in blows, and in the end Kobi quit. He didn't tell the man responsible for the area why he didn't want to do evening shifts, of course, because he didn't tell anyone what had happened to her in Eilat. Not even friends. And certainly not the girls. Mali didn't know what to tell them when she returned from Eilat, but Kobi was adamant that they couldn't tell them a thing, and in the end they said that Mommy was sick with the flu and needed to rest, and Daniella and Noy stayed another two days with her parents. She still didn't feel that she was back to herself when they returned home, and in the first weeks she had crying and panic attacks that she couldn't control and hated herself for this, and Kobi took the care of them entirely onto himself. And despite her efforts to hide it, it seemed to Mali that Daniella, who was less than three then, actually felt something. She stopped crying, as if she had matured all at once, and also cuddled with Mali much more and invented the affection game that the two of them had played since: Mali lies on the sofa in the living room, mainly in the afternoon, and Daniella strokes her hair for a long time, speaks in a whisper, and sings lullabies to her as if her mother were the baby daughter, and Mali pretends to be asleep.

At the bank they knew everything, because of the circumstances of the assault and the extended leave she received, but no one spoke to her about this, other than Aviva. And Mali never spoke to her parents about what happened, either; she could only speak about it with Gila. Contact with the Eilat police dwindled, and every time Kobi called them in order to find out if there was anything new, they told him that the investigation was ongoing. Only in May, two months after the rape, did she think for the first time that the assailant was still free, and this sent her trembling. So they began sleeping with the lights on and locking the door even when they were home. In July she was urgently called to Eilat in order to participate in a lineup, even though she repeated to them that she hadn't seen the attacker's face, and among the black men who were placed before her at the station she didn't see any with a drooping left shoulder. Because he spoke in English, the police were certain that the assailant was a foreign worker or an illegal refugee or perhaps the Swiss tourist, but she thought that the English could have also been a deceptive move and the detective agreed that this was a possibility. They tried calming her, telling her that her room in the hotel was chosen randomly because there was easy access to its balcony from the emergency staircase, and that fingerprints as well as two cigarette butts were found on it, the assailant apparently remained there during the time he was waiting. And only a year and a half after the rape did a different detective from the Eilat police call her and admit that the investigation was stuck. Then they were inclined to think that the assailant was the Swiss tourist and they managed to locate the cabdriver who took him from Eilat to Ben Gurion Airport, and the driver said that the passenger didn't utter a word during the four-hour trip. But the man was questioned by the Swiss police and denied any ties to the attack and said that he returned to Switzerland because he received a message that his mother was sick, and the Swiss police believed him and refused to continue investigating. The pictures of the Swiss man that the detective sent her through e-mail in order for her to look at them another time didn't help: he wore jeans in them, but his face could barely be seen and the deformity in his body wasn't detectable. Most terrible of all was that a year and a half later she was no longer certain that she remembered things well, not the clothes he wore that evening, and not even his smell, which she thought would never dissipate. Only the face of the woman she saw in the mirror remained.

She saw it in the mirror almost every morning.

Despite this, in her thoughts, over the course of a few weeks, it was the Swiss tourist who had followed her that evening, at the party in the hotel and perhaps even before then. She was unable to free herself from him, as if even having freed her hands and legs from the ropes and having removed the scarf from her mouth, she was still there, bound hand and foot to the same bed. When she joined a meeting of a support group for rape victims, at the advice of the police, jealousy was awakened in her over the fact the other women knew who had attacked them, so she didn't go there anymore. No one cast doubt as to whether she had been raped, but the fact that the rapist had never been found and took with him the ropes and the scarf, made it as if the rape, even in her eyes, was less real, and on the other hand prolonged it endlessly. So she, too, stopped searching for the Swiss tourist and began searching for the attacker among the bank employees and among the clients who arrived for meetings and among the men who sat next to her at the café or looked at her from their cars at a traffic light. And only during the last year did it seem to her that the ropes around her hands and feet were no longer so tight. And when she looked in the mirror she sometimes saw in it again something from what had once been her face.

Mali succeeded in falling asleep that night only in Daniella's room, on the pullout bed.

She went into her room after covering up Noy and sat down on the bed that Daniella opens in order to lay her dolls on it, and Daniella turned to her in her sleep, reached her hand out to her hair, and a short time after this Mali fell asleep. Her sleep was deep, apparently, because she didn't hear the key turning in the lock nor the door opening, and she woke up only when she felt Kobi next to her.

He sat on the bed and looked at her. She asked him, "What are you doing here?" as if this was no longer his home, and he said, "I just returned."

"Where were you?"

He didn't give her an answer to this question, not that night and in fact not afterward, either. They left the room so that Daniella wouldn't wake up, and sat facing each other on the living room sofa. She said to him, "You left me alone all night. How could you do that to me?" From outside came a faint morning light, and a garbage truck was at work in the street. On Kobi's clothes was the smell of alcohol and cigarette smoke, and his eyes were red. She asked him, "What happened to you?" and when Kobi said, "Mali, I need help," she responded immediately, "Help with what? Help going to Australia? Do you need money for a plane ticket?"

Kobi didn't understand what she was talking about, and when she said to him, "I spoke to your dad this morning," he fell silent.

"What happened to you?" she said, "tell me what happened already. Don't you see you're torturing me? I can't live like this any longer, Kobi. I didn't do anything to you, right? I didn't do anything to you."

He looked to her lost and hopeless. But what he told

her she couldn't have anticipated. And even in retrospect she thought that there was no way to know that he was lying. He said, "Mali, the police are looking for me," and she looked at his red eyes.

Actually the collapse was much greater than she had thought.

6

The news from the forensics lab arrived at the beginning of the second day of the investigation, when Avraham was on his way to the funeral. Rain wasn't falling and the car window was open, and when the telephone rang Avraham closed it and lowered the volume on the radio. "Do you want the good news first or the bad news first?" Lital Levy asked him and he answered, "You've known me long enough, no?"

The good news was that from the traces of skin and blood that were found under Leah Yeger's nails and between her fingers they succeeded in producing a man's DNA. The bad news was the DNA produced wasn't located in the database, nor did it belong to a relative of the rapist David Danon. He immediately asked her about Leah Yeger's son, because from the moment he opened his eyes in the morning he thought about the testimony the son gave to Shrapstein at the station yesterday. "Did they check if it could belong to a relative of hers?" he asked and she said to him, "Of whose? Do you mean of the victim?

Don't think they checked. But they certainly could check.
You want me to ask?"

It was usually like that, as Ilana always said: the second day
of the investigation is the key day.

On the first day every angle is possible and every testimony or finding that is added to the case can become the
start of a new investigatory lead. On the second day the
possibilities dwindle because a few suspects have already
been cleared and angles of investigation that appeared
reasonable the day before are ruled out, and on the other
hand, new testimony and findings merge with stories that
have already started developing, filling them in with details and granting them force.

On the same morning, while Avraham was on his way
to the cemetery, Commander Eyal Shrapstein was busy
gathering testimony from foremen who worked on the
street, overseeing renovations, and later on he stopped by
to question one of the workers, a resident of an Arab village
in the north by the name of Adnan Gon, who was absent
from work on the day of the murder and the next day as
well, and had been questioned in the past on suspicion of
vehicular theft and aiding with the break-ins of homes.
Ma'alul and Esty Vahaba called to the station the private
investigator whom the Danon family had hired in order
to gather incriminating evidence against Leah Yeger. And
Avraham was the only official representative of the Israeli
police at the funeral and for the most part kept his eyes on
her son. He arrived early and waited among those gath-

ered in the courtyard of the funeral home, at the salvation
gate. The morning was warmer than the previous mornings, almost springlike. Avraham squeezed the daughter's
hands when he saw her and told her he was sorry for her
loss, but he didn't approach the son and watched him from
a distance while he greeted the mourners. His wife and
grown children stood next to him. What surprised Avraham when he understood that he had identified her son
were his proportions, which Shrapstein hadn't described
in the interrogation report.

Erez Yeger was a broad, tall man, over six feet two,
and his hands were gigantic.

A little after ten the burial society workers rolled the
corpse on a stretcher to the funeral yard, and the small
crowd gathered around it in a silent circle. Under the
sheets the body looked so small to Avraham, as if it were
the body of a small child. He was surprised when Leah
Yeger's children chose not to speak in her memory, and
only an older woman, a friend apparently, spoke at length
about the lovely years of her life, the years of raising the
children and the shared trips abroad, before the suffering
she knew in recent years. "Now you're going to Yossi, who
you loved so," she said at the end of her speech, "and at
least you'll no longer have to miss him."

The friend didn't mention in her speech that Yeger had
been murdered, as if she had died under natural circumstances. Nor was the rape mentioned except by implica-
tion, when she spoke about "the bad years." Nevertheless
it seemed to Avraham that all around him things were
being whispered about the murder, and that the funeral

mourners were staring at him. And for some reason, the police photographer who was asked to document the crowd of mourners, mainly photographed Avraham.

Afterward the short procession marched behind the stretcher through the paths of old and new graves to the burial pit. In the distance Chinese workers were crawling inside giant beehives that were being erected to house the dead who were yet to come. And it grew hotter and hotter.

Because there were few men in the crowd, Avraham, too, grabbed a shovel and helped to cover the hole into which Leah Yeger had been lowered. And when the rabbi began saying the prayer of the orphans for the dead, the kaddish, he found himself mumbling the opening sentences together with him, *Yitgadal veyitkadash shemei raba, bealmah divrah chirutei*, and then he suddenly bit his lips and stopped because he was not an orphan.

After the body was interred, Leah Yeger's son fell on her grave, and Avraham waited until his wife and other mourners lifted him up and carried him to a nearby water fountain and rinsed his face, before he himself placed a stone on the narrow mound of dirt. Among the people who helped lay her to rest Avraham was the only one who knew almost nothing about her, and despite this he was supposed to try and understand the circumstances of her death, and he attempted to recall her face as he saw it in the picture that hung in the investigations room, and not the beaten face with the gaping mouth that he saw at the scene.

The gap between the testimony of Leah Yeger's son during questioning, when he said he wasn't in contact with his mother, and his behavior at the cemetery, bothered him. And when the son bent down and collapsed on the mound of dirt, almost in the position in which Avraham found his mother in her apartment, he suddenly thought how much he didn't look like his mother. Perhaps he looked like his father?

Leah Yeger, daughter of Hannah and Yaakov Greenberg, was buried next to her husband, Joseph Yeger, who was born in 1951 and died three years earlier, before his time. Avraham couldn't manage to remember if he had seen his photograph in her apartment.

Leah Yeger's phone log was waiting for Avraham in his office when he arrived, with the information that the assailant's DNA indicated that there were no family ties between him and the victim. On the list there were no calls from Ami Danon or from other numbers delivered by the rapist's relatives, but two of them in particular shocked him. The day before the murder a lengthy telephone call took place between Leah Yeger and her son, in contradiction to what the son said to Shrapstein in his testimony. According to the log, Yeger called her son during the morning hours, and he didn't answer. A brief time after this the son called her and their conversation lasted approximately seventeen minutes. The second number was the last one on the list and it shocked Avraham even more: on the day that the murder took place and exactly during the presumed time of the murder, two o'clock, a call was carried out from the telephone line in Leah Yeger's apartment to the police.

The attempt to call was made from the apartment's land-line, but the call was disconnected before it was answered.

Avraham circled the son's telephone number with a blue pen, and immediately dialed the call center in order to clarify how they deal with calls that are disconnected before they are answered. "Do you call back if the call is disconnected?" he asked the operator, but she didn't understand his question. "The number shows up for you on some sort of screen, no? Can you see which number called?" he asked again, and the operator explained that she at least doesn't return calls that are disconnected unless an attempt is made again a few times. "Do you know how many kids call and hang up?" she asked. But someone did get back to Leah Yeger, even though a no-tation of the additional call didn't appear in the log, be-cause a policeman was apparently sent to her house. He asked Lital Levy to check if there wasn't an additional call that was mistakenly dropped from the list and who were the operators at the call center in the afternoon the day before yesterday. He debated whether at that moment to call Erez Yeger in for additional questioning. According to the DNA he wasn't the man who attacked his mother, so why did he lie to Shrapstein in his testimony and say that he hadn't spoken with her for a few months?

When Eliyahu Ma'alul entered his room Avraham was still busy with just those two phone calls. Their con-versation yesterday had been forgotten, at least by Avra-ham, but Eliyahu remained standing while informing him about the testimony of the private investigator hired by the Danon family. He said it was hard for him to believe that the investigator was involved in the murder or knew anything about it. According to him, the family employed him only during the trial, and he swore to Ma'alul that he didn't tap Yeger's phone nor illegally obtain any document or evidence. "So what did he do? What exactly did they pay him for?" Avraham asked, and Ma'alul said, "Mainly he followed her. And photographed her. But nothing came of it. They hoped to get evidence that she was meeting with men and to base their line of defense on the fact that according to this the sexual relations were consensual. And he hasn't been in contact with anyone from the family since the end of the trial."

Avraham told Ma'alul about the findings sent from the lab in Jerusalem and Leah Yeger and her son's phone call, which Erez Yeger hid from Shrapstein in his testimony, and Ma'alul thought that they needed to call the son to the station immediately, despite the funeral, and asked Avraham if in Shrapstein's eyes the son was a suspect in the murder, but Avraham didn't know. He didn't tell him in his office about the phone call that was carried out from the apartment to the call center but instead waited until they left the building and sat down on the stairs leading to the station.

"I thought you quit smoking," Ma'alul said to him and still didn't look him in the eyes as he always had, and when Avraham said, "I really did quit," Ma'alul asked, "So why are we here?"

The reason was Benny Saban and the policeman who went down the stairs and disappeared.

Avraham told Ma'alul about the conversation with

Saban and his request that he not concentrate on the neighbor's testimony about the policeman who was in the building a short time after the murder. Now, when in the list of Leah Yeger's calls there appeared an attempt to call the police, it was no longer possible to ignore it.

Ma'alul's large eyes opened wide while he listened to him. And when Avraham finished speaking he told him in a whisper, "Don't you even dare think about that, Avi. I won't let you, do you hear? What, are you crazy? We'll investigate that testimony like all the other testimony. And definitely now. They got back to her from the call center and someone was sent there and didn't do what had to be done, we'll report that exactly like we're supposed to. And if you're scared of Saban, let me—I'll take that on myself, okay? It'll be on me. I can't believe you're even considering this. And Benny Saban can go to hell."

The conversation with Ma'alul encouraged Avraham because he felt that Ma'alul had forgiven him over the insult of his reprimand, but when he returned to his room he nevertheless picked up the phone receiver in order to call Ilana Lis. But then had second thoughts and hung up. Shrapstein called in order to update him on the testimony of the workers at the construction sites near the scene, and Avraham told him that Erez Yeger lied to him during questioning. Only while they talked did Avraham understand that if the son was involved in the murder then it was possible to understand the disconnected call to the police as well: had he injured his mother during an argument and then got frightened, dialed the police immediately himself and then changed his mind and fled? Maybe even *she* called when it seemed to her that the argument between them was liable to deteriorate into violence, but hung up in order not to put her son at risk? On the other hand, there were unambiguous findings from the lab that determined Erez Yeger could not have been the assailant.

Avraham spread out on the table the pictures taken at the scene as well as the paper he wrote on there, and read the sentence he wrote down in pen while gathering testimony from Leah Yeger's daughter: *He locked the door behind him?*

Why in fact did he write it? Perhaps because he thought that locking the door indicated that the murderer didn't flee from the apartment in a panic. He stuck around there. For a few minutes even. Tried to revive his mother and digest what had occurred. Had he called the police with the intention of turning himself in? But hung up when it occurred to him that he could disguise the murder as a burglary? He knew where her wallet was, and that's why the scene was so orderly. He didn't have to search. He locked the door behind him, because each delay in finding the body would enable him to get farther away from the place. Avraham read the question he had written again and again and then added additional questions next to it, to some of which it seemed to him there were now answers:

Why did she open the door for the assailant?

Was she waiting for him? Did she know he was coming?

Why didn't he take anything other than the wallet?
Exactly when and how did he leave?

Exactly as he had done in the hours after the murder,
he imagined Leah Yeger drinking coffee in the kitchen
when the knocking came from the door. Then she sets
down the mug and gets up from her place. She walked
slowly in the direction of the door, a distance of five or six
steps, and Avraham opened the desk drawer and removed
the pipe that Marianka bought him and chewed the end
of the mouthpiece. The door to Leah Yeger's apartment
opened in his imagination, and he thought that he was
able to see the man of large proportions who stood on the
other side.

He called him immediately, but the phone was answered by a woman. She said that her husband was out
driving, and when Avraham identified himself she added,
"Just a moment," and a short time later the voice of Erez
Yeger could be heard. Avraham asked him to come to the
station immediately, and when the son asked him why, he
merely said, "For further questioning."

"We're already in Haifa. It's urgent now? People are
coming to our house to pay condolence calls."

He wanted to see him at that moment and to gather
testimony himself, but perhaps there was logic in postponing the interrogation. He didn't know almost anything
about the son other than that he was a superintendent of
a high school, and postponing the interrogation for a few
hours would enable him to gather additional details and
verify his alibi and perhaps even clarify with Erez Yeger's
sister what the reason was for the dispute between her

mother and her brother. "Can you arrive first thing to-morrow morning?" Avraham asked, and when Erez Yeger said, "Yes, but can you tell me what's so pressing? Are there developments in the case?" he didn't answer.

The cafeteria was almost entirely empty when Avraham ate a late lunch there, alone. Only Efrayim Bachar, from the traffic division, sat at the other end of the large room and spoke out loud on the phone with his daughter, while chewing on toothpicks, and signaled hello to Avraham with his head.

Avraham ordered a salad and two sandwiches for him-self and ate quickly, and in his head the thoughts about the son and the phone call to the police mixed together. If he was feeling more energetic, for the first time since the investigation was opened, this was because he was no longer waiting in his office. Again he thought about Benny Saban. During his years in the police he more than once saw policemen turn a blind eye on testimony or findings, but never before this had he been explicitly asked to ignore testimony. And in these moments it seemed to Avraham that the neighbor's testimony was telling a story that was simply impossible to deny: a policeman who tried to con-ceal his identity arrived at Leah Yeger's apartment a few minutes after two, even though according to the register no patrol was sent to the building before four thirty. He was determined to report the conversation to Ilana, even though she wasn't on active duty.

On his way back to his office Avraham stopped in front

of Lital Levy's desk in order to ask if there was anything new. She said no, and then looked at her desk and handed him a sheet of paper. "I forgot to give you this before. A list of people who were looking for you two days ago, when you were off," she said, and he asked, "When was I off?" before he remembered. He glanced at the paper on the way to the office and meant to put it on a stack of files that were on the desk when he saw the name Diana Goldin and next to it a telephone number. He returned to Lital Levy in order to confirm that he read the name correctly.

"Do you know who took the call?" he asked, and Lital Levy said, "I did."

"And did she tell you why she called?"

"She asked to speak with you and when I told her you were off she said it wasn't important. Do you know who she is?"

He called the phone number that appeared on the paper but didn't get an answer and left Diana Goldin a message. Ilana Lis, on the other hand, answered him and his voice shook when he said to her, "Hi, Ilana, how are you? It's Avi."

She recognized his voice and he thought that she was happy to hear him, despite her requests. After all, for years, even when she left the station and transferred to Tel Aviv district headquarters, they spoke on the phone almost every day and updated each other on their investigations. He didn't think Ilana could disconnect from police work after twenty years in investigation departments. He didn't know if she was at her home or in the hospital, but he was too embarrassed to ask. Before she started with the treatments he did some checking on the Internet and to his delight discovered that she wouldn't be hospitalized for long weeks but rather just for a series of intensive treatments, between which she could recover at home. When he asked her again, "How are you?" since she hadn't answered him, she only said, "Couldn't be better, Avi. And you?" And he got down to business in order to cover up his embarrassment. "I need your help with something," he said. "May I visit you when you're home and feeling okay?"

"It can't wait?" Ilana asked, and he said, "It can wait a few days. But no more."

"On the condition that we don't talk about any cases, as I asked. If it's something like that then let's take a pass."

"It's not exactly that, Ilana. It's something else," he said, and didn't lie, because then he did think that they'd speak only about Saban's request.

Diana Goldin tried to call him back while he spoke with Ilana, and when the conversation ended, his phone rang again. He was unable to imagine why she was looking for him, and even when she explained, it took him time to understand. He said to her, "Diana? Thanks for getting back to me. Police Superintendent Avraham. I was on a day off and saw that you were looking for me, correct?"

Diana said that it wasn't anything important. She wanted to return to a policeman who had been at her place a few days earlier the umbrella he had forgotten, and because she didn't remember his name and didn't have his phone number, she called the station and asked to speak with Avraham. When he asked her, "When was the officer with you?" she said a few days ago. Last Thursday. "And in regards to what matter was he with you? Did you call for him?" Avraham asked and didn't expect that his question would frighten her.

"What do you mean what matter?" she asked quietly. "In regards to the rape. What other matter could it be?"

He didn't want to worry her more than he already had and so he said he'd get back to her in a few minutes. He asked Lital Levy to find out who was the policeman sent to her home. The idea that there was a connection between the two incidents, between the two policemen, occurred to him only when Diana Goldin's rape file was brought to his room and he studied it, but even then, when the idea expressed itself for the first time for an instant, he dismissed it immediately. There was a different killer in his thoughts during those hours, and there was a simple explanation for the policeman who was observed at the crime scene. And only when he sat across from Diana Goldin and gathered her testimony did he sense that perhaps he was mistaken when he hurried to rule the connection out.

He rose from his seat and welcomed Diana Goldin warmly when she entered his office an hour later. Her hair was gathered in a ponytail and her face was small and beautiful as he remembered. There was anxiety in her gaze, and he thought that perhaps he shouldn't have insisted that she come to the station immediately. But Lital Levy told him that according to her checking, no police officer was sent to Diana Goldin's home in recent days and Avraham didn't want to wait. When he studied the rape file before Diana arrived, he couldn't help but think about Leah Yeger.

Diana Goldin was assaulted in September 2012.

She was raped in her apartment by an actor who was then her partner at a small theater that put on plays for children. She was thirty-two years old and resided in Bat Yam, and Avraham was the detective who investigated the rapist, over many hours. He was also present for the confrontation between them in the interrogation room on the second floor, when the actor continued to deny what Diana said. She turned to the police a few weeks after the attack, and therefore they didn't have good physical evidence, but Avraham believed her—and so did the court.

He asked Diana, "How are you?" and when she immediately said, "Can you explain what happened?" he didn't answer. He hoped that he'd calm her when he asked if she still performed in plays, and she told him that she had established a new theater company for children's plays in Hebrew and Russian and that she performed in them by herself, or with her dolls, mainly at daycare centers and libraries. About Michael Lan, the actor convicted of her assault, she didn't know a thing other than that he was still serving his sentence. Avraham still hadn't decided what exactly he would say to her, but Diana asked immediately, "What, he wasn't a cop?" and he asked her, "Do you remember when he was there?"

"Almost a week ago. Two days ago I noticed that he forgot the umbrella at my place and then I called you because I didn't have his phone number. He was there last Thursday."

"And can you explain to me why he came to visit you?"

He called her a few days before then, she said. Introduced himself as a detective in the investigations department of the Ayalon district and asked to set up a meeting. They agreed to meet on Thursday morning because she had a performance in the evening, and he said that he'd call the day before their meeting in order to confirm that it would take place and that he hadn't been forced to cancel because of other urgent matters. He suggested they meet at the station, but said that he could also come to her home so that she wouldn't have to visit a place that she definitely has unpleasant memories of, and she agreed because it was more convenient.

"He didn't explain why you needed to meet?" Avraham asked, and Diana said, "Of course he did. Otherwise I wouldn't have met with him." According to what the policeman said, Michael Lan had appealed his conviction, and prior to it being tried in court, where she would probably be asked to testify, he had been appointed to again gather detailed testimony from her.

When Avraham looked at Diana he recalled that the thing that had surprised him when he first met her was that despite the assault there was something smiling in her face, almost clownish, as if even when she wasn't standing on a stage in front of children she remained a performer. But now she wasn't smiling. According to the inquiry Lital Levy made with the Tel Aviv district attorney's office, Michael Lan had not appealed. And the main detail that Avraham tried to understand from Diana's story was if the policeman sent to her knew the name and details of the rapist.

"That's what he called him from the beginning, Michael?" he asked, but Diana didn't remember. Then she added, "Maybe not, I don't think so. Maybe he called him the rapist at the beginning."

"And he knew your address?"

"He asked if the address had changed and I said no. The second time he called, a day before the meeting, on Wednesday, he asked if the address was the same address, and I think I gave it to him."

She said the last sentence quietly. Avraham poured her a cup of water, and she asked him, "Why aren't you saying that he wasn't from the police?" And Avraham answered, "Because I don't know. It's reasonable to assume that he was from the police, but I'm trying to clarify on behalf of whom he was sent."

Diana covered her face in her hands. When she removed them she said, "But what does that mean? Explain to me who he is," and Avraham continued trying to calm her. "As I told you, I don't know," he said. "The police is a large organization with many departments and divisions, and one doesn't always know what the other one is doing. This happens a lot, I can assure you. It very well could be that he was a policeman who was sent to you to complete an investigation, but for now we haven't managed to find out on whose behalf. Can you describe him to me? What did he look like? That could help."

The policeman was around Avraham's height, perhaps a bit taller, stocky, and his hair was light. Diana called the uniform he wore "regular": dark pants and a light blue shirt, with a pin in the shape of the police logo and a dark lace around his shoulder. She didn't notice if he had a rank nor did she remember his name, maybe because he didn't tell it to her, and she suddenly thought that she hadn't even asked him his name, and again she covered up her face and folded in on herself.

"Why would someone do a thing like that?" she asked, and Avraham saw that she was suffering not only because she understood what had occurred, but also because she was angry at herself for not being more cautious, and so he again said to her, "Diana, I'll say to you once more that it could be that the man was a police officer on an assignment. Do you understand me? And even if he wasn't, you had no way of knowing that he wasn't sent by who he said he was," and she interrupted him and again said, "But I didn't even ask him his name, don't you get it?"

Avraham waited for her to reveal her face. What he didn't say to her throughout their entire conversation, other than that he already knew that her rapist Michael Lan hadn't appealed, was that if someone had been sent to her to complete the details of the investigation it would have been a policewoman—and not a policeman.

"Do you remember how much time he spent with you?" he asked, and Diana said that he stayed for a long time. Maybe two hours.

"Why?"

"Because he wanted to know everything. You understand? Every detail. From the beginning."

"What, for instance? What kind of questions did he ask you? Can you tell me exactly how the conversation proceeded?"

The policeman wanted to know how long she had known Michael Lan and what kind of ties there were between them before the assault. And if she had a partner at the time of the rape. And then he asked about what happened that day, when they returned from a performance at the city library. How she invited Michael into her apartment in order to talk about the next project and how they drank too much vodka and got a little drunk, and how Michael suddenly asked her to dance and she agreed for some reason, even though his request seemed strange to her, and how when she felt him up against her she asked him to stop and freed herself from his embrace and turned off the music. Michael had a girlfriend, whom Diana knew well and liked, and when he clung to her in order to continue dancing despite the silence, she grabbed the phone and told him that if he didn't stop she would call her. And he also asked her about the clothes she wore that evening and if Michael tore them or if she got undressed herself, and about what happened afterward on the couch in the living room and what she said to him during the assault and what Michael said to her when everything was over. And he recorded everything, from the first moment.

"What does that mean, recorded?"

"With his phone. He showed me that he was turning the app on."

"And while he was listening?"

"What about while he was listening?"

"What did he do?"

"Nothing," she said. "He looked at me. Sometimes he

checked if the device was working and also wrote in a notebook he had."

"Did you get the impression that he was familiar with the details of your case?"

"He asked me to tell everything as if I were telling it for the first time, so I don't know. Maybe not. He said that it's necessary for the investigation."

"And did he say anything about himself that you remember? Something about his station? About his exact position with the police?"

Diana was unable to recall.

"And at no point did he try to harm you?"

"By hitting me? No."

"You didn't feel threatened during the conversation?"

"Not at all."

"You were home alone while he was with you?"

"Who else would be there? I live alone."

"And you don't remember other details that could help us to identify him?"

"Other than what I told you? No. It might be that he spoke with an accent."

"A Russian accent?"

"Not Russian actually. English maybe."

"And did you feel that he was trying to get you to say something specific? That he was trying to force something out of you?"

Avraham had no other questions, but Diana didn't want their conversation to end, perhaps because she was suddenly scared to remain alone outside the station. The piece of paper with the questions that Avraham wrote at the start of the day was sitting on the table in his room—*Why did she open the door for the assailant? Was she waiting for him? Did she know he was coming?*—But suddenly he was no longer sure he knew the answers as he had previously thought. And despite this, at the brief meeting that was set for the investigation team toward evening, Avraham avoided mentioning the testimony he collected from Diana Goldin, because he wasn't yet convinced that the connection between the two incidents was anything but coincidental.

He walked Diana out of his room and asked Lital Levy to escort her to the Computer Unit so they could draw up a facial composite of the policeman, even if it turned out in a little while that there was no need. Before they said good-bye she asked him, "You don't want the umbrella?" and Avraham took it from her hand and looked at it. She held it on her knees throughout their entire conversation, and he hadn't even remembered that it was the reason she had called.

7

For a few days Mali was sure that Kobi had told her everything that morning, before the girls woke up, and in his
way he did indeed try to tell. The woman he spoke about
and the circumstances of the injury were different, but
there was a seed of truth in what he told her, as if he nevertheless wanted her to understand.

❦

At a quarter to eight Mali called the bank and informed them
that she'd be absent from work. She waited for Kobi to
take Daniella and Noy in her car to day care and school.
When she tried to catch a cab on Ben Gurion Boulevard,
she still wasn't certain that this was the right thing to do
and hoped that when she returned she would succeed in
convincing Kobi to consult with someone, perhaps even
a lawyer. She immediately suggested that they do this together when he told her what happened, but Kobi wasn't
ready to listen. "What would a lawyer tell me? Just to turn

myself in to the police," Kobi said. "And there's no chance I'm going in there."

The taxi driver listened to the news on the radio but also wouldn't stop asking her questions. He asked if she was going to work and where she works, and her answers were confused. He wasn't from Holon and had arrived in the city following an earlier ride, and she directed him on the way to the center. When she got off at the corner of Jabotinsky Street and Krause and started walking down Krause, Mali saw that the cab was standing in the spot where they had stopped, and she turned onto one of the smaller streets and waited until it disappeared. And she didn't see the car in the place where Kobi said it would be. She crossed the street and made her way back, and only then recognized the old blue Toyota Corolla on the other side of Krause and crossed over again. She didn't waste time examining the car but instead opened the front door with the naturalness of someone leaving for work. The car didn't start immediately, and Mali placed her bag on the seat next to her and tried again. It had ignition problems and had sat there for three days without moving, most of the time in the rain, and it was necessary to try again, patiently and without getting stressed. The SUV parked in front of her was empty, and there was almost no traffic on the street. And no one looked at her while she tried to start the Corolla again and again until the trilling of the engine could be heard.

Mali wasn't used to driving a large car. She turned right on Sokolov and left at Shenkar, and only when she reached Fichman Street did she realize that she was about to pass by the police station, the same station that she'd find herself inside of a week later, but how little she knew then about what was likely to happen; how little does a person know about what will take place in his life? The night without Kobi and the memory of Eilat brought back the fear, and it didn't leave her throughout that entire day. The Swiss tourist again lay in wait for her in the darkness without her knowing where. But her anger at Kobi dissipated after he revealed to her that the police were looking for him and asked for her help. The danger of the collapse was palpable, but it wasn't taking place inside him or inside her but rather there was an external threat against the two of them, a threat they had to fight, and something was tensed in her in order to protect him. Or them.

A traffic patrol car pulled out of the parking lot and traveled behind her. At the intersection the cars stood next to each other at a red light, and Mali didn't look to the right so that the cops wouldn't see her. Her phone rang in her bag, and only when she arrived home did she see that it was her sister, Gila, who seemingly felt how much she was in need of help. When the light changed she accelerated too quickly, but the patrol car turned right. And from among all the things Kobi had asked of her, the hardest thing was not to reveal his story to anyone. She knew what Gila would say and heard her voice even without them speaking, and nevertheless she wanted to tell her. And only when she parked the car in the parking lot under the building did she dare to examine the car, without really lingering next to it and without bending down toward the bumper, and she didn't see any signs of damage or abrasion. Under the

front windshield wiper there was a ticket and a few leaf-
lets that the rain had turned into papier-mâché, and she
tossed them into the garbage can in the stairwell on her
way to the elevator. Her phone was ringing again.

She didn't answer Gila throughout the whole day because
she didn't know what to tell her. She couldn't say that
on Monday, on his way back from a job interview, Kobi
struck a pedestrian with his car who had charged into the
street without looking. That was their anniversary. The
day when a storm raged outside. The roads were slippery
and the visibility was poor, and Kobi drove quickly and
thought about the failed interview when the woman went
out into the street between two parked cars. He didn't
notice her in time to be able to stop, but turned the steer-
ing wheel a little to the left at the last moment. Despite
this, he heard the body hit the car.

Mali's heart beat rapidly as she listened to him in the
early morning, when he came back. Everything that had
frightened her in recent days took on a different meaning.
She had no reason to think that he wasn't telling her the
truth, because the accident bestowed an explanation on
everything. On his closing himself off when he returned
from the interview, on watching the news that same night
and reading the newspapers the next day, on the message
he left his father about the trip to Australia, in which it
seemed to Harry that he had cried. Even on the gun that
was lying on the table in the utility room on the roof that
same day, though they didn't speak about that.

In the papers there was no item about a hit-and-run in Holon, and this relieved both of them. Kobi didn't even know if the woman was hurt or how severe her injuries were because he fled from there quickly, without slowing down, and only saw her lying on the ground in the car's rearview mirror. Mali googled "woman injured in accident in Holon" but didn't pull up any results from the last week, just more and more items about the murder of the old woman. For a moment she thought about calling the hospital and asking if on Monday a woman struck by a car downtown had been brought to the emergency room and in what condition she was, but she didn't call that day. Nevertheless she didn't stop thinking about her. Was she still hospitalized? And from the moment she imagined the woman on the street, it was for some strange reason the girl with the black hair and the black nails who sold her the umbrella at the mall.

Kobi continued driving, without knowing to where but not in the direction of their apartment, because he feared that a driver who saw the accident would follow him, and so he decided to park the Toyota in the place he was at that moment and continue home on foot or by cab. When Mali asked him, "Why didn't you stop?" he just said, "I was afraid. I fled without thinking." If someone wrote down the license plate number and the police came to them, he would say that the car had been stolen. But because three days had passed since the accident and no policeman had yet arrived, he thought they could retrieve it, and asked Mali to do this because he didn't want to return to the place where he had abandoned it, panic-stricken.

The second thing that Kobi asked of her was to say that they were together on Monday afternoon, if someone asked. He knew this would be hard for her because she didn't know how to lie, but he said there was almost no chance she'd need to. Every moment that passed since the accident minimized the possibility that they'd reach him or that the injury to the woman was severe. And if, despite this, the police arrived, Mali would need to say that their car had been stolen the day before and that he had waited for her outside her work and that they traveled together to pick up the girls from day care and school. They hadn't yet reported the theft simply because they hadn't gotten around to it.

When Mali returned home Kobi was calmer. He said, "Was it there?" and asked if she saw anything unusual around the car, and Mali shook her head. "There aren't any scratches or dents on it, either," she said.

In his eyes and in the way he wandered around the apartment she saw that he wasn't yet entirely at ease, but as the hours passed the tension passed to her. He prepared lunch for them while she again searched for news about the accidents without him seeing. Gila called her almost every hour, left her messages and asked her to call back, and Mali still didn't answer. When they sat down to eat, Kobi tried to talk about other things.

"Did the girls say anything about me not being home?" he asked, but when she asked him suddenly, "Why did you decide to tell me?" he fell silent. Afterward he said, "I didn't know what to do. And I didn't have anyone else to tell. Would you rather me not say anything?"

But he nevertheless called his dad first. And planned to travel to him without her knowledge. "Did you seriously plan to flee to Australia?" she asked him, and Kobi said, "On the first day, I did, yes. I didn't know what to do." He didn't say it to her and she didn't ask, but she thought that since the accident there were certainly also moments when suicidal thoughts came to him. Chills went through her when she saw him again in her imagination sitting alone on the roof, that same night, she imagined him weighing the gun in his hand.

"And now? Do you still plan to go?"

"No. I think it's not necessary now."

What she actually should have done was encourage him to go. Or tell him about the pregnancy during those hours when they were alone in the apartment. Before Eilat they spoke about another child, but after that it wasn't possible, and from a financial perspective as well it was hard to think they'd manage with another baby. The fear that returned at night and the adrenaline that flowed in her body in the morning hours changed into a deep, emptying sadness. She told him that she wanted to sleep a bit before Daniella and Noy returned home, and turned off the cell phone, because Gila kept calling. Before she fell asleep she thought that she was doing exactly what he had done in recent days: hide, conceal. As if she had caught it from him. Her sleep was long and deep, and Kobi went instead of her to get the girls, and that was good, because she was too tense, and even when they returned she tried to avoid them, and Kobi sat with the two of them in the living room and watched television.

Shortly before sunset, when Mali went up to the roof to hang laundry, she looked at the water heaters and antennae spread out before her. She thought about the sentence that Kobi said to her at noon. *I didn't have anyone else to tell.*

She was still certain that they needed to consult with a lawyer, or at least with one of their friends, but after Eilat she didn't want to speak to anyone else, either. There were days then on which she couldn't get up in the morning and live. When she tried to get dressed or put on makeup it was as if she were dressing a doll or another woman, and only when she looked at Kobi did she sometimes remember that she was still Mali Bengtson and that she had two girls and a home and a job. Once, she asked Kobi how he could do it, how he hadn't despaired and given up on her, and that was one of the few times he spoke with her about his mother. During her illness his father, Harry, was almost never home, and Kobi actually took care of her completely by himself. "Harry escaped because he couldn't see her suffer," he said, "but I had nowhere to escape to. And beyond that, she had no one else in Australia. He would return once or twice a week from the university in order to confirm that she hadn't yet died, and you could smell his lovers on him."

Evening descended and it was chilly on the roof, though it was no longer rainy but almost springlike instead.

Mali remembered the portrait photograph of Kobi's dead mother that she saw in his room, and she, too, got mixed up in her imagination with the woman who was still lying on the street after the Toyota had struck her. If it weren't for the storm, would the accident have happened? The woman wouldn't have fled from the rain and rushed to cross the street, and even if she had burst out at him between parked cars, Kobi would have noticed her.

If only the storm would have arrived one day before then or one day after. Or if Kobi's interview had gone differently. If they had been just a bit luckier.

She never had any luck, but she didn't expect anything else for herself. It was Kobi's life that was supposed to look different. Her job was okay and she was grateful for the patience they demonstrated toward her at the bank, after Eilat. She got used to the apartment they rented, too, even though it wasn't a home. When they moved there they decided not to invest money in it because they hoped to save for a place of their own, and the walls remained naked. They didn't buy new furniture, either, and they used what they brought from the previous apartment and those that the owner's son had left behind. She was used to walking around her apartment as if it were someone else's house, but Kobi never stopped dreaming about the place they'd buy. And Gila, too, didn't stop asking her when they were finally moving to a real home.

Daniella called her from below, but Mali wasn't yet ready to go downstairs. And she kept her cell phone turned off.

There was something similar between Kobi and Gila,

and perhaps this is why they didn't get along, she suddenly thought. Like Gila, Kobi, too, once had confidence that he could get everything he wanted from life. Mali and Kobi were officially a couple again when they returned from Australia, and he started the course at Mossad and returned from there full of stories. She never saw him as happy as he was during that period. He talked about tracing exercises and bursting into houses and simulated assassinations of random women and men in the street, and he was certain that he'd finish it with distinction and be accepted to the job thanks to his English and his Australian passport. When he stopped talking about the course, almost at once, she thought it was because he wasn't allowed to talk about it; only a few weeks after this did she learn, almost accidentally, that he was thrown out. He hid this from her for around two months and pretended that he was heading out to the course each morning, but when he started working as a security guard at the mall he was forced to reveal it to her because he was worried that someone would see him and tell. This was temporary work, and when they got married, almost a year later, he prepared her for the fact that they'd need to travel because he was trying to get work as a security officer at the embassies, but that never happened, either.

Gila was already divorced then, not yet twenty-five and already with a three-year-old son, and swearing that she'd never ever marry again. She thought that Kobi was closing up Mali in the house and distancing her from friends, but in a weird way the conversations with her sister actually brought Mali closer to him, because it seemed to her that the main problem Gila had with Kobi was that he didn't earn enough money and wasn't successful like the men she went out with.

And after Eilat even her sister was forced to agree that Kobi took care of her like no one else would have.

When Mali came down from the roof the three of them were on the sofa in the living room, and this was the last time she saw them together like that. Daniella sat next to him and Noy lay on his other side, her head on his knees. He asked if he should make dinner for everyone, and the girls asked for hot chocolate. Harry lay at their feet, his head leaning forward on his front paws, and even though he didn't move, it looked as if even *he* had another chance.

After the girls went to bed Mali checked that the door was locked and that the lights were on and got into bed early despite the afternoon nap. Kobi got into bed a short time after her, closed the door and turned off the small lamp. When he lowered the straps of her nightgown and caressed her neck, she closed her eyes, but his fingers were unable to wake and excite her as they sometimes could. She felt and didn't feel his hands on her arms and on her thighs when they had sex. And despite the darkness suddenly there was no fear in her, just sadness. Was it only because of the woman who lay in the street in the rain and waited for help? Or did she already understand some of what was likely to happen? She turned on the small lamp and tried to fall asleep when Kobi asked, "What are you thinking about?" and Mali said to him with eyes closed, "Her."

"Who?"

She even thought about going to the store where she bought him the umbrella in order to verify that the woman who lay in the street wasn't the girl with the black hair. Did cars stop next to her after Kobi fled, and did drivers get out in order to help her? Maybe she managed to call an ambulance herself, or did one of the passersby phone for her instead?

And there were two other things Mali thought about without telling Kobi. When she asked him in the morning where the accident was, Kobi hesitated before answering, and she didn't understand why. If he had told her the name of the street, it would have been easier to search for news about the accident and to know what happened to the woman. The second thing was the umbrella he was looking for. The accident provided an explanation for what happened on their anniversary and for watching the news and reading the newspapers and the message for Harry. But it didn't explain the umbrella.

Kobi said to her, "If you're worried about the police, you can relax," and she asked him, "How can you be so sure?" Even though she wasn't thinking about this. She wasn't looking at him when he said, "Because three days have passed. If they haven't arrived by now, they won't. And I did everything that needed to be done."

When she fell asleep she still didn't know she would do this, but the next morning, from the phone at the bank, she called Wolfson Medical Center and checked if on Monday a young woman had arrived at the emergency room who had been injured in a car accident in Holon.

The nurse who answered transferred her to the emergency room reception desk and when she was asked who she was, she said without planning to in advance, "I saw the accident and wanted to know how she was." The clerk asked Mali to wait a moment before she said to her, "Look, I'm not finding anything here, but can you leave me a name and phone number and we'll get back to you if we find anything?" And Mali almost hung up and then said for some reason, "My name is Michal Ben-Asher," but gave the clerk her real telephone number. From that moment on, she waited for them to call her from the hospital, but eventually it was somebody else who had called.

8

Only at the end of the third day of the investigation was the team updated on the testimony of Diana Goldin about the policeman who had visited her apartment. Until then Avraham kept this new lead to himself and breached a few more standards of police protocol, guided by an inner certainty that grew stronger as the day progressed. In the evening, after a second visit to the scene, he summoned the members of the team for an urgent meeting and announced to them that he had in his possession the end of a thread leading to the killer.

The night before this he stayed awake until almost two. He drank black coffee on his porch, ate too many dry cookies, and thought only about the policeman who went down the stairs and disappeared. The main thing he was unable to understand was *why* the policeman questioned Diana Goldin and recorded their conversation. And why he didn't try to attack her, even though they were alone. Diana told him that the policeman requested that she tell him everything, *As if I were telling it for the first time*, and that was probably the key. Despite the growing certainty that the policeman questioned her on his own, the first thing Avraham asked of Lital Levy when he arrived to the office in the morning was to check again with all district department heads if a policeman was sent to Diana Goldin with the task of completing an investigation.

Shrapstein didn't understand why Avraham asked to be present at the questioning of Erez Yeger in the early morning, but in retrospect this was the right decision. Three days had passed since the murder, and he decided that he wouldn't continue observing the investigation from the window of his office on the third floor. The weekend was approaching and after it was the short vacation he requested because of Marianka's parents' visit, and he had to update the team about the new lead that day, so that they would be able to continue working on it in his absence. All the other leads in the investigation led them nowhere: Ma'alul and Esty Vahaba exhausted the investigation of the rapist's family and were convinced that no one among them was involved in the murder. And the worker who Shrapstein detained for twenty-four hours, Adnan Gon, had an alibi. He didn't come to work on the day of the murder because of the storm. And even though the day before, Avraham had pictured Leah Yeger's son at the entrance to his mother's apartment, now he was certain that Erez Yeger wasn't the person who had attacked her, and not only because of the DNA tests, which determined that Leah Yeger's assailant wasn't a relative.

When Avraham entered the interrogation room on the second floor with Shrapstein, he saw the son up close for the first time. Erez Yeger walked from side to side in the room, ungainly and very tall. He wore a thick, checkered sweater that, without his knowing, played perfectly into the investigation's plan. He watched the two policemen while they sat down in their places and afterward sat down across from them. Shrapstein spread out the summary of his investigation from two days earlier on the table, and when he stretched his fingers over it he seemed to Avraham nervous, perhaps because Erez Yeger lied to him in his previous questioning and perhaps because of Avraham's own presence in the interrogation room.

"Do you know why we brought you back here?" Shrapstein opened. Avraham sat at the edge of the table and examined Yeger's facial expression.

"You said there were developments in the investigation."

Shrapstein looked at the papers laid out before him and not at Erez Yeger, when he nodded. "There are definitely some developments," he said. "Important developments even. Do you want to know what the developments are?"

Shrapstein smiled as if to himself and turned the gold ring on his finger, and Erez Yeger looked at Avraham. Did he recognize his face from the funeral? Avraham hadn't said a thing since he entered the room, not even his name or rank.

"Soon I'll tell you about the developments, but first

there's something I want to clarify with you," Shrapstein
continued. "During the previous questioning you said to
me that there hadn't been communication between you
and your mother in recent months. Can you confirm this
statement?"

"Yes."

"And you continue to claim that there wasn't communication between you two?"

Yeger's face reddened, but he only nodded. Why had
he lied? From his experience Avraham had learned that
most of those questioned don't lie because they believe
they'll succeed in deceiving the investigators, but rather
because they're ashamed of what they're hiding.

"Go ahead and explain to me why there wasn't communication between you. Can you do that?" Shrapstein
asked, and Yeger answered, "I told you already. I didn't
want any communication with her."

"Correct. That's what you said. And that satisfied me
during the first round of questioning. But now, following
the important developments, your answer doesn't satisfy
me. I would like you to please elaborate on the reasons."
Yeger didn't respond, and when Shrapstein said, "Should
I write that you refuse to elaborate on the reasons for the
conflict between you?" The son immediately answered,
"There was no conflict between us." He again looked at
Avraham, who signaled to him with his hand to turn his
gaze to the officer questioning him.

"What was it? Money? A dispute over your father's
inheritance?"

"I told you that there was no conflict between us."

The heat in the room was working at full power, and Yeger was already sweating inside his checkered sweater. Underneath it he was wearing a warm white undershirt. His face and palms were damp. When he asked to air out the excessively heated room, Shrapstein explained to him that the window didn't open. But Erez Yeger wasn't the man who sat opposite his mother next to the kitchen table and afterward strangled her and left her body on the carpet, and only at that moment did Avraham suddenly understand why he was certain of this. If it were him, the scene would not have been as ordered as he found it. Leah Yeger arranged her apartment for *an official meeting* and not for a meeting with her son. And it wasn't possible that she had told no one about this meeting. Earlier that morning Avraham phoned Leah Yeger's daughter and asked her if she was sure that her mother hadn't told her that she was supposed to be questioned again by the police about the rape, and the daughter said that she didn't know anything about it. But maybe the son knew? Avraham wanted to ask him about this immediately, but Shrapstein continued laying his trap around Yeger. And he wasn't up-to-date on Avraham's new lead.

"So what if you told me that there wasn't a conflict," Shrapstein continued quietly. "You also said that your last conversation was a long time ago. Isn't that right?"

Yeger placed his palm on the table and then lifted it and moved the hand onto his forehead in order to wipe the sweat from it and looked at Avraham when he responded to Shrapstein, "That's what I said. Yes."

"You're kidding me, right?"

"No."

"What do you think, Avi? That he's kidding us?"

Shrapstein rose suddenly from his place, and Yeger followed him with his gaze as he approached him. He erupted once he was bent over Yeger, his mouth right above his head, and it was impossible to know if this was a real outburst or part of Shrapstein's interrogation plan. "Do I look retarded to you, Erez? Or maybe the policeman sitting here next to me looks retarded? You're lying to me like I don't have a record of your mother's phone calls and like I don't know when the last time you talked was."

Yeger again looked at Avraham in order to test with his expression if the things Shrapstein said to him were correct. And then of all times, when Yeger walked into the trap that Shrapstein had prepared for him, Avraham opened up an exit door for him inside it. He said to him, "Erez, we're asking you if you spoke with your mother not because we're suspicious that you're involved in the murder but rather because we want to know if she told you that she expected to be questioned by the police." And Yeger said, "I don't know what you're talking about."

Shrapstein turned and looked at Avraham, and in his eyes then there was still only misunderstanding. Avraham knew that his interference disrupted Shrapstein's interrogation plan and that he should have prepared him for this in advance, but only during those moments did he understand what he wanted to hear from the son. "I mean questioning about the rape she went through," Avraham continued. "According to the phone log you did speak with your mother on Sunday, twenty-four hours before the murder. And it doesn't interest me why you're lying but only if she informed you during your conversation that a policeman was supposed to come to her for questioning the next day."

"She didn't say anything to me about a questioning," Yeger said. And then added, "Because I didn't speak to her."

Shrapstein didn't relent. He remained where he was standing, over Yeger, and said to him, "Let's go back to the phone conversation. Explain to me why you're hiding it. And try to stop lying." But Avraham continued asking questions as if he were the only detective in the room, and Yeger spoke only to him.

"So tell me something else, Erez," he said. "If your mother were to set up a meeting or make an appointment with a doctor, where would she write a reminder for herself about this meeting?"

"I don't know. What do you two want from me? I told you from the beginning that we weren't in contact."

"We conducted an examination of her computer and we saw that she didn't keep an electronic datebook. But she certainly had some other datebook, no? Older people write things like this in a set place, because they tend to forget."

This was the moment that Avraham was waiting for. Yeger was silent and then said, "She had a calendar, I think. In the kitchen. She would write dates of birthdays and other things there, but I don't know if she still has it." Avraham tried to recall if he had seen the calendar at the scene.

"Are you sure that the calendar is in the kitchen?" he asked, and Yeger said, "I think so. That's where it used to be."

Shrapstein left the interrogation room and slammed the door behind him, but Avraham continued asking questions.

"Other than this calendar she didn't have another place, a datebook perhaps?"

If Leah Yeger kept a datebook it's possible it was in her handbag that was stolen, but it was also possible that it was someplace else.

"I don't know if she had a datebook. I think she did. Maybe my sister knows."

"And do you have any idea where she put her datebook? Did she usually keep it in a purse?"

"Don't know."

"So try to remember."

"But I told you, I don't know. You didn't ask my sister about it?"

Shortly after this, when he was in the car on his way to the scene, Avraham called Orit Yeger, and she confirmed that in the kitchen her mother had a calendar on which she wrote reminders for meetings and events. She saw it for the last time two weeks before, and even wrote there a reminder herself for her daughter's Purim party. Her mother also had a datebook, with phone numbers and addresses, but Orit Yeger didn't know where the datebook could be

and if it was reasonable to assume that it was in the handbag that was taken from the scene.

Before he opened the door to her apartment Avraham
put gloves on his hands, and right as he turned on a light
he noticed that the calendar was not hanging on the wall
in the kitchen. The apartment hadn't been opened for
two days, and in it stood warm air. Nothing had been
moved in the rooms, and the sights came back to Avraham, the birds on the carpet, the lamp, the painting of the
two women in the field, the table set for a meeting. Leah
Yeger waited for a knock at the door, but the man who
stood behind it wasn't her son but rather a policeman. And
suddenly he understood that he didn't need to look at her
body anymore in order to understand her death, as he had
sensed, but to think instead about Leah Yeger's life in this
apartment before the knock at the door was heard.

She didn't tell her son about the policeman who had
contacted her and asked to arrange another round of questioning, because the relations between them had been sev-
ered. And she didn't say a thing to her daughter, either.
Did she include anyone else in her life? On the refrigerator
in the kitchen was a picture of her with her daughter and
granddaughter and next to it an old picture of her son
with a tall man who apparently was his father.

But her son didn't visit her, for reasons he was hiding.
Nor his children, her grandchildren. There was a set day
when she picked up her granddaughter from day care and
brought her to her place, and on Fridays she would go to
her daughter's for dinner, but during the rest of the time

she was forced to live alone in the apartment where she was raped, the apartment where her husband died of a heart attack. Was this the reason she agreed to meet with the policeman? That other than him no one wanted to listen?

Avraham sat down for a moment on the chair in the kitchen. How much time had passed until Leah Yeger understood that something wasn't right? In the living room, next to the television, there was a cordless phone, but Leah Yeger didn't use it because the policeman would have noticed, so Avraham walked the length of the hallway. He peeked into the bedroom and then continued to the office and there saw the device. On the writing table was an old telephone, but the cord wasn't plugged into its socket on the wall. He immediately called Orit Yeger.

"Do you know if your mother used that phone in the office? Was its cord always in the socket?"

"What phone?" she said, but seemed to remember it a moment later saying, "Oh, wait, yes. It was."

In contrast to his first visit to the scene Avraham knew exactly what to look for, but this time, too, he wasn't alone there because Leah Yeger was the one who guided him. Next to the phone, under a pile of documents, he found the datebook she had apparently hidden. In the square for the day when the murder occurred—*Monday, February 23*—only numbers were written, in tiny handwriting, with a red pen: *2:00*.

This wasn't much, but it was all Avraham needed. He returned to the station within less than five minutes and asked Lital Levy to call an urgent team meeting. Saban entered the conference room first, and when he asked Avraham, "Where's her son? Did you arrest him?" Avraham had no doubt that Shrapstein had told him about the events of the morning. Avraham nodded and said to him, "Soon," because he was waiting for Eliyahu Ma'alul and Esty Vahaba, who entered after him and grabbed seats around the table. Ma'alul noticed the facial composite that was drawn with Diana Goldin's help and that Avraham had placed on the table next to the umbrella and asked, "That's it? Did we catch our killer?" And Saban looked at the computerized drawing in amazement. He asked Avraham to start the meeting because his time was short, and Avraham looked mainly at him when he began by saying, "We have a new lead in the investigation."

He was certain about so few facts, and to most of the questions presented to him in the meeting he didn't have answers, but the feeling that accompanied him since yesterday and guided him in the investigation from the morning hours was one of real certainty. Saban asked, "So it's not the son?" and Avraham said, "No. I believe Leah Yeger was murdered by a policeman who set up a meeting with her for the purpose of an investigation."

Saban straightened up in his chair and placed his cell phone on the table. And Avraham continued. "Yesterday evening I received new testimony that I didn't manage to tell you about, since this morning we were in the interrogation room with the son. Another rape victim, Diana Goldin, testified that a few days ago a man was at her place who introduced himself as a policeman working in

the Ayalon district and questioned her about the rape she
went through. According to inquiries we since made with
all the departments in the district, no policeman was sent
to her with this task. I believe this is what happened to
Leah Yeger as well."

Saban was flustered by what Avraham said. "But on
the basis of what are you determining this?" he asked.
"Just on the basis of that neighbor's testimony who . . ."
He suddenly went quiet, and Avraham took advantage of
this in order to continue.

"We have the testimony of the neighbor who saw a
policeman in the building after the murder. And today I
found in the apartment of the murder victim her appointment book with an entry for the time at which the murder
took place. So we have two policemen that we cannot
locate, at scenes tied to rape victims, at a distance of a
few kilometers and separated by a few days. Diana Goldin
wasn't assaulted by the policeman because he succeeded in
deceiving her until the end, but I believe that Leah Yeger
understood that he wasn't who he said he was, and therefore she tried to call the police. He figured this out, and
then a struggle between them began, at the end of which
she was murdered."

Ma'alul pointed at the composite drawing. "That's the
man?" he asked, and Avraham nodded. Esty Vahaba also
studied the composite and her gaze was serious.

"In my estimation," Avraham continued, "the policeman's methods are very sophisticated. He makes arrangements by phone with the rape victims and confirms that
they're not suspicious of him by means of two phone calls.

This at least is what he did in the Goldin incident. He offers to meet them at the station in order to neutralize any suspicion. I assume that if they are suspicious of him or ask too many questions on the phone about who he is exactly and the reason for the questioning, he cancels or doesn't show up. He comes to the meeting dressed in a uniform and asks them to describe the rape they experienced, ostensibly for reasons tied to the investigation or legal deliberations on the matter. At the meeting with Diana Goldin he took notes and also recorded everything she said to him on a cell phone."

Saban held his cell phone in his hand when Avraham finished speaking, and then said, "This sounds like a dangerous lead to me, Avi. Beyond that, even if we suppose that there's a connection between the incidents, how do you intend to find the suspect?"

The facial composite that was drawn with Diana Goldin's help was lying on the table. Avraham explained that the policeman forgot an umbrella at her home, thus they will have fingerprints that can be compared to prints from the murder scene. It would also be possible to compare the log of incoming phone calls to Leah Yeger with the list of calls made in recent weeks to Diana Goldin. Other than that, this weekend Diana Goldin will go over the photographs of every policeman in the district, and, if need be, over the photographs of all the policemen in the country. "Why of policemen? Do you think he's really a cop?" Ma'alul asked, and Avraham said, "I think so. Or an ex-policeman. Otherwise he wouldn't have access to information about rape victims." In addition, Avraham planned to identify the suspect in the footage of security cameras in the area where the murder was carried out. To go over camera after camera and look for the policeman who, according to the testimony of the neighbor, didn't get into a patrol car but instead left the scene on foot. Until they find him.

"And then what?" Saban asked.

He hadn't thought about this beforehand but immediately said to Saban that then it would be possible to publicize the facial composite or a picture of the policeman in the media, and Ma'alul smiled at his words but Saban did not. "You're suggesting that we publish a photograph in the newspaper and say that the man in the picture is perhaps a policeman who perhaps harassed rape victims and perhaps murdered a woman, without being certain that this is correct? Did you fall on your head, Avi? This is just what the police need with everything that's happening here already? For every policeman in the country to become a suspect in the harassment of rape victims and murder? You're out of your mind."

After the meeting, when Avraham was left in his office with Ma'alul, he understood that maybe he had been mistaken, but when he returned from Leah Yeger's apartment he didn't have an organized plan for continuing the investigation, there were only preliminary thoughts about the next steps. He didn't know enough about the policeman other than that he was the man Leah Yeger was waiting for. And he also hoped that the man wasn't a real cop, but otherwise he wasn't able to understand the fact that he had in his possession information about the women who had been assaulted, because even among police, access to rape files is limited to detectives who dealt with them directly.

Saban left the meeting room without saying a word and returned after speaking with someone on the phone. He said, "We aren't publishing anything, Avi. No composite sketch. No photograph. We'll continue checking this angle, but we'll do it very, very discreetly, are you with me? And beyond that, we have another suspect that you actually released from custody. What do you intend to do with her son? From my perspective he's the central suspect," And Avraham planned to respond to him when Esty Vahaba interrupted. "Maybe it's possible to do this without publishing photos," she said. "We can speak to other rape victims and find out if they've encountered the policeman or if a policeman contacted them. It could be that he didn't do this just twice."

Saban opposed this suggestion as well because he didn't want to provoke anxiety among rape victims and thought that if too many women were questioned that it was liable to leak to the media, but there wasn't any other way, and Avraham insisted. He looked at Saban from his new place at the head of the table, the place where Ilana Lis had sat, and said quietly, "That's a good idea, Esty. We'll look for a photo of him in security cameras and even if we don't find it, we can speak to the victims, with the composite sketch. And Erez Yeger won't flee anywhere. We'll see to that. In any case, we'll question him again at the beginning of the week. But according to the findings, the assailant is not a relative and I'm telling you he's not the murderer, and that

our central lead from this moment is the policeman who
went down the stairs and disappeared."

He stayed in his office at the station until after midnight that
day. Read the summary of Diana Goldin's testimony again
and again, and examined the photographs from the scene
under the strong light given off by the desk lamp. The
window was open but he felt no need for a cigarette, and
he didn't even put the unlit pipe in his mouth. Leah Yeger's
picture was lying before him on the table.

Marianka called him a few times during the day, but
he answered her only at ten in the evening. She'd hoped
that he'd return early, but when he was detained she prepared the apartment herself for her parents' visit and reminded him that at four thirty in the morning they were
supposed to be waiting for them at the airport, in the
arrival hall where he hid from her a few months before.
Afterward he stood for a long time by the window and
watched the cars passing in the street. He thought that
despite the confrontations with Shrapstein and Saban, he
had led his first murder investigation in the right direction,
and he wanted to call Ilana Lis despite the late hour; this
wasn't so she'd give him support so much as an opportunity to swap ideas about the policeman's motives. When
he had remained alone with Ma'alul before, Eliyahu said
to him, "That was a hell of a meeting, Avi," and Avraham
said to him suddenly, "You were right about what you said
to me, you know? That I was dealing in bullshit and that I
had someone to rely on."

Ma'alul no longer turned his gaze away, and there was a smile in his dark eyes. "Forget it; I have," he said. And perhaps because they were close again and because Avraham couldn't speak with Ilana, he said to Eliyahu, "I wasn't stressed because of Saban but because I didn't truly understand how to conduct a murder investigation. Until today."

"Like any other investigation, Avi, no?"

"No. Not exactly."

The findings from the lab helped, as did the testimonies gathered from those interrogated, but the main thing was to bring Leah Yeger back to life. For the last time that same day Avraham saw her in his imagination sitting next to the table in her kitchen, when the knock came from the door. If she had told her son or daughter that a policeman was supposed to question her in her apartment, Avraham would know now with certainty that he wasn't mistaken, but her son had cut off his relations with her and apparently she wasn't close enough to her daughter to tell her, either. She made arrangements for the meeting and tidied up the apartment because she didn't have many visitors. And she wasn't suspicious of the policeman until he made some kind of mistake. She planned on telling him how she was attacked and perhaps was even happy about the visit because she wanted to talk. When she heard the knock she got up from her chair and hurried to the door behind which stood the policeman, who in the meantime looked around in order to verify that no one saw him. *What was he searching for with Diana Goldin and Leah Yeger?* This, Avraham still didn't understand and didn't even have a guess, and he said to himself that he had to think more about *him*, and not just about her. Was *he* surprised when she opened the door for him and he saw her face? Or had he already looked at it before then in pictures from the investigation file?

Because he wanted to know everything. You understand? Every detail. From the beginning. That's what Diana Goldin had said.

"Why, Leah, why didn't you tell anyone he was coming?" Avraham whispered as if to himself, and then tried to concentrate again on the policeman who waited behind the door. A few hours later, while he was waiting with Marianka at the airport, this was the question still echoing inside him.

PART TWO
The Killer

9

When they returned from the airport with Bojan and Anika
Milanich, Avraham didn't recognize his home. Throughout the apartment tablecloths that he didn't know they
had were spread out, on which were placed vases he had
never before seen, with enormous flower bouquets. In the
small office, which for three days would be transformed
into her parents' bedroom, Marianka had placed a small
basket filled with grapefruits.

Avraham's eyes were red because he hadn't slept at
night, but he saw Marianka's excitement while they ate
breakfast on the porch. His cell phone was sitting at his
feet, on the floor, and he tried not to check too frequently
if any new messages had been sent to him. Marianka told
her parents that he was in the middle of a murder investigation, and her mother pretended to be interested in the
case, but he couldn't tell them much because he hadn't
revealed most of the details even to Marianka. And every
time he looked away or went to the kitchen to help Mar-

ianka with the food, her parents whispered to each other in Slovenian.

And despite this, they did not succeed in hiding the point of the visit from him.

Bojan and Anika Milanich detested him, and he knew this well before then.

When they met during the summer that he spent with Marianka in Brussels they were still friendly, but when they heard about her plan to travel to him in Israel, the friendliness disappeared. She didn't tell him everything they said, but Avraham felt their disgust with every look and every meeting. She spoke to them by phone once a week, usually on Sundays, and she told him that they had come to terms with her move, but he didn't believe it. When he asked, "So how is it that they're coming here suddenly?" she said, "In order to be with us—what do you mean? And also in order to get to know you."

Why, if this was the case, were they sitting forlorn on the porch of his apartment and barely saying a word?

Anika Milanich didn't touch the omelet that he and Marianka prepared and only drank coffee with milk. She was fifty-one years old and looked no more than forty. In Slovenia she was a teacher at a music academy, and in Brussels she gave private lessons on the piano. Her favorite composer was Chopin, and the pieces that she loved to play more than anything were the mazurkas. When Avraham was invited to their house for the first time, she asked him which mazurka was his favorite and he didn't know what to say. She was tall and smartly dressed, and when no one was watching her smile twisted up into a grimace

of disgust. Marianka told him once that one of her students at the academy became a world-renowned pianist
and that her mother tried to set them up, even though he
was gay. Bojan Milanich, holder of a black belt in karate
and an instructor at a theological seminary, sat next to
Anika and looked at the skies of Holon. He was a solid
man with a rock-hard potbelly and broad shoulders, and
Avraham was certain that he was willing to kill every man
who came near Marianka with a yoko geri kick, even if it
was Glenn Gould. He was fifty-three years old, and even
though everyone said that Marianka reminded people of
him, Avraham insisted on seeing no resemblance.

After breakfast Avraham did the dishes in order to let the
three of them be together. He hoped that after this the
tension would dissipate. They rode in his car to Tel Aviv,
and when they walked the length of Rothschild Boulevard, from the national theater to the old neighborhood
of Neve Tzedek, the sky was blue. Marianka showed them
Tel Aviv as if it were her home, pointing at the buildings
she liked, talking about the restaurants and cafés and the
sea, but Bojan walked quickly ahead of everyone with his
gaze fixed on the ground, and Avraham saw how Marianka's face fell. They returned to Holon early in order to
have time to rest, and in the evening, when they walked
from their apartment to his parents', Marianka pointed
out that this was the neighborhood where Avraham grew
up. When Anika said, "You love this place if you returned
to live here," Avraham answered, "Yes," and afterward,

"No," and then tried to say something else but was stopped because of the English. Holon wasn't elegant like Brussels, or picturesque like Koper, the port city where Marianka was born and which for now he had seen only in photo albums, but it nevertheless was his home.

His mother tried so hard to make the dinner festive. She wore the clothes that she bought in autumn for his promotion ceremony and dressed his father in a white oxford shirt over his T-shirt, and the apartment was sparkling clean. The television was turned off for the first time in years, and all the lights were on, and even the wool blanket everyone sat on so the sofa wouldn't get dirty was removed. At first she invited everyone into the living room but she was unable to bear the tension and urged them to move to the kitchen table because the chicken was ready. His father sat at the head of the table, his eyes staring at the empty plate and a bib wrapped around the collar of his shirt, but when Avraham looked at him he saw another man who wasn't sitting there. Avraham touched his father's shoulder, as he had begun doing in recent months, and then bent over and whispered in his ear, "We have guests. Marianka's father and mother," and a smile lit up his father's eyes as he nodded his head.

Marianka told her parents in advance about the stroke his father had suffered and about the fact that his condition was deteriorating, but despite this it seemed to Avraham that Bojan and Anika were looking at his father the way they observed the streets and buildings they saw on their way, with contempt and pity. His mother said that his father no longer understands or feels a thing, but Avraham knew she was mistaken. Did his father not see how beautiful Marianka was in her black dress? And the fear in her eyes that dinner, too, like breakfast on the porch or the walk through Tel Aviv, would be a failure? And did he not hear how Marianka tried to start up a conversation every time silence descended over the table?

Avraham hoped his father didn't see the nauseous expression that was strewn across the faces of Bojan and Anika while they ate. They answered the questions his mother asked in faltering English, about Slovenia and the move to Belgium and afterward about classical music and the principles of the Christian faith, the way one answers a child. In their home, dinners were entirely different, boisterous and with many guests, at the end of which Anika would sit at the piano and Bojan would force Marianka to dance at least one mazurka with him, and Avraham thought that the bitterness he felt toward them was also tied to the fact that they were younger than his parents and full of life.

At meals in their house bottles of wine were opened and gulped down one after the other, whereas his mother brought to the table one bottle, white and bland, which had been opened a few months ago at a meal in honor of Avraham's birthday and kept in the refrigerator. When he was helping to clear the plates for the entrée, his mother said to him in the kitchen, "They don't like the food," and Avraham said to her, "What are you talking about? They said that everything is delicious." Bojan and Anika brought her a gift of a green tablecloth and a pair of candlesticks, and she asked him in a whisper, "Do you think that they expect me to put them on the table?"

On that same Friday, Avraham felt that if he didn't find the
policeman within a few days, he would never be caught.
And that soon no one other than him would care who
murdered Leah Yeger.

In the papers there wasn't a single item about the
murder that had taken place only four days earlier, nor
was there anything about the storm, which had been forgotten as if it never was, and most of them dealt only with
the coming elections. Like almost every Friday since the
start of winter, stones were thrown in the Arab neighborhoods in Jerusalem, and district policemen reinforced the
Jerusalem police in order to prevent disturbances after the
prayers at the mosques. In the station's log no unusual incidents were recorded that day other than a report on a
stabbing at a club in Bat Yam, and when Eliyahu Ma'alul
and Esty Vahaba went to watch footage from security
cameras and traffic police cameras in the area where the
murder occurred, they were almost alone at the station.
Avraham called them at every available moment in order
to find out anything new, even during the dinner at his
parents', from the room that was once his room, but they
didn't have anything to tell him, and Ma'alul asked that he
stop calling. Ma'alul brought sandwiches and a thermos
with black coffee with him from home, and he and Vahaba
watched the footage late into the night, but the policeman
who went down the stairs and disappeared wasn't to be
seen in any of it. Diana Goldin arrived at the station on
Friday afternoon and with Vahaba went over photos of the
district policemen, but didn't identify anyone.

And on Saturday as well, until the afternoon hours,

nothing happened. Avraham hoped that in the morning, while drinking his first coffee, he could go over his notes and continue thinking about the policeman, but Bojan and Anika got up before him, and since Marianka was still sleeping, he prepared coffee for the two of them as well and they drank it together in silence on the porch. Despite the disturbances, they insisted on traveling to Jerusalem to visit the holy sites. Ma'alul announced in advance that he would remain home on Saturday, and Esty Vahaba arrived at the station near ten in order to continue watching footage. Avraham called her twice, and they concluded that if she didn't find a picture of the policeman she would begin, once Shabbat ended, reaching out to rape victims in the district with the computerized facial composite, but at noon Vahaba called.

They were standing in the square in front of the Church of the Holy Sepulchre when Avraham heard the ring from his coat pocket and then saw the phone number and asked them to go in without him.

And even though at that point it wasn't yet a positive identification, because the picture still needed to be sent to Diana Goldin and presented to the neighbor, Vahaba was convinced. At 2:28, a short time after the murder, a policeman could be seen passing by the cameras of a Bank Hapoalim on Sokolov Street, not far from the scene. Avraham held the cell phone close to his ear because a tour guide was speaking in the square before a group of pilgrims from Poland. Three policemen secured the entrance to the church but none of them recognized Avraham.

The policeman was cautious and didn't stop at the

kiosk or supermarket in order to buy a pack of cigarettes or to hide from the rain, as they had hoped. But for an instant he passed in front of the bank's external security camera facing the street and was recorded by it. And to his misfortune, not long before then, the bank underwent a renovation, and sophisticated, up-to-date cameras were installed that recorded his face in profile, but clearly, and Diana Goldin immediately confirmed that it was him.

A brown leather jacket covered his light blue shirt such that it was impossible to see if there was a rank on it. Avraham asked Vahaba to send the picture immediately to all department heads in the district so that they could try to identify the policeman walking quickly down Sokolov Street without looking to the side. He also asked her to show the picture to the neighbor from the second floor, but he didn't answer. Then he called Ma'alul in order to inform him that the picture was found and that it was of excellent quality. Ma'alul promised that he'd join Vahaba in the evening and asked him, "Are you coming in, too?" And Avraham answered without hesitation that he would.

His fingers shook when he tried to enlarge the pictures that were sent to his cell phone and look at the sharp face.

The policeman was short and stocky, as Diana Goldin had described. In his right hand he held a small bag. Avraham searched for his gaze in the picture, as if he'd find answers in it, but the policeman wasn't looking at the camera lens. He didn't know how long Marianka and her parents had been delayed in the church, but when they came out Marianka asked him, "Why didn't you come in?" and then she realized that something had happened.

When he said to her that they'd need to return early to Holon she asked him, "Now?"

His cell phone was back in his coat pocket, and he didn't take it out. And anyway, it was impossible to do more with the pictures than what he had done. If he had received permission from Saban to do it, he would post it that same day on the police Facebook page or ask that it be broadcast on the television news in order to receive the public's help in the search. For a moment the thought occurred to him to post the picture without permission. After all, they only needed one person to recognize him.

Because of the despair in Marianka's eyes Avraham suggested that they eat hummus at a restaurant in the Old City, but Anika tasted one warm chickpea and left the entire serving on the plate. Avraham already knew that he'd go to the station when they got back, so he strove to be friendly and talkative. They had only one more day together, and he tried, for Marianka. He asked her father about his work at the theological seminary and when he started practicing karate and about immigrating to Brussels, but Bojan answered him with few words, as if against his will. He actually ate all his hummus as well as the portion that Anika left. But the whole time it seemed he wanted to say something else.

Marianka kept quite throughout the entire meal, and when they ordered coffee Anika, of all people, turned to him and said, "Are there developments in the murder case?" And Avraham said, "Yes, it seems so."

"So you certainly want to go back, no? I feel that you aren't with us."

Bojan signaled to the waiter that they would like the bill, and Avraham looked at Marianka when he said, "I have no choice," and Anika said to him, "Police never actually get a vacation."

He tried to smile when he said to her, "Sometimes they do."

"I mean a time when you don't think about your work. You certainly take your investigations everywhere."

Avraham hoped that the waiter would come quickly with the bill, but he passed before them with five plates of hummus on the way to another table.

"Why do you actually love it so much?" Anika asked, and Avraham tried to understand what she meant.

"Why did you decide to become a police detective? You certainly could have done other things."

Avraham was still thinking of how to answer when he heard Marianka saying, "Avi needs to be near pain," and then saw her dad nod, like a senior doctor who confirms the diagnosis of a junior one. This wasn't true, but Avraham knew that this is what Marianka thought, because they spoke about it sometimes. He tried to explain to her that since he was a boy he dreamed of being a policeman because of his addiction to detective novels and his sense that he could prove that the fictional detectives were wrong and that the people convicted were innocent. No one knew this was the reason, other than Marianka. Not Eliyahu Ma'alul and not Ilana Lis and definitely not his parents, from whom he hid his dream to join the police until the day when he was accepted to serve and informed them that he wouldn't be a lawyer. When he said, "I think

I became a policeman in order to save people in danger,"
Avraham sought out Marianka's eyes, but she was looking
in a different direction, and on Bojan's face rose a forgiv-
ing smile, as if his answer were incorrect.

Avraham actually didn't have much to do in his office during
those hours. When Shabbat ended, Vahaba began showing the policeman's picture to rape victims in the district,
but Ma'alul still hadn't arrived. Avraham tried calling the
neighbor from the second floor, but he still wasn't at home,
and then he looked again and again at the footage in which
the policeman could be seen passing by on the street. Perhaps because he was alone in his office and because he had
watched the policeman so many times, Avraham suddenly
realized that in his head he was talking to the policeman
in second person, as if he were sitting across from him in
the room. *How did you obtain details of rape victims?
And what did you want from them?* He wrote the questions in pen on a clean sheet of paper. When he sent Ilana
Lis a brief text message: *Maybe we can meet anyway?* she
invited him to come to her home on Monday. And Benny
Saban sounded like he had woken up from sleeping when
Avraham called him and Benny asked, "What picture are
you talking about?"

He informed Saban about the fact that a high-
resolution photo of the policeman had been found, and
suggested that they post it on the Facebook page or in the
media, and Saban asked to get back to him. But when he
called again after a few minutes he announced to him in

a tone even more aggressive than the one he used in the meeting on Thursday that there was no chance the picture would be published. Before saying good-bye Saban asked him, "You're off tomorrow anyway, no?" and Avraham said, "Not sure yet. The guests are going early Monday morning, but in any event I'll be available all day. Everyone knows what they need to do and they'll keep me up to date, and if they need it, I'll come in." Esty Vahaba and Eliyahu Ma'alul were supposed to go through all the sexual assault victims in the district until another woman contacted by the policeman was found, and to report to Avraham after each inquiry was carried out. And they did call him every hour or two, but by Sunday evening they still had no news. None of the women they presented with the photograph identified the man in the picture, and none of them was questioned or received a request from a policeman she didn't know. Avraham spent these hours on visits to churches and monasteries with Bojan and Anika Milanich, because he didn't want to leave Marianka alone. First in Nazareth and afterward at the Sea of Galilee, in the place where Jesus apparently walked on water. His cell phone didn't stop ringing, and Marianka stopped trying to start a conversation involving everyone, so they wandered from site to site silent and expressionless, as if they belonged to a forlorn Trappist order, counting the hours remaining for them together. Toward evening, when they returned to Tel Aviv and sat in a restaurant on the boardwalk, Avraham even thought about ignoring the ringing of his phone, but finally answered and heard Ma'alul saying in an agitated voice, "Avi, are you alone? Can you speak for a moment? It's very urgent."

Marianka looked at Avraham when he went out of the restaurant to the parking lot.

"What happened? Is everything okay?"

"Definitely not, Avi. You have no idea what went on here today, when we weren't at the station."

Through the glass windows of the restaurant Avraham saw that Bojan was speaking to Marianka, and she looked upset, exactly like Ma'alul sounded.

"What happened?"

"Shrapstein brought Yeger's son in for additional questioning. And arrested him. We just returned to the station and Saban informed us that we're not to continue presenting the picture of the policeman to the victims, because Erez Yeger has been arrested and the investigation is now focused on him."

Avraham was stunned. And remembered that Saban asked him yesterday if he was taking vacation and didn't try convincing him to cancel it.

"What exactly did he arrest Erez Yeger for? We know that the assailant isn't a relative."

He absentmindedly put his hand in his coat pocket in order to take out a pack of cigarettes, when Ma'alul said to him, "That's the thing, Avi, he's not her son. I mean not biologically. He's adopted, apparently. Her daughter revealed this to Shrapstein during questioning early this morning, and he brought Yeger in for questioning as a precaution and arrested him immediately. His alibi doesn't hold water, either, because he was released from reserve duty a few hours before the murder and could have reached Holon. Didn't you know that he wasn't her son? And in the meantime, he's refusing a polygraph and DNA test. He's taken a lawyer and is maintaining his right to remain silent."

Avraham took the phone away from his mouth. He recalled a thought that passed through his head at the funeral when Erez Yeger fell on his mother's grave mound: *He doesn't resemble her at all.*

"Avi, can I ask you something?" Ma'alul said, and Avraham answered, "Yes." He knew what Ma'alul wanted to ask even before he heard his words.

"I'm with you on this policeman, but isn't it possible we're mistaken?"

He didn't immediately respond. Before Diana Goldin entered his office he indeed was able to imagine Erez Yeger standing on the other side of the door.

"I'm not saying that we'll stop checking out this angle," Ma'alul continued, "but the son is a logical suspect, don't you think?"

But Leah Yeger wouldn't have written down a meeting with her son on the calendar that was taken from the scene nor in her datebook, and there was also the testimony of the neighbor about the policeman who came down the stairwell and the picture of this policeman that was found! And besides this, the neighbor didn't see anyone else leaving the scene of the murder. Ma'alul listened to him and then said, "But maybe there's an explanation for that, you know?" And Avraham fell silent. "Her son does reserve duty at an air force supply base, and it could be that the neighbor got confused between a police uniform and the uniform he was wearing, do you get it?"

Marianka looked strange to Avraham when he returned to the restaurant.

Her eyes were red as if she had cried and washed her face. And how did all that Ma'alul told him not weaken Avraham's confidence? If he had been alone he would have gotten into his car and gone to the station, but the time was almost ten and he didn't even leave Saban a message when he called him and didn't get an answer. Before they said good-bye Avraham told Ma'alul, "Anything could be, Eliyahu. And there's certainly a reason why the son lied. But I think that they simply don't want the investigation to head in the direction of the policeman, don't you understand? In any case, I ask that tomorrow you and Vahaba continue showing the photo to the remaining victims. And if we need to I'll find a way to publish it, with or without Saban agreeing, you'll see."

When none of them asked him why he left the restaurant for such a long time, Avraham already understood that something had happened. The waitress came to their table and Marianka didn't order anything for herself and then said, "Do you want to share what you have to say with Avi as well? He deserves to hear what you think." Both she and Anika looked at her father, and Bojan spread a napkin over his lap and indeed began to speak.

At the start of his speech Avraham still wasn't listening to him attentively because he was thinking about the things he'd need to do when he arrived at the station the next morning. But after this the words sharpened in his ears, and he couldn't believe what he heard. And even though Bojan's remarks were directed at Avraham, he looked only at Marianka while he spoke.

"As you can imagine for yourself, and as we already told Marianka, we didn't come here for nothing," he began. "We missed her and were also happy to meet your parents and visit places that we had only read about until today, but the reason why we're here is to try to convince Marianka to return home. We had misgivings before we came, but now we are certain that this is what she must do. We have no intentions on hiding anything from you, and therefore we now say this to you as well."

Next to Avraham's plate was a glass of red wine that he hadn't ordered, and he sipped from the glass and waited. Marianka sat next to him and played with her fork but didn't look at him. "Why convince her to go back?" Avraham asked, and Bojan said, "Because she made a mistake when she came here. We told her our opinion beforehand and we said it again now. She has nothing to do here. We all started building a new life for ourselves in Brussels. She had a good job with the police and a chance to advance, and here she is alone and far away from people who truly are concerned for her." Bojan was silent for a moment and then looked at Marianka and continued. "We know that you won't admit this in front of us," he said, "but we feel that you are very miserable here. You're throwing your life in the garbage, and we think you know this and want to ask Avi as well to understand and help you come to the right decision. It is important for us to say that we are not opposed to the relationship between you, but we understand that there's no chance that Avi would leave his job and come to live with us in Brussels."

Avraham didn't say a thing. Marianka raised her eyes from the table and looked at her mother when she quietly asked, "Do you really think I'm miserable here?" And Bojan smiled.

"I look miserable to you?" she asked her mother again, but Anika didn't answer.

"Definitely. You are miserable because you're alone and far from the family and the life that you built for yourself and that we helped you to build," Bojan said. "And we see this, even though you try to pretend. You're squandering your talents and your life in a place where you have no one. Avi has a job and a family and he can't take care of you. And you won't find work that is appropriate for you without knowing the language. And you aren't a Jew, either."

Avraham needed to interrupt and stop him then, but Marianka and her father looked only at each other, as if he and Anika weren't sitting at the table, and Marianka said, "But I *am* happy here, don't you see? I love Avi and we have a home. For the first time I have my own place. It's true I don't yet know what to do with myself, but I'll find something."

"And if you don't find anything?" Anika suddenly asked, and Bojan signaled with his hand that he wanted to continue speaking and said, "It is important to us that you hear these things, because no one else loves you enough to say them to you. And I don't know what you mean when you say that you love Avi, but you thought that you loved other men as well before him, right? And at some point those loves ended. In any case, our obligation as parents is to inform you that we won't support your life here. We won't be able to come back because that would be an expression of support for your choice. And it is important to us to emphasize that we have nothing against Avi, just the opposite, we respect him, and actually because of that we hope that he will understand and help you to leave."

He had to say something, if not for himself than at least for Marianka. And maybe he just needed to take her hand and get out of there. He tried to smile when he said, "I understand your concern for Marianka, but I want you to know that she's in good hands. We're thinking about our shared future, for now we haven't made any decisions, and if it gets hard for Marianka we'll think about that together. I can promise you that I only want what's good for her." Everyone was silent when he finished, as if he hadn't said a thing.

Bojan continued looking only at Marianka. The waitress served the appetizers and on the table a short candle burned. "I don't know if you're a believer, Avi," Bojan said. "We are. We *all* are. And a day before we came here I saw from the window of my office a sight that was for me a sign that we are doing the right thing. On the street opposite the window there was a run-over dove, and suddenly I saw another dove land next to it and begin to peck at its corpse. I tried to understand what I was seeing, until I realized that it was impossible to know if it was kissing it or saying good-bye to it or perhaps actually eating its flesh. Do you understand what I mean?"

Avraham didn't understand, but Marianka did. And he couldn't help but recall the birds on which he found Leah Yeger's body. If the conversation had taken place at another time, and not minutes after Ma'alul informed him that Saban and Shrapstein were trying to wrest control of the investigation away from him, perhaps Avraham would have responded differently, especially when Marianka put down her wineglass and smiled at her father and then said to him, "You're an idiot, you know? I now finally understand how much of an idiot you are."

"I'm trying to say to you that your good intentions don't change the situation, Avi," Bojan continued as if Marianka hadn't said a thing to him. "I believe you that you want only good for Marianka, as you say, but she is the one run-over in the street now, and you're pecking at her flesh, even if it seems to you that those are kisses."

Anika touched Bojan's hand, as if to signal to him that he had gone too far. Or perhaps she actually did this in order to support him? Marianka was the one who got up first and left the restaurant, and Avraham simply went after her. And only later on, when they returned to their apartment, did he ask her, "What the hell was that crazy fable about the dead birds?"

Marianka asked him to open the car door and got inside and sat in the passenger seat and burst out laughing.

"Let's go," she said to him afterward, and when he

asked what her parents would do, she answered, "Doesn't matter. Let them go back on foot."

They stopped in a parking lot not far from there because Marianka wanted them to go down to the beach, and when they sat facing the dark water she said to him only, "I'm sorry," and he asked her, "About what?"

"That you heard all that. I should have known that this is what would happen. You were right."

So why did he feel that *he* needed to apologize to her? To apologize for bringing her to Holon and for not responding to her father and mainly for hiding from her everything he was going through since the investigation opened and for truly leaving her alone. They didn't talk almost at all about her parents that night but about themselves instead, about her and about him, and Avraham managed to tell her everything he hadn't said in recent days. He told her about the conversation with Ma'alul and about Erez Yeger, who wasn't his mother's biological son, and about the fact that she was raped in her home by a man she knew and about the policeman whom he was sure asked to question her for reasons he still didn't comprehend. When Marianka asked him why he hadn't shared all this with her before then, Avraham told her the truth. That he had no idea. And then he added, "Maybe in order to protect you from something," and she said, "To protect me? From what? And why do you think that I need protection?"

The next day, at four in the morning, they said goodbye to Bojan and Anika in the street, across from a cabdriver who had come to take them to the airport, without hugging.

Avraham couldn't go back to sleep, and even though he wanted to stay with Marianka all day, he went ahead and left for the station early. When Esty Vahaba called him toward noon he was in the car, on his way to Ilana Lis so that she could advise him on how nevertheless to publish the picture of the policeman who went down the stairs and disappeared, only Vahaba said that she thinks there's a woman who perhaps knows something about the policeman.

He slowed down and asked her, "What? He visited her, too?" and Vahaba said, "No, she didn't say anything, but she was quite shocked when I showed her the picture, I think. And I have a feeling she didn't tell me everything she knows."

That was the first time Avraham heard the name Bengtson.

10

The policewoman called Mali on Monday morning.

She was in a meeting with a new client when a number she didn't recognize appeared on the screen of her cell phone and she didn't answer, but the second time she said, "Excuse me," and stuck an earbud into her right ear. She inserted the other earbud when she heard the voice on the other end of the line. A woman asked to speak with Mazal Bengtson, and Mali said, "Speaking." And she was sure that the policewoman got to her because of the phone call to the hospital's emergency room a few days before. She got up from her seat without apologizing to the client and hid her mouth with her hand while she spoke. The policewoman asked if they could meet, and when Mali said she was at work, the policewoman asked her where she worked. She was sure that the policewoman already knew—just as she must now know who was responsible for the accident—since the phone call to the emergency room was made from the office, and therefore she said, "In Holon. On Shenkar Street."

"I can come to see you there," the policewoman said. "And this won't take more than five or ten minutes."

Mali asked Yana if she could take the client instead of her and immediately went to the women's restroom. A cleaning lady was mopping the floor and Mali waited for her to leave before entering one of the stalls and calling Kobi.

During those days, the two of them had so many opportunities to try and alter their fate, but they didn't.

She asked herself endless times what Kobi would have done had he been awake and answered the phone, and she would have told him that the policewoman was on her way to her in order to question her about the accident. *Would he have told her the truth then?*

During the weekend the two of them had hoped that everything was behind them, or at least tried to hope, and maybe that's why she was so unprepared for what happened. Kobi pretended he was in a good mood, but she saw him continuing to take deep inhalations, as if he were suffocating. The weather improved, and on Saturday he suggested they take the girls to the amusement park in Tel Aviv, like they promised them at the start of winter. Mali preferred that they stay home, but after Daniella and Noy heard about the plan, there was no chance that they'd relent. Kobi woke early and went up to the roof to work out. When she was making pancakes he came up to her from behind and wrapped his arms around her stomach and asked, "Are you coming with us or staying here?"

She couldn't tell him why she wasn't going on the rides, but perhaps hinted at it when she said that she was nauseous and had a headache and was scared she would throw up. There weren't lines at most of the rides and Kobi took Daniella and Noy on the Devil's Tunnel ride, which disappointed them, and then on the roller coaster and the bumper cars, and went around with them again and again on the giant octopus whose metal arms spun around high above the treetops. Mali looked at them from below. At the outbursts of horror and laughter on the girls' faces. How they held Kobi's hands. She took pictures of them with her phone, because Kobi asked. And over the weekend she did think about the woman who he struck with his car. She was sorry about the phone call to the hospital and hoped they wouldn't call her back as they had promised, though on the other hand she wanted them to call in order to say that the woman had been released. It didn't occur to her even for a moment that he had lied.

She would look at the pictures from that day at the park only much later, and then she would be unable to stop looking at them. Especially at a picture she took when the three of them were on the roller coaster: Daniella and Noy embraced in his arms in a green car climbing toward the end of the track, a moment before the drop.

In the weeks to come Mali met the policewoman many times, but that morning she didn't know that her name was Esty Vahaba. She was very short and younger than Mali, and smoked a cigarette during their conversation. She asked

Mali for an identification card and then crossed her thick legs and placed a plastic clipboard on them and sat bent forward while she filled out the forms. Vadim, the bank's security guard, watched them while they walked away from the bank and sat on a bench. The policewoman placed a paper cup on it and when she drank from it later, coffee spilled onto her fingertips.

Mali watched the cars that passed by them, as if Kobi could have been in one, and recalled the policewoman who questioned her in Eilat. She was older than Esty Vahaba and good-looking, and stared at the computer screen while over and over she asked Mali questions about the wine she drank at the party and her relationship with Kobi and if she was 100 percent certain she hadn't invited a man up to her room. When Vahaba asked, "You were assaulted a few years ago in Eilat, correct, Ms. Bengtson?" Mali didn't understand why she was mentioning this and how it was connected to the hit-and-run accident. The policewoman's cigarette disturbed her because of the pregnancy. But then Vahaba said, "I ask that you keep secret the things I'm going to tell you, because we're talking about confidential information from an investigation in its earliest stages, and we're not sure about anything, okay?" And only after Mali nodded she continued. "We suspect that there's a policeman, or a criminal who dresses up like a policeman, who works in the area and harasses women who were victims of rape. What I want to check with you is, has a man like this contacted you or been with you?"

Mali immediately said, "No," and at first sensed only relief. The policewoman put out her cigarette on the end of the bench, as if she sensed that the smoke was bothering her. "Are you sure?" she asked, and Mali said to her, "Yes."

"Do you remember when was the last time you gave testimony?"

It took her time to answer, because she didn't remember. And while she was trying to remember she suddenly heard the words that were said before, *A criminal who dresses up like a policeman.*

"I don't remember exactly when. A while ago. Maybe a year."

"And no one from the police has contacted you since? Maybe in the last few weeks? Not even by phone?"

"No."

"And are you perhaps in contact with other women who were assaulted who you know were recently reached out to in this way?"

Did Mali already know then? In contrast to the woman who gathered testimony from her in Eilat, Esty Vahaba looked at her when she spoke. Her eyes were large and opened wide, as if unnaturally. On her forehead, above her left eye, was a scar. She paused before bending over again toward the clipboard and writing a few lines on the form. She remained sitting in her place when she said to Mali, "There is a gag order on this investigation in order not to create panic among women who've been attacked, so I'm asking you again to keep the details I'm providing you with secret, okay? And if a man who introduces himself as a detective from the police contacts you and asks to gather testimony, or if you remember that this indeed happened or hear about someone who this happened to, you'll inform me immediately, right? We're afraid that he did this to a few women and that he'll do it again."

She accepted the policewoman's card, putting it in her coat pocket without looking at it, and as she rose from the bench she felt something twisting and turning in the pit of her stomach. No one had contacted her. The things the policewoman said, about the panic among women who had been attacked and about the fact that the policeman had done this a few times, were what caused Mali to understand with certainty.

"Do you know who this man is?" Mali shouldn't have asked, but she did need to know.

The policewoman still sat on the bench, as if it was hard for her to get up. She said, "We don't know his name, but we have a good picture of him, and we'll find him soon." And Mali asked her to see it nevertheless.

Vahaba stared at her with her big eyes and then removed the photograph from a gray folder that was resting on her knees. And Mali looked at the photograph momentarily, no more than a second, before everything went dark. She asked Vahaba, "When is the picture from?" since this was her final hope, but the policewoman said to her, "From last week."

Daniella and Noy were at day care and school, and during the first few minutes Mali didn't know what she would do with them after she picked them up. At eleven she had an additional meeting, and she sat across from the customer as if nothing had happened. She explained to him why the bank was refusing to provide him with the mortgage that he had requested, and he raised his voice. How much time passed before she understood that *there had been no accident*? She imagined herself suddenly in the delivery room, without Kobi and without anyone else next to her. The spasms in the pit of her stomach turned into nausea, and when she went to the bathroom and tried to vomit, they thought at the bank that the reason was her confrontation with the customer.

For the second time in a few days she needed to explain everything from the beginning to herself: the job interview and what happened on the day of their anniversary, Kobi's disappearance in the days after and the message he left for his father on the phone, and the car that wasn't in the parking lot. Now there was also perhaps an explanation for the umbrella and for Kobi's desperate searching for it. And perhaps also for watching the news and reading the newspapers. Kobi wasn't lying when he said that the police were looking for him, but he lied with regards to the reasons. And she never lied to him. Never. Even though there had been no accident, the young woman he hit with his car was still lying bloody on the street and no one was coming to help her.

When Kobi woke up he tried to call her because he saw that she had called him many times, but she didn't answer because she still didn't know what to say. He sent her a text message, *Everything okay?* and she answered him, *Yes, in a meeting.* Maybe that first lie gave her the idea? The policewoman's card was in her pocket, and Mali thought about calling her and she also could have called her sister, Gila, to set up a meeting with her, but when she picked up Daniella and Noy from day care and school, she had already decided to return home and also that she wouldn't say a thing to Kobi for now. The girls sat in the back, and Mali looked at them in the mirror while driving and asked Daniella why she was quiet. Noy rehearsed the song they were preparing in class for the Purim party. When she saw Kobi's car in the parking lot she immediately remembered last Monday. *This was the day on which he was discovered, apparently.* The car wasn't there then when they returned home, but she smelled his aftershave in the elevator and discovered that the door to the apartment wasn't locked, and when they went inside she heard that he was showering. His clothes were thrown onto the bedroom floor, but she didn't see the policeman's uniform.

The table was set for lunch when they came inside, and ravioli was cooking on the stove. When Kobi opened the door for them he said to her immediately, "Why didn't you answer me after the meeting? I tried you a few times." Mali answered that she had back-to-back meetings and that she called in the morning because she was worried that she wouldn't manage to get the girls, but in the end it worked out. Her eyes avoided his eyes, but in a strange way she wasn't as frightened as she had been before the meeting with the policewoman, only confused. And she didn't touch the meal. Noy told Kobi about the preparations for the Purim party at school, and Daniella remained quiet and, like Mali, didn't eat a thing. Mali felt that something inside her was also growing stronger or hardening, perhaps out of anger. After Eilat it was as if she had left her body, and even when she returned to it this was a partial return, and during those hours at home, after the conversation with the policewoman, it was also as if the parts that had been broken had joined together again.

Kobi asked her, "How was work?" and Mali said to him, "Good." And before then she wouldn't have been able to lie to him like this. When she went to the bathroom and kneeled before the toilet she managed to throw up. Kobi hurried after her and waited beside the door, and when she came out he asked her, "Are you throwing up?" She said that she ate something spoiled rotten at work and that she feels better. Because she didn't want to remain alone with him, she didn't go into the bedroom. She did homework with Noy and let Daniella watch television, and when Daniella fell asleep on the couch Mali sat down next to her and stroked her hair. At five Kobi asked her if she was feeling okay and if he could go work out, and she said yes. Maybe all she had to do was ask him, "Why'd you go back to it," and he would have told her? Only when she saw his car leaving the parking lot and driving off did she hurry to the bedroom and start looking. She looked for the uniform among his winter clothes and in the underwear drawer, and afterward up above among his summer clothes and in the box of costumes, but they weren't in the bedroom nor in the utility room on the roof, not even in his drawers, which she opened for the first time.

The nausea disappeared, and she didn't stop looking, even though she didn't know what she would do with the policeman's uniform if she found it.

The first time that she saw Kobi wearing it, Mali was lying in their bed, trying to fall asleep.

Kobi came into the bedroom then and turned on the main light and his eyes were red, as if he were crying. She asked him, "What is that?" and Kobi sat down on the edge of the bed in silence and she asked him again, "Kobi, why are you wearing those clothes? You're scaring me."

This happened a few weeks after Eilat.

The cut on her neck hadn't closed up all the way, or at least that's how she felt, even though no one other than her noticed it anymore, and her wrists also hurt sometimes like they did the morning after. In the mirror she was still the other woman then. And Kobi was the person who, thanks only to him, would sometimes remember who she was. He didn't explain why he was wearing the uniform and began speaking only after she stopped crying. But when he spoke she again burst into tears, and he hugged her and she stopped.

Everything hurt then as though her flesh were peeled off and she tried to tell herself that he was bleeding as well, and if she would only place her hand on his wound it would pass. When he asked her to come with him to the kitchen and sit across from him by the table, she agreed, because she had no other choices. On the table were his cell phone and a pad of yellow paper and a pen, as if it were an investigation room.

Toward evening Mali looked for the police uniform among the dirty clothes at the bottom of the laundry basket and even in the girls' rooms, although by now it was clear to her that she wouldn't find it. When she returned to the bedroom in order to search the box of sheets under the bed, she saw their picture on the wall and wanted to shatter the glass and tear up the photograph. Nothing that she was about to do had yet occurred to her during those hours, but she did imagine herself again in the delivery room, without him, without knowing where he was, and afterward there also appeared in her thoughts a picture of the four of them together in her car: she was driving and Daniella and Noy were sitting in the backseat and next to them the baby in his special car seat, and the passenger seat was empty.

At six thirty, when knocking could be heard at the door, she was on the roof. She thought that Kobi was early and forgot to take a key with him, and because she didn't want to see him she didn't go down right away, but Daniella called from downstairs, "Mom, it's for you," and when Mali came down the stairs she saw the policewoman who questioned her in the morning and felt how her knees weakened.

Behind Esty Vahaba stood another policeman who Mali didn't know then.

11

Only at the end of questioning Mazal Bengtson, truly at the last moment, did Avraham bring control of the investigation back into his own hands. Before then, for a few hours, he sensed that he was again being hesitant as he had been on the first day of the investigation. He watched Shrapstein lead Erez Yeger into the interrogation room, and he didn't intervene when Shrapstein tried to get Yeger to admit that he murdered his mother. And he listened to the things Ilana Lis hurled at him without responding. Until almost the last moment, he also sat in Mazal Bengtson's empty living room barely involved in the conversation. Bengtson again said that no policeman had contacted her, and Esty Vahaba's feeling, that Bengtson hadn't told her everything during the first questioning, seemed so unconvincing to him.

⊶———⊷

The apartment was on the seventh floor of an old residential building: 8 Uri Zvi Greenberg Street.

The door was open when they entered the building before six thirty in the evening, and the stairwell remained dark even after they turned on the light. The narrow elevator gave off an odor of cigarette smoke and animals, cats perhaps. And Avraham was forced to stand too close to Esty Vahaba. On the mirror were two stickers, one with the telephone number of a plumber and the second of an exterminator, and Avraham read them in order not to look at himself in the mirror and see what Ilana Lis saw.

Vahaba knocked on the door twice before ringing the bell. A four- or five-year-old girl, with light hair and blue eyes, opened the door for them and then immediately called for her mother, who looked entirely different. Mazal Bengtson was tall and dark complected, and her hair was black. Perhaps thirty-five years old. She wore a gray fleece and slippers, and to Avraham it seemed that they had interrupted her while cleaning. She didn't ask them why they had come, and this should have grabbed his attention, but during those moments his thoughts were still in Ilana's apartment.

The girl who opened the door for them remained standing in the doorway to her room and looked at them from there throughout the conversation, as if to watch over the mother. Mazal Bengtson led them to the living room, offered them coffee or tea, and went to the kitchen to boil water, as those being questioned sometimes do when policemen show up at their homes with no notice, in order to relax. At night, when he recalled the conversation with her, Avraham thought how much Mazal Bengtson didn't resemble her daughters. Like Erez Yeger and the woman who wasn't his mother. He looked at the apartment while they waited for her. The blinds in the window facing the street were closed, and the feeling in the almost empty living room was claustrophobic. In its center were two black leather couches and a small glass table, and a flat-screen television hung on the wall opposite them. The rest of the walls were bare, except for one small photo that was hanging on one of the walls, as if by accident. The two of them sat on one of the couches, and Mazal Bengtson set their mugs of coffee on the glass table and sat down across from them on a stool. Throughout most of the conversation Avraham gazed at the photograph of the deer skipping through dense forest, fleeing from the hunters' rifles or the camera. Under the photograph was a small bookshelf and in it were two rows of books, mostly in English, and this, too, should have attracted his attention, but at that time he didn't remember the English accent of the policeman who questioned Diana Goldin, and even if he had remembered, it's reasonable to assume he wouldn't have made a connection between them. On the couch a woven blanket was spread out, like at his parents' apartment, and something about it and the bare walls caused him to think that they hadn't been living in this apartment for a long time or that it was a temporary refuge of sorts that they planned on leaving.

And he actually didn't even want to be there. He joined Esty Vahaba because that was the only way to make progress on his angle of the investigation, and because he didn't know what to do when he returned to his office from the terrible visit with Ilana Lis.

Since the morning hours, everything had worked against him. He hoped that Erez Yeger would agree to their giving him a polygraph and DNA examination in order to prove he wasn't the assailant, but despite the advice he received from his lawyer Yeger refused and didn't say another word to Shrapstein in the interrogation room. Nor did he explain why he hid from the detectives that he was adopted or the phone call with his mother the day before the murder. Through the interrogation room window Avraham heard Shrapstein threaten the handcuffed Yeger that if he didn't agree to the tests, that the police would publish the news that a relative had been arrested on suspicion of involvement in the murder. Avraham thought this was just an interrogation technique, but while he was eating lunch Ma'alul informed him over the phone that Ynet.com posted an article saying that the police were close to solving the case.

It took the page time to open because the Internet connection at the station was slow, and when Avraham read the piece he couldn't believe it.

The headline read, "Police Close to Solving Holon Murder," and in the body of the article it was written that in less than a week the investigation team succeeded in arresting a suspect in the murder of Leah Yeger, a member of the victim's family, and that in a few more days an indictment would be brought against him and the gag order would be lifted in its entirety.

Avraham immediately called Benny Saban, but he

didn't answer. And when he hurried to his office he discovered that he wasn't at the station. When Vahaba came in to update him about the testimony she gathered from rape victims, it seemed for a moment so pointless, since, after all, the investigation was nearing its end. Vahaba, too, saw the article on Ynet.com for the first time in his office. She wasn't certain that further questioning of Mazal Bengtson would yield additional information, but it seemed to her that Bengtson was the only one from among all the women she spoke with who perhaps knew more than she told her. Bengtson's rape case was handled by the Eilat district, and Vahaba explained to Avraham that she had decided on her own to also speak to women who weren't attacked in the district but resided in it, and Avraham looked at her with admiration when he asked to read the file. "But why would she hide something?" Avraham asked, and Vahaba said, "I have no idea. But she asked to see the photo and I think she was surprised when she saw the policeman in the picture."

Bengtson's fair girl who stood in the doorway to her room also looked at them with a frightened gaze when Avraham said to Mazal Bengtson, "I am Police Superintendent Avraham, commander of the Investigations Branch in Ayalon District. As Esty told you today, we are in the middle of a very sensitive investigation concerning a policeman or a man who presents himself as a police detective and gathers testimony from rape victims, and we came to share with you additional details from the investigation that would perhaps help you to recall if you recently met with this man."

Mazal Bengtson's gaze passed back and forth between him and Esty Vahaba, and she also didn't stop sending fleeting glances in the direction of the girl standing by the door, but Avraham did not attribute much importance to this.

"May I ask you a few preliminary questions? I understand from Esty that you were assaulted approximately three years ago, correct?"

"Yes."

"In Eilat."

"Yes. In a hotel."

Avraham didn't recall from the rape file that he read beforehand in his office if Bengtson was married or divorced, and on the door he didn't notice any sign with names. He felt that she wanted them to leave so she could continue cleaning the apartment. Perhaps she also didn't want to return to the assault that she certainly had tried to forget. Avraham opened his notepad and searched for a pen in his pockets, and when he didn't find one he asked Vahaba. "You told Esty today that you don't remember the last time you gave testimony to the police. We have it written that you were questioned in 2013. Is that correct?"

"It could be. If that's what's written."

"And do you recall who questioned you then?"

"Always the same policewoman."

"Yifat Asayag from the Eilat police?"

"Yes."

What was he supposed to ask her actually? And for what purpose? Did he think that she'd suddenly tell him that the policeman had been in her home and before he took off left her with a full name and a telephone number? He tried to get rid of the doubts that arose in him following the meeting he had before this with Ilana Lis and to concentrate on the woman sitting in front of him, but nevertheless it was as if he didn't see her. Mazal Bengtson was a good-looking woman, but he didn't notice this because of the fleece she wore or the gloomy living room, and only when he would meet her again would he notice this. On a finger on the left hand was a wedding ring and on the other hand was a second ring. And Avraham remembered what he read about the night when she was attacked in Eilat.

She was alone there, in the framework of a professional conference. And the man who attacked her was never found.

One of the theories of the investigation team was that the assailant was a tourist who was staying at the hotel and fled Israel that same night or a refugee who entered the country a few days before from the Sinai desert. A different theory was that Bengtson invited to her room a man whom she met at a party in the hotel but wasn't willing to admit this. What bothered the team was that no traces left by the attacker were found on the clothes she wore when being questioned that night, and only when they told her that did Bengtson say that after the attack she took off her pajamas and put on the clothes she wore to the party.

How old then was her daughter who watched them from the door? And did she know anything about all this? Despite his efforts to concentrate, Avraham's thoughts wandered to the conversation with Ilana. He heard himself say to Bengtson, "One of the details we discovered is that the policeman makes phone contact with the victims and confirms over a few conversations that they aren't suspicious of him before setting up a meeting with them. Perhaps you recall something like this? Someone who tried to set up a meeting with you?" Bengtson thought for a few seconds before she said no.

"This means you're certain that since 2013 no person introducing himself as a police detective contacted you, not even by phone? Perhaps you want to see the photo again?"

All that was so unnecessary, or at least this is how he felt.

Avraham fell silent and grabbed his warm mug and looked at Esty Vahaba, who was sitting next to him. When the girl came near to them on tiptoes, as if they wouldn't sense it, Bengtson said to her, "Daniella, go back to your room, okay, sweetie? We'll finish soon, right?" Avraham nodded.

Only when Ilana opened the door for him earlier that afternoon did Avraham think about the fact that this was the second time he was visiting her home overall. And that she had never been in his apartment.

The previous time had been during the shiva for her son who was killed in a training exercise. Avraham didn't come alone then but rather with a delegation of policemen from the station, and they stayed less than an hour because the house was full of visitors. But he remembered

everything. The well-lit living room and the shelves loaded
with books and especially the strange art objects, dark
clay masks and colorful pictures in which nothing clear
had been painted, and wooden sculptures that Ilana and
her husband had brought back from their travels around
the world and which were scattered throughout the house.
Even Ilana looked the same to him, at least at first glance.
She wore a loose-fitting dress and over her long red hair a
scarf had been wrapped, but her blue eyes looked at him
with exactly the same glance, which at least at the start
of their meeting Avraham felt contained affection. They
didn't hug but only shook hands. And when he asked,
"How are you?" Ilana said to him, "You see, everything's
okay. I'm still alive."

Did Avraham only understand then how much he
missed her? How much he longed for her presence at meetings of the investigation team? He wanted to talk with her
from the moment he left the murder scene, because almost
from his first day with the police she accompanied each
case he investigated. And in each one of the team meetings he'd led since the murder he thought about what she
would do were she sitting there instead of him. There was
complete silence in the apartment, not even noises from
outside could be heard, and he wanted to ask Ilana what
she does before her husband returns from work, when she
added, "I finally have some vacation. I'm taking advantage
of the time in order to read books I never got to," as if she
really could hear his thoughts. On the giant wooden table
in the dining room, next to a plate with dates, he saw the
book *The Man Who Mistook His Wife for a Hat*, opened

and facedown, and for some reason he thought that she put it there for him and that she hadn't read it beforehand. Hadn't she told him once, many years ago, that she'd read that book? He didn't know if or how to ask her about the disease and the treatments. When they sat at the table it seemed to him that he noticed in her pale face signs of her disease and that she wasn't telling him everything. She had grown thin, and when she led him to the living room she walked with difficulty. Finally he asked, "How do you feel?" and Ilana said, "Excellent. The surgery was successful and I have two more rounds of treatment, and afterward I'll return to work." But she didn't look to him like someone who could soon return to work. When she asked him, "What's with you?" he was struck by a strong desire to tell her about Marianka and her parents' visit and his father's deteriorating condition, and at the same time he felt the exhaustion building up in him in recent days, and thought that if he placed his body atop the thick pillows scattered on the sofa, he'd fall asleep. He said, "I'm fine."

"And how is your girlfriend? Is she managing here?"

That was what it was like from the first day he told Ilana about Marianka. She refused to call her by name.

"Yes. Quite well actually."

"What is she doing? Is she working?"

"She found work at a health club. Giving karate lessons. And she's looking for other things."

"Wasn't she a cop there?"

"Yes. She was. But she was also a karate instructor."

Afterward Ilana said that you wouldn't know by looking at him that his girlfriend is a fitness instructor, and

Avraham laughed. He was sure she had changed her mind and wouldn't refuse to help him when he asked to share his troubles with her, and when she questioned him about working with Saban, it seemed to him that he was right. "What did you want to consult with me about?" Ilana asked, and Avraham said that everything had changed since the last time he called.

"We have a hell of a case. You must have heard," he said, and Ilana was quiet for a moment before asking, "Do you mean the murder of the old woman? I heard on the radio before that it's closed."

"They arrested the wrong man," Avraham said immediately, and Ilana asked, "Who did the arresting?"

"Saban. And Shrapstein was with him."

"And why the wrong man?"

"Because it's someone else. It's not her son."

Was he mistaken when he felt that Ilana was listening to him with great interest? He updated her on the details of the investigation she wasn't familiar with, told her that Leah Yeger had been raped in the past, and about the testimony of the neighbor and Diana Goldin and about the photograph of the policeman. Ilana didn't interrupt him once. He was now head of the Investigations Unit and Ilana was on leave, and they were at her home and not at the station, but it was exactly like their conversations once were, especially when Ilana left the living room and returned with an ashtray and a pack of Marlboro Lights. Avraham hesitated before saying to her, "No, thank you. I quit," and she looked at him, surprised.

"Are you sure? Is it because of the athletic girlfriend?"

He felt better when he finished talking, and when Ilana asked him, "So how can I help you with this?" he said, "I don't know. You tell me. I want to convince Saban to publish the photo of the policeman, but I don't know how. He's scared of the damage it's liable to cause, and you can imagine that that's the last thing the police need right now, but I have no other way to get to the killer. Do you have any idea how I should talk to Saban? Or maybe I can speak to someone above him?"

Ilana exhaled the smoke too close to him and said, "I think that in this matter Saban's right. To publish a photograph like that when you know so little about the suspect and his involvement, it's an irresponsible act. And I also agree with him about the damage it's liable to cause. Understand, Avi, you see before you this investigation, but whoever's above you has to see the larger context. There are other investigations, and the police have other tasks in addition to solving a murder. That's exactly the responsibility of a district commander."

"But I have no other way to get to the policeman, Ilana. And I think I'm not mistaken and that it's him, and once we know who this is we'll be able to verify it through the findings from the scene. Will you at least agree that everything points to him?"

Ilana set the cigarette down in the ashtray and Avraham almost reached out his hand to it.

"How could I know?" she said. "I haven't seen the investigation materials and I haven't read the testimony and I have no way of helping you with this. I have no idea how trustworthy your witnesses are, and most important, I haven't questioned her son. It sounds to me like you could be right, but I'm sure you'll succeed in catching him even without publishing a picture in the newspapers. I trust you."

Avraham placed the handbag that was by his feet on the table and said, "I have everything here, Ilana. The materials are here." It was forbidden to remove the file from the station, but he had to bring it. Ilana put out the cigarette and asked him suddenly, "Avi, what do you really want?"

There was anger in her gaze, and he didn't understand why.

"You know you're not allowed to share the materials in the file with me because I have no official position with the police right now, and I'm happy about that. And I asked you not to involve me in any investigation. That doesn't make me feel good and doesn't give me comfort, trust me. I want to detach myself from all this. And you don't need me."

"I'm not trying to give you comfort, Ilana," he said. "And I'm telling you that I do need your help. Saban is only occupied with how he and the police look, and above him as well they apparently don't like it that I'm searching for a cop."

Ilana interrupted and said to him, "I've known you enough years and I think you're doing this because you think that if you include me I'll feel better. But let me decide what's right for me, okay? And don't help me, Avi. Not like this at least."

That wasn't the reason he was there, and he told her again that he was in need of her help.

"I told you, I can't help you."

"I think you can."

"How?"

"Think with me about a way to get to him. If not with the help of the photograph then another way. And also about his motives. Why would a policeman do a thing like that?"

For a moment Ilana looked at him with interest. Avraham recognized the flash in her eyes when a certain detail in an investigation sparked her imagination. This was exactly like before she got sick, in her old office at that Ayalon district station or in the new one at the Tel Aviv district headquarters. She and him and a cigarette burning in an ashtray between them and smoke exhaled toward an open window. The intimacy between two detectives who knew that thanks to the cooperation between them an endless number of past cases had been solved. "You don't have a motive?" Ilana asked.

"I have theories."

"Such as?"

"Revenge perhaps. He wants to get back at the police for something. If he's still a policeman it could be that he's frustrated. And maybe it's someone who was fired from the service."

Ilana said, "Could be," and went to the kitchen to empty the ashtray in the garbage, and Avraham thought this was a sign that she'd look at the materials, but when she returned the intimacy had faded, and Ilana again refused to discuss the case with him. He insisted again, until she suddenly asked him, "Do you want to know what I really think?" and lit another cigarette.

He said that he wanted to know.

"So I think that Saban is right."

"Right about what?"

"This photo, like I told you, cannot be published. Period. And the investigation of the son can progress at the same time as you look into the matter of the policeman, I don't see why not. Do you remember what we always said? That you have to listen to all the possible stories simultaneously? That the most severe mistake we make is to lock into just one story *because it suits us*, and not listen to other stories?"

He heard the hint in what she was saying, even if she hid it in different words.

"You think I locked into the story *because it suits me*?"

"That's not what I said, Avi. I said that—"

"But that's what you think?"

"I told you that I think you've got the right angle. But that it wouldn't hurt to check other angles at the same time."

"Why do you think this story suits me?"

Ilana was silent. And she put out the cigarette, even though she had just started smoking it. Only when he asked her again did she suddenly say to him angrily, "Maybe because you resemble this cop a little, no?"

He thought she was kidding, but in Ilana's eyes there was something else, which he didn't recognize, when she continued speaking. "Don't get insulted, please. I mean that cops will do anything in order to catch people who break the law and put them in jail. That's our goal; do you agree with me? Something else is guiding you, just like with this cop. He's not questioning the women in order to catch their assailants, right or not? He does it for other reasons. For *his own* reasons. And you're like that, too. I'm not sure I understand what's guiding you, Avi, what you're looking for exactly, and the truth is that I always thought this is what prevents you from being the exceptional detective you could have been. But maybe it's still not too late for you to change."

When Avraham was on his way back to the station and heard again and again in his head the things Ilana said to him, he understood that she didn't mean to hurt him and had simply hurled at him the rage that had built up in her for weeks at the disease that had spread throughout her body and about the fact that she had to resign from her position that she loved so much and that she wouldn't dare to admit, even to herself, that she wouldn't be returning to. And he also remembered what Marianka said to her parents, about the fact that he's a policeman because he needs to be close to pain. But when he heard Ilana's words for the first time he froze and didn't respond, and then he rose and put the investigation materials in the file. Ilana said, "So you are insulted? But you wanted to hear the truth," and Avraham said quietly, "That's not the reason the story *suits me*, Ilana. The story suits me because it's the only possible story according to the evidence and because all the other stories aren't reasonable. But thanks for the help." He didn't wait for her to walk him out, and as he walked toward the door he heard her call out from behind him, "Did you come so I'd say amen to everything you said, Avi?" And he tried to smile when he turned around and said to her, "I didn't come for that, Ilana. I came in order to see how you were doing."

He had no more questions for Mazal Bengtson, and he waited for Esty Vahaba to finish questioning her as well so that he could return home. Vahaba bent over toward the glass table and said to Bengtson almost in a whisper, perhaps so her daughter wouldn't hear, "I want to be completely honest with you, Mazal. There's a reason we came after you already gave me testimony this morning. I felt after our conversation this morning that perhaps you're scared to say that you did meet with this man. That perhaps it's unpleasant for you to admit this. And I wanted to tell you that you have nothing to be ashamed of and that you have nothing to fear if that happened. You're not the only one who fell into his trap and agreed to give him testimony. There's no way to know that he's not an on-duty policeman if that's how he presented himself. But if you know something, then you have a way to help us in preventing him from harming other women."

Bengtson listened and then again said that she hadn't met the policeman, and that if she had met with him she wouldn't hesitate to say so. And Esty Vahaba sighed and said, "But if you remember something, we're here."

This was the last moment, and were it not for the phone call from Eliyahu Ma'alul Avraham apparently wouldn't have seen a thing. His phone rang and he got up and walked away from them in the direction of the entrance and listened to Ma'alul, who said to him, "Avi, I have some good news for you. I was with the neighbor and I showed him the policeman's photograph, and he says that's for sure the man he saw. He's certain it's not Erez Yeger but rather the man in the photograph. Do you hear me?" And Avraham didn't respond to him because while he was listening he saw the picture through the open door.

For a moment he considered going in immediately, but he didn't do so.

From the place where he stood he saw only part of the naked body along with her face, for a moment. He said to Ma'alul, "Excellent, Eliyahu, but I'm here in the middle of something. I'll call you in a bit," and then he approached Bengtson and Vahaba, who got up from their seats, and asked where the bathroom was. Afterward, when Avraham tried to explain to himself why he did it, he thought that what drew his attention was the contrast between the woman he spoke with in the living room and the one he saw in the picture. Mazal Bengtson pointed toward the white door at the beginning of the hallway and Avraham waited in the bathroom with the light on until he heard her walking away and then he silently opened the door and exited.

The next room over was dark, and he passed by it on his way to the bedroom, which was lit, even though no one was in it. If she had noticed him Avraham would have explained that he was looking for a towel in order to dry

his hands. The picture that he saw earlier from the hallway was hanging over a double bed, and at first he saw in
it only the woman who sat before him and didn't manage
to attract his attention. But then he saw as well the man
whose arms were wrapped around her breasts.

12

The thought to turn him in crossed Mali's mind immediately after the police left.

When the police were at their place, Mali couldn't say a thing because the girls were there, but especially because Kobi was liable to enter the apartment at any moment. Daniella waited by the door to her room, even though Mali asked her to wait in her room, and Mali watched her daughter and the door because she was actually scared that Kobi would return and see the police and that they, too, would see and recognize him. This is what gave rise to her fear and not their questions, maybe because she felt that she would be answering them soon enough. She didn't believe them that they came because something in the previous conversation caused Vahaba to be suspicious that she hadn't revealed everything, and she was sure they knew more about Kobi than what they told her. And the strange thing was that in the meantime she continued lying. She had already lied to Kobi that day when she hid the policewoman's visit to the bank from him, and she continued to

lie in the evening when she didn't tell him that the police
had been in their home. And that night she lied to Gila
just as she had lied to the two police officers who had
presented to her Kobi's picture in uniform. She had been
such a bad liar since they were girls, and all of Gila's efforts to teach her how to lie without blushing or without
bursting into tears had failed, and now she suddenly didn't
collapse, and despite the lies she felt for the first time in a
long while that she was doing what she needed to do. As if
the lies were necessary in order for it finally to be possible
to speak the truth.

It was easiest for her to lie to the detective who came with
Vahaba to their apartment. He didn't look at her while she
spoke and didn't listen to her answers but instead looked
at the photo Kobi took during a hunt he organized with
his father, as if he could see something in it that others
didn't see. Mali thought the detective's face was familiar,
maybe because he went to school with her or served with
her in the army, but she was unable to recall where they
had met.

He was the one who spoke at the beginning of the
conversation. He asked again when was the last time she
had been questioned and if anyone had tried to contact
her since, but his questions were asked indifferently, as if
he wasn't waiting for the answer, and Mali managed to
answer without her voice shaking. She attributed his indif-
ference to the fact that they knew everything about Kobi
and she didn't understand why they didn't ask her directly:

Is your husband the man who dressed up as an officer?
What would she have said had they asked her this?

Afterward the detective was silent and looked like someone who had lost interest in her, and the one who addressed her was mainly Esty Vahaba. In her of all people, even though she wasn't high ranking like the detective, there was something calming and trustworthy, and Mali felt an inexplicable intimacy with her, which grew in strength in the weeks that came afterward. And the sentence Vahaba said at the end of their conversation played an important part in the decision Mali made. "You have a way to help us in preventing him from harming other women," Vahaba said to her before they went, and this thought remained with Mali.

That evening she felt that she was doing it mainly for Kobi's sake. In order to save him. And also for their sake, for the sake of Daniella and Noy and the baby, whose presence she felt during the conversation with the police as if it heard her trying to calm her from inside. But the thought about the women who Kobi sat across from and forced to talk to him also pursued her in the coming hours. She remembered the woman whom she saw in her imagination lying injured in the street, and then again the night on which Kobi came back to their apartment wearing the uniform.

Mali asked him then, "Can you explain to me why you're wearing that uniform?" and Kobi sat down on their bed with his back to her and hid his head in his hands. Afterward he said, "I can't take it anymore," and she asked, "But where were you?" Then he told her.

Neither of them went to sleep that night.

She told him everything he wanted, just so that he would stop and not do it again to any more women. His cell phone rested on the dining room table, and Kobi spread out the stack of papers next to him and she sat down across from him and refused to stop, even when he suggested that she give up because she was sobbing. Daniella woke up once during that night and came to them in the kitchen, because of Mali's crying, and Mali took her back to bed, stayed next to her until she fell asleep, and continued to cry without a sound. Kobi promised her then that he would never do that again if she told him everything.

He returned home a few minutes after the police left, and since he didn't ask a thing about them she thought she had been lucky, and it hadn't occurred to her that perhaps he saw the squad car parked in front of the building and waited for the police to go away. The mugs of coffee that she made for them had been forgotten on the table in the living room, but Kobi didn't notice them, and Mali thought that she had managed to get rid of them without his paying attention. His face was damp and the stubble on his cheeks hurt when he kissed her on her cheek. And when he discovered that the girls hadn't eaten dinner, he offered to shower and then make something for them. He placed the bag with the sweat-drenched workout clothes on the floor in the corner of the bedroom, and it remained there like that, soaking in the smell of his sweat, until she opened it three days later. Mali took advantage of him being in the shower to get dressed, and when he came out she was by the door and said that she'd try not to return too late. Kobi looked surprised when he asked where she was going, and she answered him while looking for the keys in her purse so that their gazes wouldn't meet. That evening she didn't look at him, simply because she was scared he'd see. Daniella and Noy waited for dinner in the kitchen and Mali kissed them before leaving, and suddenly she thought they were liable to tell him that the police had been in their home. But she couldn't tell them a thing in his presence. When she looked in the mirror while going down in the elevator, she thought she should approach the police already that evening. The face she saw in the mirror was again her face, as if it had been brought back from a faraway time, and she looked at it until she felt in the soles of her feet the thud of the elevator stopping. And while she was still on the way she decided not to tell Gila everything but rather tell her about the hit-and-run accident as if it had truly happened.

Gila had no hesitations. Mali knew that this is how it would be, and perhaps that's why she decided to ask her for advice.

In the text she sent her, Mali wrote only: *I have to meet you this evening. Even if you're not free*, and when she sat down across from her in the café Gila immediately asked her, "What happened to you? You scared me like crazy," and Mali said that a few days earlier Kobi had hit a pedestrian with his car and fled and asked her to help him hide the accident from the police, but today policemen came to their place and suspect Kobi. When Gila spoke, Mali felt just how far apart they were from each other and how what had happened in recent years had separated them. Gila was full of life that evening, more so than usual, and perhaps there was some schadenfreude in her as well. Even externally they no longer resembled each other. Gila ordered another cappuccino and afterward asked Mali to step out to smoke a cigarette, and said aloud, even although there were people in the street, "It's clear you have to tell them, I don't see any question here. And if you want I'll do it instead. Do you understand that if you keep cooperating with him they could accuse you of obstruction of justice? And what would you do with the girls then? Ask Mom to take care of them?"

She was oblivious of that until then, and the thought of Daniella and Noy in the house of her mother and father frightened her. Suddenly Mali again saw herself alone in the delivery room, the baby was almost out, and she was shrieking, but no one else was there other than them, and she understood that even if she wasn't accused of a thing, she would remain alone, at least for a few months, the period of the pregnancy and the time following the birth, and this was the only time that day when she couldn't choke back the anger that rose up in her. She didn't answer when Gila asked, "You told him that he has to confess and he said that he wasn't ready?" nor when she said, "I don't understand you, Mali, how much do you think you have to suffer because of him? Do you want Dad to say something to him? Or should I speak to him?"

A sharp pain shot out from her abdomen, as if someone were stabbing her through it again and again. She tried to erase the picture of the birth using the other picture that had appeared that morning, in which she was driving a car and the girls sat in back with the baby, and the seat next to her was empty. "Do you know what happened to the woman he hit?" Gila asked, and it took Mali some time to understand who she meant.

"Was she killed? Was she seriously injured?"

"Of course not," Mali said, panic-stricken. Then she lowered her voice and added, "I don't know what happened to her. I searched but didn't find anything."

"So make him go, and tell him that if doesn't do it you'll go instead. And explain to him that if he turns himself in that'll help him afterward, don't the two of you get that?"

But Mali didn't go to the station that night.

The time was late, and she didn't want Kobi to get suspicious. And despite this she waited around in the car under their building because she was hoping that Kobi would be asleep when she got back, until a neighbor passed by there and saw her. Was this what she thought that night? That if she presented herself to the police and explained to Esty Vahaba what happened, then they would understand them and be lenient with the punishment? Kobi would never enter the police station and willingly confess. When she would return home in the evening hours in a few weeks, or even in a few months if they're not lucky and the punishment is severe, Kobi wouldn't be there, and she would always enter a dark apartment and grope with her hand for the switch in order to turn on the light. She would lock the door alone and would need to get used to sleeping alone at night, despite the heavy hand. The bed she would get into would be empty, and in it she wouldn't find the familiar body that had hardened but preserved the memory of the soft body that Kobi had when they met.

He wasn't sleeping when Mali opened the door.

All the lights in the apartment were on, and she heard Kobi get up from the bed. His eyes were soft when he said to her, "You came back late," and she tried to smile when she answered, "That's how it always is with Gila, you know." All this was so hard, harder even than speaking the truth and recognizing it, but what she had started was already impossible to stop. Kobi asked, "Do you want me to warm you up something?" and Mali said that she ate. And when he tried to hug her she said that she had a headache, and he asked her, "Is everything okay? Did something happen at work?" And Mali shook her head. The apartment was silent, Daniella and Noy were sleeping, and this was another opportunity, almost the last, to tell him about the baby and the police and to beg for him to go to the police station himself. They didn't speak much in bed, other than about Harry. She remembered that Kobi said that tomorrow everyone would need to say good-bye to him because there was no point in waiting.

She forcefully closed her eyes and felt Kobi continuing

to look at her in the weak light given off by the reading lamp. And despite her efforts, like every time she forcefully closed her eyes, she felt the hand coming from out of the darkness and trying to crush her throat, and for a moment she had trouble breathing, but this time she succeeded in fighting against it. Is this what it would be like every night until Kobi was released and came back? He placed a hand on her hair and caressed her, and she said, "Not now," and even though she lay with her back to him she felt his eyes still touching her.

The next day, while the three of them ate breakfast in the kitchen, Daniella suddenly asked them, "Mommy, why did they come to us yesterday? The people from the police?" But Kobi was still sleeping and didn't hear.

Noy asked, "What people?" and Daniella said, "The man and the woman who talked with Mom yesterday," and Mali didn't even remember what she explained to them that morning and how they switched to talking about the costume that she'd buy Noy for Purim.

That afternoon, Mali traveled from the bank to the police station. She turned off her cell phone so that Kobi wouldn't call while she was there. In the morning she told him that her mother would bring the girls back from day care and school, and Kobi said to her, "Why your mom? I can get them myself." She walked quickly down Fichman Street, as if she had another destination and passed by the station building without looking at it. Three policemen sat on the stairs leading to the station, smoking.

She still didn't know what exactly she'd say to the police, even though throughout the day, between meetings and even during them, she repeated the sentences she woke up with that morning. *I came so that you'd help my husband. He's the man who dressed up like an officer, but he didn't mean to hurt anyone.* She planned to ask to speak with Esty Vahaba because she felt that she'd understand. *It's my fault he did this, and he didn't mean to do any harm. And he needs help. We have two small girls, and we'll soon have a baby.*

She turned right and began walking away from the station, but in the distance there was nothing to calm her and the buses that passed shook the street. Maybe she wasn't at peace with the sentences she wanted to say because it wasn't really her fault? Also the picture of the birth alone kept on hurting, she and the baby crying in the room without anyone to hear, and the thoughts about the darkness that would welcome her when she opened the door.

And this was the last evening.

Mali remembered that darkness descended after six and that she continued walking away from the station. She walked slowly and only sometimes, when someone walked too close to her, did she increase her pace. But she wasn't afraid, and when she reached the park near the old public library and heard the voices of high school students coming out of it, she sat down on a bench. The lamps in the park weren't on, and the only light reaching the bench came from the street.

One of the girls came up to her and asked if Mali had a cigarette for her, and only then did Mali understand that in this very park, years ago, she kissed Kobi for the first time. She stole a cigarette from Gila for him and was scared to smoke, even though she wanted to try so badly, but after he smoked she surprised herself when she leaned toward him and kissed him in order to know what the taste was and because Kobi wouldn't have tried to kiss her himself. She returned to the car and drove to the mall to buy Noy a *Frozen* costume as if the lives of the four of them would continue as usual, and when she returned home she again had to lie to Kobi as she explained why her phone was off. The girls were already asleep, and that was good, because she didn't have to speak with them. Kobi told her that in the afternoon they said good-bye to Harry in the garden. He carried him in his arms in the elevator and they did a last walk in the building's garden and afterward let him eat salami, and Noy took a picture with him alone on the roof because Daniella refused. They didn't cry, because Kobi explained to them that the next day he was taking Harry to a hospital in order for them to perform surgery, but he did say that Harry was old and might not return.

Lying in order to finally tell the truth. And to save him.

Kobi didn't touch her at all that evening. Even though they walked right next to each other in the same apartment, it was as if they were in different, separate spaces, each one preparing him- or herself for what was soon to come. She got into bed alone, as she would need to get used to doing, and in the silence that was in the apartment she heard him from the living room speaking to his father.

He said in English, "Dad? It's me, Jacob," and afterward she heard him say, "No, I'm not coming. I just wanted to assure you. Everything's okay. You don't have anything to worry about. I'm sorry about the message I left you. Everything worked out, so don't worry about me, okay? And how do you feel, Dad? You feel okay?"

Something in his English was so natural, and she could sense the taste of the tobacco that was on his lips then, as if the English returned to him something of its taste, and after the taste came the sights from the public park and from the morning in January 1991 when he waited for her and her father.

Kobi? It's Mali from class. The war started.

His sleepy voice when he said to her, with the accent he had then, *Now? In the middle of the night?"*

Suddenly she wasn't sure she'd be able to go to the police station the following morning, but she did go. Kobi was in their bed when she awoke, a bit before six, and didn't feel her getting up. She opened the blinds in the living room and saw that rain was falling and so put the jackets for the girls on the couch in the living room, so they wouldn't forget them, next to the costumes, and when Daniella again said she wouldn't wear the costume, Mali didn't insist. Noy asked if they were going to come to the Purim party at school and Mali said yes to her, because she really hoped then that it wouldn't take more than two or three hours.

13

During the first few minutes, Avraham didn't say a thing about the picture that he saw in the bedroom, despite the excitement. He got into the squad car parked on the street and drove off in silence. The coming hours and what he had to do in them rolled around in his thoughts, and he forgot that he wasn't alone. Only when Esty Vahaba asked him, "So what do you say?" did he remember that she was sitting next to him and answered her without taking his eyes off the street, "It's her husband."

Vahaba looked at him. "Whose husband?"

"Mazal Bengtson's husband. That's the policeman."

When they stopped at the light he saw the surprise on Vahaba's face and told her about the photograph hanging over the bed. He paused opposite it for a moment and then regained his composure and walked softly back to the small bathroom and flushed and turned off the light before closing the door behind him. Mazal Bengtson and Vahaba were waiting for him in the living room. And the girl who stood by the door to her room throughout the questioning wasn't there. He wanted to stay and continue the investigation but preferred not to arouse suspicion and to put his thoughts in order before deciding how to proceed. He said to Mazal Bengtson, "Thank you very much for your help," and her gaze avoided him when she answered, "It was nothing. Sorry I couldn't help more." On the mailbox for apartment 13 there was no name, but Avraham took a letter from the national insurance out of it and on the envelop saw his name for the first time: *Yaakov Bengtson.*

The man he was looking for.

The man who set up an appointment with Leah Yeger and knocked on the door to her apartment, wearing a uniform. Who strangled her and left her on the rug in the living room, and then was seen going down stairs and disappeared.

He wasn't a cop.

At night, after the emergency team meeting that he called, Avraham couldn't stop thinking about Bengtson, even though during those hours he didn't know many details about him. Marianka slept, and Avraham walked silently through the apartment and turned on a light just in the kitchen. On the table was a small basket with fruit, and the refrigerator was full of food, some of which they bought and some of which they cooked in preparation for Anika and Bojan's visit, but he defrosted a frozen roll in the microwave, as in the days when the refrigerator was empty. He prepared a cheese sandwich and made black coffee, despite the late hour, and sat down to eat on the porch with Mazal Bengtson's assault file. He read again about how she was attacked in Eilat by a man who wasn't caught.

A bit after 1:00 a.m.

In a room on the seventh floor of the Royal Club Hotel in Eilat.

What amazed Avraham during the team meeting that he'd organized after returning to the station with Vahaba was that no one other than him raised the question of the motive, whereas now that was the only thing he thought about. Before then, when he assumed the assailant was a policeman or a man who was fired from the ranks of the police, he thought the motive could have been frustration or revenge. But Bengtson wasn't a policeman. And why in fact had his wife lied? Avraham had no doubt there had to be a connection between her unsolved rape and the crimes committed by her husband.

Absentmindedly, he found himself conversing with Bengtson, as if they were sitting across from each other in the interrogation room.

Is this what you did? You searched for whoever attacked your wife? Did you believe you could catch him alone? Or perhaps you were trying to prove something to the police who were unsuccessful in catching the rapist? He didn't think much about Mazal Bengtson that night, and in retrospect he should have been thinking about both of them, or about the connection between them, a connection that he was far from understanding even when everything was over.

Ma'alul was on a bus on his way home when Avraham and Esty Vahaba returned to Fichman Street, and Avraham asked him to get off at the next stop, catch a cab, and return to the police station. Saban was called from talks about another case. And Avraham informed Marianka that he'd be late because of developments in the murder case, and heard the disappointment in her voice when she asked, "So when will you get back?"

He didn't know. And didn't ask Lital Levy to summon Shrapstein to the team meeting as well, but no one commented on his absence. When everyone grabbed their seats around the conference room table, Avraham recalled his visit with Ilana Lis. When he left her apartment he was debating whether to go home and leave control of the investigation to Saban and Shrapstein, whereas he now sat at the head of the table and his powers had returned to him, and he waited for silence to fall over the room. Saban, as usual, set his cell phone on the table and touched it when Avraham said, "That's it, we located the policeman," and then paused in order to note Ma'alul's response and facial expression. In the center of the table was a bowl of clementines that remained from a previous meeting, and Eliyahu reached out his hand in order to take one when Avraham began speaking. Saban waited for him to continue.

"Beyond that, I think we also figured out his connection to women who were rape victims," Avraham said. "We're talking about a man whose wife was assaulted a few years ago in Eilat. Her name is Mazal Bengtson, a resident of Holon, and the man who attacked her wasn't caught. Her husband, Yaakov Bengtson, is the man we're looking for. And he isn't a cop."

Avraham said the last sentence mainly for Saban. The eyes of the district commander woke up when he asked him, "How do you know?" And Avraham said, "We were with them now. The credit goes to Esty, who spoke with his wife this morning in the framework of the questioning she conducted with rape victims and felt that she was hiding information. She suggested that I join another round of questioning at their place and I saw his picture there. Afterward we made an inquiry with human resources. We don't and have never had a policeman by the name of Yaakov Bengtson."

Ma'alul peeled the clementine and placed two segments in front of Lital Levy, who sat next to him. When the cleaning woman entered without knocking and asked if it was possible to wash the room, Avraham signaled to her with his head that it wasn't yet. All this wasn't as celebratory as one might think the meeting in which the solution to his first murder case was presented would be, but this didn't bother him. When Saban asked, "And you're absolutely certain that this is the same man from our photograph?" Avraham nodded.

In the photograph in the bedroom Bengtson wasn't in fact dressed, but it was impossible to mistake the face—especially the eyes. Both photographs were black and white, and in both of them Yaakov Bengtson was shot in profile, and his pale eyes were identifiable in both of them. Avraham was sorry that he didn't photograph the picture with his cell phone in order to show them, but he didn't think about this when he was there. Saban put his phone into his pants' pocket and asked, "But you showed her the picture, no?" and Vahaba answered yes for him.

"And what, she didn't identify him?"

"She said she doesn't know him," Vahaba answered. "But understand that she is the one who requested that I show her the photograph we found on the security tape when I questioned her this morning. And when I showed it to her, it seemed to me that she knew something. That's what made me suspicious."

"So do we assume that his wife knows and that she is cooperating with him? Or is she protecting him?" Ma'alul asked, and Avraham didn't answer immediately, because this was one of the things he still didn't know. This question continued to bother him at night as well, on the porch, during the phantom conversation he conducted with Yaakov Bengtson, and even then he didn't have an answer.

Did you tell your wife you were continuing to chase down the man who raped her? That you dressed up as an officer and questioned women and that one of them you killed because she apparently understood that you're not a cop?

"I have no idea. I assume that she identified him and lied. This at least has to be our working hypothesis," Avraham said, and when Ma'alul asked, "Just a moment, Avi, did you also tell her that he's suspected of murder?" Avraham looked at Vahaba because he didn't know what she told her that morning. Vahaba said, "What do you think? Of course I didn't tell her," and Avraham exhaled with relief.

Ma'alul and Saban thought he had to call Bengtson in for questioning that night, but Avraham wanted to know additional details about him before they met. The questions he wanted to ask were only beginning to be formulated, and the right questions were the key to the right answers.

Saban said, "You did nice work, Avi. And Esty, same thing. And do you see that it was possible to find him without publishing in the papers and embarrassing all the policemen in the country? In any case, I think it's necessary to question him quickly and at the same time not abandon the angle of the son. Is that acceptable to you? What do you intend to do now, Avi? Do you want to bring him in?"

Avraham shook his head.

His working hypothesis was that Bengtson knew that the police were on his trail. Vahaba presented the photo from the security video to his wife that morning and revealed to her many details of the investigation, even if she said nothing to her about the murder. If Mazal Bengtson shared information with her husband, he'd know that they're onto him and would definitely be ready for this when he was called for questioning. Therefore it would be better for now to put him, or the two of them actually, under surveillance, and wait.

"Wait for what?" Saban asked, and Avraham said immediately, "Wait until we've gathered firmer information and evidence, and until we know better who he is and why he did what he did."

This was the plan of action he had formulated since he saw the photograph. Later he would think that perhaps he had made a mistake, but on the other hand, it was impossible to summon Yaakov Bengtson in for questions without preparing. Avraham asked Ma'alul to put together a profile of him with the help of all the information he could manage to collect. He wanted to clarify whether Bengtson had a prior record and if his DNA and fingerprints were located in the criminal forensics database, and if so to have them compared to the findings taken from the murder scene. He wanted to know where Bengtson worked and what car he had, and if it was photographed in the area of the scene on the day the murder took place. He even asked Ma'alul to find out if Bengtson has a Facebook account and what kinds of material he posted there. Ma'alul wrote down these things in his notebook and said to him, "No problem, Avi. You'll get it by noon tomorrow." Esty Vahaba was asked to gather additional information on Mazal Bengtson.

When Saban sighed and asked him, "Do you need anything from me?" Avraham hesitated for a moment before he answered, "Yes. Erez Yeger, the son," and Saban looked at him in amazement. "You want to release him? That's not premature? You made progress today, but you still don't know if this Bengtson or whatever you call him was involved in the murder. Only that he apparently dresses up like a cop, the son of a bitch."

That wasn't correct, but that wasn't what Avraham wanted. He knew that Bengtson was involved in the murder even if he still didn't know everything. He knew that Bengtson was the man who was seen in Leah Yeger's building, and he knew that he was the man who had set up a meeting with her. "No, I want the opposite," he said to Saban. "I want to extend Yeger's arrest for forty-eight hours and to make another announcement to the newspapers about prolonging his arrest and the additional progress in his investigation."

His objective was to try and confuse Bengtson.

A week had passed since the murder, and Yaakov Bengtson had time to cover up the evidence, certainly if he knew that the police were on his trail. And to Avraham it seemed that Bengtson knew well what he was doing. He removed from the scene everything he thought was liable to incriminate him, and the chance that they'd succeed in finding the uniform he wore that day or the cell phone with which he recorded the conversations with the women was tiny. Avraham had to try to cause him to think that the investigation was advancing in a different direction, despite the visit to his home, and in the meantime understand who he was. Only then would there be a chance that Bengtson would unknowingly lead them to the evidence, for instance the uniform he was wearing during the murder or the place where he disposed of Leah Yeger's handbag and calendar, or that he would say something to someone unintentionally. He had to try to cause him to sleep at night, while they were awake, ready for any move he'd make.

Saban listened to his plan, and after he saw that Ma'alul was nodding as well he approved it.

And perhaps if Avraham had summoned Bengtson for questioning immediately he would have received answers to the questions he continued asking him without a sound, on the porch, in the dark.

Do you, too, wait for the morning to come in order to act?

Toward two he went to bed, laid down next to Marianka's thin body, and she moved away from him in her sleep. All this was so strange: He was in the apartment where he had resided for many years, in the bed on which he had placed his heavy body at the end of a day of work for more than ten years, and nevertheless the feeling was different. He stared into the darkness and listened to the humming of the refrigerator in the kitchen but nothing put him to sleep. Marianka turned to him and without opening her eyes said something he couldn't hear, in a language he didn't understand. A short time afterward he poured himself a cold glass of water and returned to the porch because it was clear he wouldn't sleep.

The report that he requested from Eliyahu Ma'alul was e-mailed to him the next day at noon.

And from the first line it was clear that pieces of the puzzle were falling into place. *Yaakov (Jacob) Bengtson was born in Australia in 1975*, Ma'alul wrote, and this explained his accent that Diana Goldin mentioned in her testimony. *He arrived in Israel in 1990, received citizenship because his mother had Israeli citizenship, was drafted into the army in 1995 as a lone soldier, served in the Nahal and was discharged in 1998 with the rank of first sergeant.* He had no criminal record. His first visit to the police station was when he submitted a complaint against an employer who had allegedly harassed him, but the case was closed for lack of public interest. The second was when he gave testimony about the rape of his wife to the Eilat police.

Avraham asked Lital Levy not to forward him calls other than those from Ma'alul and Vahaba. He read the report in his office, twice, while eating lunch. He didn't hear from Saban throughout that day, and the conversation with Ilana had been forgotten, because everything happened so quickly during those hours and exactly as he had hoped. In the margin of the report that he had printed, Avraham began writing down for himself by hand questions in advance of Bengtson's interrogation, some of them questions he formulated at night and some of them that expressed themselves during the reading. And the more he read about Bengtson, the more Avraham felt how much he longed to sit across from him in the interrogation room. Since the morning there had been a policeman and a volunteer from the district detective staff in front of the building at 8 Uri Zvi Greenberg Street, but Yaakov Bengtson hadn't left his apartment. His wife, by contrast, dropped off her daughters at day care and elementary school and continued in her car, a Suzuki Alto, to a branch of Bank Discont on Shenkar Street.

When Ma'alul called Avraham and asked, "So, did you read it?" he immediately asked him, "Tell me, do you have any idea if he has a valid Australian passport?" and Ma'alul promised to find out. What especially drew his attention was the fact that Bengtson tried a few times to receive work in the security services and was rejected, usually because he didn't pass psychological evaluations. *In*

1999, Ma'alul wrote, *Bengtson passed a security examination with the Shin Bet as well as the evaluations, and
was accepted to an agents training course with the prime
minister's office, but he was released a few weeks after the
start of the course due to unsuitability. In 2002 he tried to
get accepted for police work but was rejected on the basis
of the first round of psychological evaluation.*

He wasn't a policeman but *wanted to be.*

When Avraham read that Bengtson's last place of
work was a security company that guarded construction
sites near the Green Line, and that he was fired from his
job following a conflict with his supervisors, he added in
the margin of the report the question: *He's not working
somewhere else now?*

Ma'alul didn't have a definite answer for this when
they spoke in the afternoon.

"And do we know why he didn't pass the psychological evaluations?"

"Unsuitability. I asked that they transfer the reports
to me, but it's uncertain that they keep them, and even if
they did, they have to find them in the archive. But listen,
Avi, I spoke with two of his former employers and both of
them tell me that he's very borderline. Or unstable. One of
them is the man who Bengtson filed a complaint against.
He has a tendency for confrontations and outbursts, and
it was impossible to know when he would come to work
and when he wouldn't and in what mood. You don't want
us to bring him in yet?"

He thought that it wasn't yet time. It was necessary
first to obtain evidence that tied Bengtson directly to the

murder, in addition to the testimony of the neighbor who confirmed that he saw him on the stairs, and it seemed to him then that they had time to obtain it. Ma'alul said, "Are you sure, Avi? So he won't flee on us to Australia." But there was no chance he'd flee, because he was under surveillance. "What's with his car?" he asked. "Did you start searching for photos of the vehicle from the area of the murder scene?"

"Not yet. I'll start now."

"And Facebook?"

"He has quite an active page, but in recent days he hasn't posted anything. This maybe also says something, no? Other than that there's nothing special there. Pictures of his daughters and clips of Thai boxing."

"Nothing against the police?"

After the conversation with Vahaba, who called him a little before three, he felt that they were even closer to him.

Mazal Bengtson had worked at Bank Discont for sixteen years and was considered an exceptional employee. Vahaba couldn't go to the branch where she worked and gather testimony from her coworkers for fear of being discovered, but she spoke discreetly with Mazal Bengtson's immediate supervisor and he told her that she was absent from work one day last week, that she hadn't requested extended time off, and that to the best of his knowledge she wasn't planning a trip. Vahaba also spoke by phone with the detective from the Eilat police who was responsible for the rape case, and the detective told her something that possibly had a connection with regards to both members of the Bengtson couple and the police. As Avraham read

in the file, during the rape investigation they examined the
possibility that Bengtson was assaulted by a man she knew
at the party and invited to her room, even though she refused to admit this. The detective had no evidence for an
invitation of this sort, but a few things gave rise to the
suspicion—the fact that the complainant was apparently
drunk on the evening of the assault, the time that passed
between the assailant leaving her room and the reporting
of the assault, and the clothes that she afterward claimed
she had changed into. Similarly, the investigation looked
into the possibility that it was the husband, Kobi Bengtson, who assaulted the complainant, and he was asked to
prove where he was during the time of the rape. His alibi
convinced the detective and the possibility was dismissed.
According to their examination, during the assault Bengtson was with the couple's daughters in their apartment in
Holon.

*Did you think that the police didn't seriously investi-
gate your wife's assault? Was this your problem? Or were
you hurt by the insinuation that she invited the rapist to
her room?*

Avraham didn't put the pen in his hand down during
the conversation with Vahaba, either. And when he listened to her he thought that she was the only person on
the staff for whom the investigation was as important as it
was to him. Vahaba was the one who on a Saturday found
Bengtson's picture in the security footage and the one who
felt, as she gathered testimony from his wife, that she knew
more than she was revealing. Without her it was possible
that they wouldn't have reached Bengtson and would be

exactly as far from the murderer as they had been on the
day the murder took place. And in retrospect, her feelings
about Mazal Bengtson were correct as well. Before they
hung up Vahaba said to him, "You don't think it's possible
that she's not cooperating with him? That she's concealing
the investigation and that it's worthwhile trying to speak
with her?" And Avraham said to her that it wasn't. He
thought this wasn't logical, because Mazal Bengtson lied
in her testimony. And also in the afternoon, when Vahaba
called again and there was excitement in her voice when
she said to Avraham, "Mazal Bengtson might be on her
way to the station," he didn't think she'd turn him in. The
two of them waited on the phone while Bengtson parked
her car not far from the police station and walked in the
direction of Fichman Street. But she passed by the station
and didn't enter, and then continued walking to someplace
else.

"She wants to tell us something, Avi. I'm sure of it.
She's simply scared of him. Maybe she even knows that he
murdered. Are you sure you don't want me to bring her in
now? I'm telling you she'll talk to me."

He asked to think about it before deciding, but by
then Eliyahu Ma'alul had already entered his office, without knocking, his eyes sparkling and a smile stretched out
across his face. Avraham asked him, "What happened?"
and Ma'alul said, "We have him, Avi. We're onto him."
And from everything he could have said, this was the one
thing Avraham hadn't thought of. "Bengtson got a ticket,"
Ma'alul said, and sat down across from him, and Avraham asked, "What do you mean?"

"A parking ticket, Avi. A stupid parking ticket. On the day of the murder. About two hours after. Guess where."

He guessed, but all the same asked him where, and Ma'alul placed a sheet of paper on his desk and said to him, "On Krause. Do you get it? From now on every time we say 'With God's help,' we also add 'and with the help of the city's parking inspectors.'"

The arrest warrant and search warrant of the Bengtson family's apartment were issued that evening, a little after nine o'clock. Avraham was at home and told Marianka how everything was working as they thought and what their plan was for the next day. A team of detectives was supposed to arrive at the apartment in the morning, when Mazal Bengtson was at her job and the couple's daughters were at school and day care, conduct a preliminary search there, confiscate electronic equipment, and bring Bengtson to the station. The investigation file, and in it the list of questions Avraham had prepared, was already there, in his office.

The first question was very direct: *Can you tell me what happened when you arrived last Monday at Leah Yeger's apartment?*

"Do you think he'll confess?" Marianka asked, and Avraham said, "I don't know. I still don't have any idea who this man is." On the table in the interrogation room he planned to spread around pictures of Leah Yeger's body from the murder scene and next to them he planned to place the umbrella that Bengtson forgot at Diana Goldin's apartment as well as the pictures of him, wearing a uniform, from the security video. In the middle would be the picture of Leah Yeger that was taken when she was still alive. The camera in the interrogation room would start working, and Avraham would wait silently, allowing Bengtson to look at the pictures, the umbrella, to digest his situation, to understand that he was trapped. Only afterward would he begin asking him questions without exposing the information they had in their possession about the ticket that he received and the testimony of the neighbor who saw him in the building.

And the next morning they even managed to eat breakfast together. Marianka asked him, "Are you ready?" and Avraham nodded while sipping coffee. He said that perhaps they'd be able to go out to a restaurant that evening if he returned early. Through the small window in the kitchen it was possible to see rain clouds, but that wasn't the only reason he wore the heavy blue coat that he forgot at the murder scene. This was the last day of his first murder investigation, which began a week and two days earlier, and he wore the same coat on the day it was opened as well. He wanted to sit across from Bengtson and look at him up close as he examined the pictures scattered on the table, but also thought about the next case that perhaps wouldn't be a murder case and about the fact that he'd take another day off in order to be with Marianka. Because of the rain he planned to go to the station on foot, but at seven thirty his cell phone rang.

Lital Levy sounded upset. "Avi, are you on the way? Because it looks like we need to change our plan."

He asked, "What happened?" and looked at Marianka, who set down her cup of coffee.

"His wife left alone, without the girls. This means
that he'll apparently take them to school and it's not clear
if he'll return to their apartment after that. Apart from
which, his wife is probably on her way to us."

He quickly drove to the station, and even though he arrived within five minutes, Mazal Bengtson arrived before
him all the same. Lital Levy called him again when he
pulled the car into the parking lot and said, "She's already
inside. Where are you? She told Ezra that she wanted to
speak with Vahaba and she's waiting for her at Registration. What do you want me to tell her?"

He didn't know then why Mazal Bengtson decided to
come to the station to talk and if she was cooperating with
her husband or was there without him knowing. Did he
already feel that something in the connection between the
two of them would disrupt the order of things that he had
planned? He thought he would question Mazal Bengtson
in his office, but then changed his mind, because of the
cameras. And he didn't know exactly what he'd ask her
because he'd prepared himself to question her husband
and not her.

When Avraham entered the station he saw her standing next to the registration desk.

He took a deep breath before he approached and noticed her as if by accident. And then he asked, "Are you
looking for me?"

14

In the days that followed, all the rage that was inside Mali was directed at him, not at Kobi. She saw Avraham in a dream slowly walking out of a room that resembled the room at the hotel in Eilat, and then heard an explosive sound that woke her in a fright from her sleep. Her fist was clenched and damp, because she was the one who held the gun and shot the policeman in his back. The time was 3:21 a.m. The girls were in their beds, and her father, who insisted on sleeping in their apartment, was folded up on the couch in the living room. By then Mali knew his name, but at the start of that morning, at the police station, she didn't remember what he was called and if he introduced himself when he questioned her two days earlier.

But she remembered his heavy steps on the stairs and the coat he wore, a heavy blue winter coat. When he suggested that she come up to his office, she assumed that she'd wait there for Esty Vahaba. And he actually didn't need her to tell him a thing because he knew more than her and only took advantage of her in order to confirm what he had discovered and then entice Kobi into turning himself in. To her it seemed that she was finally taking responsibility for their past and their future, but only when it was already too late did she understand what in truth happened at the station that day.

⚬══▶══⚬

Other than the rage, what stayed with Mali from that morning were sights that devoured one another and fragmented sentences, and especially so very many unimportant details. Had the rain not gotten stronger it's possible she would have stopped in front of the stairs leading to the police station and maybe even taken off, but the rain sent her fleeing inside, and she found herself standing across from the policeman at the entrance, unprepared, even though she had thought only about this moment over the last two days. At that moment, the day still had logical outlines of time and place that she thought she'd be able to control, like a girl who plays with the hand of a clock: the time was eight o'clock, and Mali believed that she'd spend no more than a few hours at the police station and would manage to get to the Purim party at the school. She planned to ask Esty Vahaba to invite Kobi in for questioning in the afternoon or tomorrow, and then to come there with him, to join him in questioning and explain what he would be unable to, or wait outside the room so he wouldn't be there alone.

Her hair was wet, and she wiped water from her forehead. Before her in line stood a man who wanted to complain that his car had been stolen overnight and Mali hoped that taking care of his complaint would never end. She looked out through the glass door. Maybe the rain had stopped and she could escape into the street. And outside it was still Holon then, cars and buses stood in a traffic jam that the rain had created on Fichman Street, and she wasn't yet lost in the labyrinth of massive forests that surrounded her afterward.

The desk sergeant asked the man to wait until the on-duty detective became available to take his complaint, and then he asked how he could help her. The business card that Esty Vahaba gave her was in her jacket pocket, and Mali removed it and asked to speak with her, and the desk sergeant asked, "I don't know if she's here. Did you arrange to meet with her today?" And she didn't notice Avraham until she heard his voice. He approached her from behind and asked if she was looking for him, and Mali told him she was waiting for Esty Vahaba. It seemed to her that he was surprised to see her there, beside the desk, but she didn't see a thing.

She did remember that when they sat in Avraham's office his first question was, "How can I help you, Ms. Bengtson?"

Before this he took off his blue coat and hung it on the door and offered her coffee. He waited for her to sit down and then left and closed the door behind him, and Mali placed her bag on the desk as if she had come for only a moment. Of all the details why does she remember those so well? Instead of remembering what shirt Kobi wore that day and how his face looked sunk into a pillow when she gazed at him that morning. Thick folders were arranged in a high pile on Avraham's desk, and it didn't occur to Mali that in one of them were kept documents from a murder investigation in which Kobi was the primary suspect. Next to them was a wooden frame and in it was a picture she couldn't see.

When Avraham returned, with a coffee mug in his hand, he asked Mali to come with him, and they left his office and went into another room, farther down the hall. A small room with a table and a computer on it and two chairs, and on one of its walls, above the table, a camera hung. It took her time to understand that he wanted to begin questioning her and didn't intend to wait for Vahaba. She knew that she'd be able to insist, because since she had decided to turn in Kobi, the woman she saw in the mirror was herself and not the woman whom she met there in recent years. Avraham asked for her identity card and filled out the details, first on the computer and afterward on paper, by hand. There was no expression on his face, and this strengthened her sense that he didn't know why she was there. When Avraham finished registering the information, he raised his head from the page and for the first time looked at her directly and asked how he could help her. And she said to him without her voice shaking, "Esty Vahaba hasn't arrived? Because I'd prefer to speak with her."

"Vahaba is on her way to the station and will join us in

a few minutes," he said. And then he asked, "Do you want to tell me in the meantime what it is you need to speak with her about?"

Mali didn't intend on answering him and wasn't afraid, not even when Avraham asked her, "Did you come to talk to us about the policeman?"

When he got up and left the interrogation room for the first time, Mali thought he had given up, but after a short time he returned and placed a folder on the table and removed from it the picture of Kobi. "Do you want to look again at the picture we showed you and tell me if you recognize this man?" he asked. She didn't look. When he said to her, "Ms. Bengtson, I ask that you look at the picture," he had already raised his voice. "Do you recognize the man in the picture or do you not recognize him?"

She began to speak because she suddenly saw Kobi.

Exactly like then, in room 723 in the Royal Club Hotel in Eilat. Kobi looked at her over Avraham's shoulder and smiled his smile, which was almost the only thing that hadn't changed in him, and this is what caused her to answer. She said, "I came because of my husband, Kobi," and Avraham brought the photograph closer to her and said, "You're not answering the question, Ms. Bengtson. Do you or do you not recognize the man in the picture?"

This was another sign that she missed, like so many additional signs. She didn't say to Avraham that the man in the photograph was Kobi, but his next question was: "Ms. Bengtson, do you confirm that that's your husband?"

There was no longer a man behind Avraham. Kobi disappeared and left her alone in the room.

Avraham gripped the pen in his hand and wrote something and then sighed and asked her, "Does your husband know that you're here now, Mazal?" and Mali suddenly said, without expecting that this is what she'd say, "Please call me Mali, if you can," and Avraham looked at her for a moment in silence as if he were thinking about the things she had said to him. And then he just said again, "Ms. Bengtson, I'm trying to understand if you're here voluntarily."

Avraham often left the interrogation room in those hours, and Mali thought that this was connected to the fact that he wasn't ready for what he discovered or to the fact that he was waiting for Esty Vahaba, as she had demanded. But it was exactly the opposite. Vahaba was outside and waited for Avraham's approval to join the interrogation, and Avraham left Mali behind in the room alone in order to continue spinning the web that she was trapped in without understanding that Kobi had entered into as well.

But this allowed her to think.

Without her wanting it she was again in the room where everything began. She heard the sound of the water flowing into the bathtub. The television turned on. The only sentence she succeeded in saying then, *I have two little girls.* The interrogation room at the Holon police was almost identical in every way to the room in Eilat where she sat when the policewoman questioned her about the clothes she changed and the party that was held at the hotel before the assault. But now she was different. Daniella and Noy were at day care and school, one without a costume and the other dressed as a princess. And she thought a lot about Kobi. About his appearance in the room and about the fact that he wouldn't be with her in the delivery room. About the months that they would be far from each other. When she imagined herself driving in the car with the girls and the baby, were they traveling to visit him in the place where he'd be? It was clear to her that Kobi would be angry at her when he discovered what she had done, but she hoped that afterward he'd understand. He would see that he would have been caught regardless and that her confession helped the police to understand him. She planned to tell him about the pregnancy and to ask him to cooperate with the police, so that even if he were punished he'd manage to be released not long after the baby was born and they could simply leave Israel and go to Australia.

The door opened again, and Esty Vahaba stood in the opening. Avraham entered behind her with a chair, but from that moment he allowed Vahaba to ask the questions and was barely involved in the interrogation. And Vahaba's voice calmed Mali, at least for a while.

"Hello, Mazal. How are you?" Vahaba asked.

She was terrible—but at the same time better than she had been for years.

"I'm happy that you came, Mazal, you know? I had a feeling that you'd come, and I think you did the right thing."

Mali imagined how the camera was documenting her, and at that moment this gave her strength. When Vahaba asked, "Do you understand that your husband is suspected of impersonating an officer and of harassing rape victims, as we told you?" Mali nodded.

"Did you say anything to him about our conversation? And tell me the truth honestly, because it's important."

"I didn't tell him anything."

"Does he know you're here now?"

"No. I told you. But I won't hide that I was here from him."

This was correct, because her fear of Kobi also disappeared from the moment she made the decision. And in its place was only sadness and longing.

"So why are you here now? Why didn't you tell us about him when we were with you the day before yesterday?"

"Because I was afraid that he'd come home. And I also wasn't sure that he did it. And I came to explain to you what happened."

"What do you mean you weren't sure that he did it?"

"I wasn't sure that was him."

"And how do you know now?"

Avraham didn't stop looking at her, but his gaze didn't frighten her. It was as if she finally succeeded in getting up from the bed in room 723 without waiting, shutting off the television that was on, and turning off the faucet of running water.

"Do you mean that you knew he was impersonating an officer even before we showed you the picture?"

"I knew, yes. But not that he was doing it now."

"I don't understand what you're telling me, Mazal. Explain to me please in a clear manner."

"I knew that Kobi once did it," she said, and her voice was clear and didn't shake.

Vahaba asked, "When was this 'once'?"

"A few months after what happened to me in Eilat. Nearly three years ago. He did it only one time."

"And how did you know about this, Mazal? Did he tell you himself what he did?"

Mali didn't answer immediately, because the questions were getting closer and closer to what was hard for her to say, even though she was no longer afraid.

"Mazal, you said that you came so that we would understand him," Vahaba continued, "and I'm trying to understand the two of you. Look me in the eyes please. I know what happened to you in Eilat. And also that your assailant wasn't caught, correct? Did your husband try to catch the rapist?"

Mali shook her head, because that wasn't the reason. Kobi never mentioned the man who attacked her.

"So what did he want, Mazal? Was he trying to prove something to those investigating your rape? To get back at the police?"

These were the things that were still hard for Mali to speak about, and mainly because of which she didn't know if she'd manage to enter the station and turn him in. She asked Vahaba, "To get back for what?"

Suddenly Avraham interrupted the conversation and said, "So what the hell was he trying to do? Why would someone dress up as a police officer and harass women who went through something like that?" And then he removed an additional photograph, of a young woman, from the folder. "Do you know this woman?" Avraham asked, and it seemed to Mali that she had seen her face. "Let me tell you who this is. Her name is Diana. She was raped in 2012. Like you, no? Do you want to know what your husband did? He contacted her and introduced himself as a police officer and set up a meeting with her. In her apartment. And forced her to tell him about the rape she experienced in great detail and he also recorded her. And then he also assaulted her. Do you understand this, Ms. Bengtson? Can you imagine what she went through? What your husband did to this woman?"

What shook her and brought the fear back to her were the things that Avraham said about the assault. She looked at Esty Vahaba in order to understand if Avraham was lying before she said to the two of them, "It can't be that he hurt her. You don't know Kobi."

"How do you know? Did he tell you everything he did, Ms. Bengtson? I'm telling you he did assault her. Cruelly even. Did he forget to tell you that? Do you want to see pictures of what he did to her? Or perhaps he told you and you're collaborating with him?"

Because of the young woman's face in the photo that Avraham placed on the table, she recalled the hit-and-run accident that Kobi made up and the woman whom she imagined lying injured in the street. *Had he tried hinting to her that he had hurt someone? Maybe unintentionally?* She didn't believe that this was true but nevertheless the fear returned, and she recalled the first night when he put on the uniform. And that was the moment in which the story burst out. Mali closed her eyes, and Avraham spoke to her from out of the darkness. "I'll ask this one last time, Ms. Bengtson. Before I accuse you of being an accomplice and obstructing justice. Tell me, please, how you knew what your husband was doing and what exactly he did tell you." But she still didn't answer him. When he came up to her she opened her eyes, because he was too close when he said, "Why aren't you talking to me, Ms. Bengtson?" And Mali whispered, "Because he did the same thing to me."

Silence descended on the room, and Vahaba asked, "What do you mean he did the same thing to you?" And Mali again said, "He did the same thing to me," before she again lost control of herself.

The hours that came after this are even foggier in her memory.

She does remember that Avraham brought a cup of water up close to her and then mumbled something to Vahaba and left, and she remained in the room with the policewoman and was unable to stop crying. Afterward she told Vahaba everything, not about herself but rather about the woman who wasn't her, whose face first appeared in the elevator at the hotel, and only now she had managed to erase from all the mirrors. She also remembered the phone call in which she asked Kobi to come to the station, even though she wanted to forget it, and then running on the stairs of the station. Later in their conversation Vahaba even tried to give her a hint as to what Kobi was truly suspected of, but Mali didn't understand that hint, too. Vahaba waited for her to drink and stroked her hair and asked her, "Do you want to tell me what he did to you?" And when her crying quieted Mali spoke about the woman who wasn't her who was raped in Eilat, and about her husband who arrived at the hospital the next morning and in the months to come didn't leave her for a moment. The woman had two small girls and her husband quit his job and stayed at home with her and took care of the daughters by himself and she wouldn't have gotten through this period without him. Throughout this time he didn't ask her a thing and only waited patiently for her to recover. And actually when it seemed that she was getting stronger thanks to him and when she decided to return to her job and he stayed home because he hadn't found another job, their hell began. One evening, after the girls had gone to bed, the husband asked his wife, "Why can't you tell me what happened there?" And when she asked him, "Where?" he said to her, "There, in Eilat."

"I don't know. Why do you want to talk about it?"

She didn't know how far things would deteriorate, and had she known, she would have responded differently. "At the police you told them everything, no?" the husband asked, and the woman who wasn't her was silent because she didn't know what to say.

When he insisted that he had to know what happened there, she said to him, "Enough, Kobi, please," but the husband wouldn't let up. "Imagine that you're at the police again," he asked, and she said only, "I don't want to."

That was the beginning.

And the end as well.

The camera fixed on the wall filmed her, and Vahaba

wrote while she spoke, and it seemed to Mali that when she finished talking that everything would be behind her and that she'd be able to go and leave behind in the station the woman she was talking about, and not see her again. Vahaba put down the pen and asked, "And what happened after this, Mali? Did you know that he did the same thing to other women as well?"

"Do you mean back then? I explained to you, he did it only one time," she said. "And he told me that night. He didn't want to do it, do you understand? I know you don't believe me, but you must know Kobi to know. I had a support group of victims and he found the list and went to a woman whose details were there. I didn't even ask him who. He told me that night and swore he wouldn't do it again. I told him everything that happened to me that night in Eilat so that he'd stop."

Something in the words she spoke drew Vahaba's attention and only in retrospect did Mali understand what. She asked, "Do you still have that list at home?" and Mali said, "Don't know. I haven't looked for it in a long time."

"Do you think you can find it?"

"Maybe."

"Have you seen it recently?"

"No."

"Maybe Kobi has it?"

Was Vahaba trying to hint to her what Kobi was truly suspected of when she asked her, "Do you remember if in your group there was a woman by the name of Leah Yeger?" A knock was heard at the interrogation room door and Vahaba left, and when she came back to the room

Avraham also returned with her, and some time after this, maybe an hour or maybe more, was the phone call.

The two of them treated her differently now, and Avraham spoke to her in a soft voice and Mali truly thought that everything was behind her, because she told them everything she knew, but when she asked him if she could go, Avraham said to her quietly, "For now, no."

He asked, "Do you know where your husband is now?" and she explained that Kobi was supposed to be at the vet and that afterward the two of them needed to meet at Noy's school for a Purim party and then take the girls home, and Vahaba asked if she could call someone to pick up the girls instead of them.

"But why? Do you want to arrest him now? You can't wait until tomorrow or the afternoon?"

There were endless terrible moments that day but that was the worst. She thought she was helping Kobi, and she had lied to him so many times that week, and even the last lie was supposed to be for his benefit. To lie in order to tell the truth. In order to save him.

"Will you arrest him at home? Is it impossible to wait until he isn't at home?" she asked, and the two of them were silent.

"Don't arrest him at home, I beg you. We won't be able to go back home. We have two small girls. You can't ask him to come to the station?" And Vahaba asked her, "How? Without telling him he's a suspect?"

And this, too, she'd never be able to forget, that the idea was hers.

"I'll tell him to come and meet me here. I'll tell him

that there are developments in the rape investigation and that you asked me to come in."

They looked at each other, and Avraham left the room, and when he returned he held out her phone to her. Vahaba sat next to her while she called, but Kobi didn't answer, and she tried him again, and again he didn't answer, and Avraham walked away from them and said, "We'll wait a few minutes and call again," but the cell phone rang before she could try. They looked at the phone and she nodded, and Avraham signaled to her with his hand to answer.

"Hi, Mali, did you call me?"

She heard children in the background and was sure she heard barks as well, and therefore she asked him, "Are you still at the vet?" and Kobi said, "No, not anymore. I'm on the way home. I couldn't do it in the end."

She lied to him in order to tell the truth, in order to save the two of them, when she said in a steady voice that she was on the way to the police station on Fichman Street. That they called the bank and asked her to go there urgently, because there's a development in the rape investigation, without telling her what development. "Can you meet me there? Do you know where it is?"

There was a moment of silence before Kobi asked, "And what's with Noy?" and Mali said, "I spoke to my mom. She'll go to her party instead of us and will take the two of them to her place."

And those were the last sentences.

Did he know where she was calling from? Or did it take him time to understand? He asked, "Are you already there?" and Mali said to him without her voice shaking,

"No, not yet. I'll be there in two minutes," and Kobi again was silent before saying to her, "I'm coming right away."

Afterward she only remembers herself running. Not like at the hotel where she barely managed to walk down the hallway until she reached the elevator.

She was sure that Kobi would arrive in a few minutes, and the police left and took her cell phone with them, but a long time passed before they returned. Vahaba set a bottle of water on the table, and when Mali asked her if Kobi had arrived she said, "Not yet," and Mali wasn't sure Vahaba hadn't lied. She didn't feel movement in her belly, even though she placed her two hands on it after Vahaba left, and she tried to feel something inside her, and then remembered Australia, because it was clear to her that when everything was over they'd go there. For a moment the two of them were again twentysomething. They walked beside each other among the eucalyptus trees that were so tall that the two of them could hide from the rain in a cave-like hollow that had opened up wide in one of the trunks. They walked and in front of them were two large dogs, their legs not making a sound when they treaded up the forest floor covered in wet brown and yellow leaves. Kobi tried to show her something at the top of one of the trees, a bird perhaps, but Mali wasn't able to see a thing.

Did all that really happen then? Did she really think about Australia while she waited for him or only after she heard the shot?

The interrogation room door was open and the corridor was long and empty and she didn't know in which direction she should run, but when she saw policemen hurrying down a staircase she ran in the same direction and didn't feel the movement of her legs, even though she hadn't run in so many years. It was easy, like she hadn't ever stopped running and she was fast like she could still catch the assailant who left the room. On the second floor many people were running, downward, on the stairs, mainly policemen in uniform, but in the commotion that was created no one noticed her. Vahaba wasn't among them, nor was Avraham.

Afterward her running came to a stop and her memory was cut off all at once. As if life had ended. A sense of time and place was lost to her for a few hours, and from out of the darkness other times and voices appeared. She ran out of the room at the hotel and would never return to it. On the forest ground lay a policeman in uniform. From another time, even earlier, the words could be heard in the voice that was once her voice, *Kobi, can you hear? The war started. Do you hear me at all?*

15

Avraham was sure that he heard the shot first, as if it were fired next to his ears an instant before it could be heard throughout the station. And even though there were policemen who reached Bengtson before him because he was waiting for him in his office on the third floor, Avraham was the first to identify the man lying on the floor in the station's entrance. Dressed in uniform. David Ezra, the desk sergeant, tried to stop up the wound in Bengtson's neck with his red hand, and people screamed, "Policeman shot!" and Avraham pushed his way through them. Did he know it was Bengtson when he heard the shot through the open window? And how did he immediately recognize that it was him on the station's floor? The gun lay next to Bengtson. Ezra was bent over him, his knees in the expanding puddle of blood. When Avraham leaned over them, Ezra looked at him in shock and Avraham said to him only, "He's not a cop." His shoes were in the red puddle when he placed his right hand next to Ezra's, and he felt the blood and the pieces of wet flesh between his fingers. The gunshot wound in Bengtson's neck was black and giving off smoke and his head was twisted on the floor in a strange position, almost torn from the body, and Avraham tried to massage his chest and called out loud, or so it seemed to him at least, "Can someone perform CPR?"

Bengtson's legs struck against the floor again and again. And like Leah Yeger's eyes, his eyes weren't closed all the way.

The ambulance left for Wolfson Medical Center within less than three minutes, and Ma'alul called Avraham from there when they arrived, in order to tell him that Bengtson was alive. And this filled him with hope. On the way to the hospital Ma'alul searched Bengtson's clothes for a suicide note or a confession, but didn't find anything. At first Avraham didn't understand why this was what Ma'alul searched for, but Eliyahu said to him, "Trust me that this is the thing we need to find right now. Can you search his car and their place?" In those moments Avraham was unable to think of what the right thing to do was. He went out to the street in order to digest it all.

Because of the ticket that Bengtson had received he knew the make of his car and license plate number, and for a few minutes he searched for the blue Toyota in the streets near the station, until he found it parked on Golomb Street. One of the rear windows was open a bit, like Bengtson's pale eyes before he was taken away, and Avraham threaded his hand inside and opened the back door. When he sat down in the driver's seat and looked through the windshield, he suddenly thought that this was the closest he'd get to Bengtson, and the thought caused him to tremble. It couldn't end like that. He asked himself if when Bengtson left his car behind and walked to the station, he knew that he wouldn't be returning to it and if so, why did he bother parking and locking the doors?

The rain let up and then grew stronger, and Avraham returned to the station dripping wet. Only when he encountered Ezra standing outside smoking, his shirt spotted in blood, did he see that his own pants and the blue sweater he wore were also covered in Bengtson's blood that had been absorbed by the fabric and gotten wet in the rain and now turned brown. Someone brought Ezra tea in a Styrofoam cup, and Avraham saw through the glass door that the forensics team was working around the large puddle of blood. The gun was still lying on the floor in the place where Bengtson had let it drop from his hand.

"So he's not a cop?" Ezra asked without looking at him, and Avraham shook his head.

"No."

"Why was he wearing a uniform?"

They stood under the awning at the entrance because the rain continued. The tumult in the station was considerable, and Avraham needed to go inside and put an end to the rumors that were passing from mouth to ear, that a criminal had shot a policeman who tried to arrest him or that an armed terrorist had infiltrated the station and fired, but he remained outside another moment in order to calm down and think.

"So who is he then?" Ezra asked. They stood right

beside each other in order not to get wet, and the steam rising from Ezra's cup of tea reached Avraham as well. "He was suspected of murder," he said. "Did you manage to speak with him before he fired?"

"Speak about what? He entered and immediately pulled out the gun. I didn't see him at all before then. And when I saw him he was already on the ground."

"And he didn't say anything to anyone? He didn't scream anything?"

"Not a word."

Ezra tossed his cigarette butt and immediately pulled a pack out of his pants pocket and lit himself another cigarette, and when he brought it to his mouth Avraham noticed that his hands had already been washed. He, by contrast, didn't wash his hands until the afternoon hours and not only because he didn't have time.

Fifteen minutes after he returned to the station he already had to provide explanations, and he realized that Ma'alul was right. The only thing that interested his supervisors was verifying that Bengtson was the murderer. They didn't want to know if he would remain alive and perhaps even hoped that they'd announce from the hospital that he died on the operating table. They questioned Avraham only about the evidence.

The Tel Aviv district commander arrived at the station with the district spokesman, and they conducted a preliminary inquiry in Benny Saban's office. The main entrance to the station was closed, and reception was indefinitely suspended. The police commissioner demanded an immediate report on the incident and the minister of internal security was also updated, even though he was on a trip to Berlin. First, it was necessary to repudiate the rumors that the man who was shot was a policeman as well as those about a terrorist who had infiltrated the station. In Saban's office there wasn't an extra chair and Avraham stood the entire time, but this didn't bother him.

"Can you explain to us what happened? Saban told me that he's a suspect of yours," the district commander addressed him, and Avraham tried to explain, to himself as well.

Everything was supposed to have happened differently.

He planned to question Bengtson during the morning hours in his office. The investigation file was ready and the evidence was arranged in order, and the questions that he prepared at night on the porch and in the day before then in his office were written down on a piece of paper. *Can you tell me what happened when you arrived last Monday at Leah Yeger's apartment? When did she become aware that you're not a policeman? Immediately when she opened the door? Or only when you sat at the table and began speaking?*

He didn't believe that Bengtson would answer his questions immediately, but he thought that when he understood that they had in their hands enough evidence to place him in the building that he'd break. He'd permit Bengtson to look at the photograph in which he was seen in a police uniform, and would place his umbrella on the table. Bengtson would break, this was clear to him when he prepared himself at night for the interrogation, and he only feared that at the last moment he'd succeed in fleeing by means of the Australian passport, and therefore a detective team stayed outside the building where he lived and was prepared to immediately implement the arrest and search warrants issued by the court.

The district commander spoke to Avraham quietly. Avraham didn't know him, since he was new to the position and had arrived from Jerusalem, and had only heard that he was thought of as an officer who likes getting down to details and is involved in investigations conducted under him, especially white-collar investigations. Saban looked at him with concern when he presented Avraham with his questions, but he didn't appear agitated and made no accusations. He wrote a few lines down himself with a pen in a notebook while Avraham spoke. The district spokesman, who sat next to him, wrote nonstop on a laptop without interrupting the conversation.

"Can you tell me what you know about the gunman and to what extent you're certain that he's involved in the murder of this woman? And how, at all, did he enter the station with a weapon?" he asked, and Benny Saban said to him immediately, "We are absolutely sure of this," even before Avraham started to answer.

At the beginning of the day he truly thought he knew all he needed to know about Bengtson. That he understood why he dressed up as a policeman and questioned rape victims and what happened when he arrived at Leah Yeger's apartment last week. Afterward it became clear that he didn't know everything. But he had in his possession much evidence for the fact that Bengtson was in the building at the time of the murder but he was missing a

last, additional piece of evidence for the fact that he was
also in the apartment, and this he would obtain easily by
examining Bengtson's DNA and fingerprints. He was also
convinced that Bengtson would admit to it during questioning and believed that a search of his place would turn
up the handbag that he took from Yeger's home in order
to disguise the murder as a robbery or the cell phone with
which he recorded her, or the calendar he took from her
kitchen. But since then the plans had changed. Mazal
Bengtson was apparently frightened by the questioning
conducted with her two days before this, and decided to
turn in her husband without knowing he was suspected
of murder. And the announcement that she was on the
way to the station disrupted his plans. He instructed the
detective team to delay executing the arrest and search
warrants until he heard from her, and he received her in
his office without knowing why she came and what to
ask her, and the uncertainty made him anxious because
he had been so prepared. Despite this, while questioning
Mazal Bengtson he still sensed that everything was under
control and that the change in plans was even working in
their favor, and he didn't think he was wrong when he hid
from her the information about the true suspicion directed
toward her husband. She entered the station voluntarily
and said that her husband dressed up as a policeman and
questioned rape victims. And she even explained, without
understanding this, how Bengtson obtained addresses and
telephone numbers of rape victims from a list of women
who participated in a support group that she had in her
possession, and when she did this Avraham felt that the

decision to postpone the execution of the arrest warrant and listen to her was the right thing to do.

But there was also one moment during her interrogation in which Avraham's confidence was weakened, and he didn't share it with the district commander. Perhaps then he should have understood that nothing would happen as he thought, because from the start of this investigation almost everything actually happened by chance. This was when they tried to understand how Mazal Bengtson knew that her husband was dressing up as a police officer and asked her about this over and over until she broke and said, *Because he did the same thing to me.* Avraham halted the questioning and left the interrogation room not only because she burst into tears but also because suddenly he wasn't sure that he understood Bengtson and his motives. And when she told Vahaba afterward what happened in their home, he understood even less. Mazal Bengtson again said, *You don't know Kobi. He did the same thing to me*, and Avraham looked at her through the glass window of the interrogation room and thought that perhaps she was right. And also that he should not have under any circumstances brought her into the interrogation room and interrogated her after what she went through. Then she suggested that she get Bengtson to come to the station. Avraham explained to the district commander and to Saban that he hesitated before deciding, but accepted her suggestion because he thought that this way Bengtson would be apprehended unprepared. He would be led to the interrogation room, ostensibly on other grounds, and only there would discover that he had entered into a trap. Mazal Bengtson had begged that they not arrest her husband at their home and her plea also influenced his decision.

Saban looked confused when the district commander lit himself a cigarette, since smoking in his office was forbidden. He handed him a coffee mug for the ashes and got up to open a window and the district commander straightened himself in his chair and placed his notepad on the table.

"How much time passed from the moment you called him until he arrived?" he asked, and Avraham said, "It took him some time."

They waited more than an hour for Bengtson, and already by then it was clear that something was wrong. He didn't arrive at the station right away, and the detective team trailing him informed them that the suspect had traveled to his home. For a moment Avraham thought about instructing the detectives to go up to the apartment and immediately carry out the arrest and search, but the temptation to surprise him unprepared in the interrogation room was too great, and there was also the promise he made to his wife. When Bengtson got into his car and drove in the direction of the station, the detective team updated them that he was on his way, but didn't notify them that he was wearing a uniform. And Avraham was relieved. He asked Lital Levy to make him another black coffee and again arranged the papers on his desk and then called Ma'alul, and Eliyahu said to him, "It's nice when the fish jumps on his own into the net, no?"

Had Bengtson noticed he was under surveillance? Or

did he know his wife planned on turning him in and had laid a trap for him? In contrast to the district commander and Saban, these were the only questions that interested Avraham, and in order to get answers to them, the doctors at the hospital would need to save Bengtson's life. He peeked at his cell phone, but Ma'alul hadn't sent him a text from the hospital. And it was impossible to call him in the middle of the inquiry with the district commander, which was getting longer and longer.

"How did he have a gun, do we know?" he asked, and Avraham said, "He was a security guard."

"And you didn't take into account that he'd be carrying a weapon when you called him to the station?"

"According to the information we received he is not presently employed by any security company."

"And do we know what the connection was between him and the victim? What's her name, Leah?"

"There was no connection. As I said, her name apparently showed up on a list of victims from his wife's support group. And he apparently set up a meeting with her, as he did in earlier instances with other victims, with the aim of questioning them. And I assume she figured out that he was impersonating an officer."

The district commander placed his burning cigarette in the mug, and Saban looked at him anxiously. "There are too many *apparently*s in your answer," he said. "I don't like that. It's enough of a mess if a murder suspect enters a police station with a weapon and shoots himself in front of civilians and police, but it's an even bigger mess if he's wrongly suspected. So let's get his DNA already, and thank God we aren't wanting for pieces of him down there, and we'll compare them as fast as possible to the findings from the scene. And did you send someone to his home to look for her handbag or that list of victims?"

"I'll go there myself," Avraham said.

"And please prepare a report about what happened, because we need to brief the police commissioner and the minister and put out a formal announcement. In the meantime there's a gag order, but we must publish something by tomorrow morning. And please emphasize in your report that the two of them arrived at the station voluntarily. Both the husband and the wife as well. And that the evidence points unambiguously to the fact that this man who committed suicide is the killer."

Saban said, "No problem, Doron. There will be a full report by tonight, right, Avi?" When the district commander interrupted and asked, "And what's with the wife? Did she see him shoot? Is she still at the station?" Avraham looked at Saban because he didn't know what to answer. He hadn't seen Mazal Bengtson since the shooting. Only when he left Saban's office did he see her through the glass window of the interrogation room folded up in Vahaba's arms. For a moment he debated going in, but in the end only knocked on the window.

"Did she see him?" he repeated to Vahaba the question the district commander had asked him.

"You didn't hear her scream? I managed to stop her two meters before she reached him." Vahaba's eyes were red.

"And does she understand what happened? Did you tell her why we were looking for him?" he asked, and

Vahaba said, "Yes. Did I have a choice? She says that she murdered him. That because of her he's dead. And she wants to go to the hospital. Can I take her there?"

What could he have told her? That he, too, wants to go to the hospital? Vahaba noticed the blood that had turned brown between his fingers, and perhaps therefore she asked him, "And how are you?" And even though he knew that this wasn't what she asked, Avraham said, "I'm heading out to their place. Can you ask her for the key to the apartment?"

That was the closest Avraham would get to Bengtson that day. He was asked to find a suicide note or a bag or a list of rape victims in the apartment that would prove Bengtson murdered Leah Yeger, but he searched for something else, exactly as Ilana had accused him of doing, but he admitted this to himself only a few days later.

He opened the door with Mazal Bengtson's key. The same smell was in the elevator that he smelled earlier in the car, a smell of wet clothes and dog hair. The windows in the living room were closed, and he turned on a light in the apartment. And he remembered the girl who stood next to the door while he questioned her mother.

There were only electric and property tax bills on the dining room table, and in the sink were two bowls with the remains of Corn Flakes and a bit of milk. Avraham turned over the bills, and on the back of one of them read a short line written out by hand: *I'll be back in the morning. Sorry about everything. Tomorrow I'll explain to you what happened*. This wasn't Bengtson's suicide note. But when had he written it? And what had he needed to explain? In this apartment no one had been murdered, but nevertheless Avraham again felt he was walking through a murder scene. The silence was exactly the same silence. Quiet rooms that no one would live in anytime soon.

Like his previous visit to the apartment, two days before this, it seemed to him that no one had lived there before what happened, either, as if the place weren't a home or as if the tenants were preparing to vacate it and leave. In the living room were the two couches covered by a blanket and the television. On one of the couches was a princess costume that seemingly had been forgotten there when the tenants rushed to leave. And the picture of the hunted deer on one of the bare walls that reminded him immediately of the other picture. And it wasn't possible, but he had a feeling that he wasn't in the apartment by himself. The stairs that he hadn't climbed the time before led him to a small room with a window opened onto the roof. A washing machine and a plastic basket full of clothes—but the handbag wasn't there, either. Nor on the table or in the chest of drawers in which a thorough search would have to be conducted.

He went out to the roof and looked down over the cement railing, and suddenly he was able to imagine Bengtson looking from here down at the detective's car parked in the street. Heavy clouds touched the roofs but the rain had stopped.

He already understood that he wouldn't be asking Bengtson the questions he wanted to ask. *Why did you ac-*

tually do it? Did you think you'd catch your wife's rapist?
Then he called Eliyahu Ma'alul and Esty Vahaba, but there
wasn't any news from the hospital.

*Or perhaps you wanted to · take revenge? But on
whom?*

The only room that he still hadn't gone into was the
bedroom. And when he turned on a light he immediately
saw the white dog. It lay at the foot of the bed and didn't
move from its place even when it noticed Avraham, just
stretched its head and turned its watery eyes to Avraham
and then placed its head on the floor again. Even though
he tried with all his might not to see it, Avraham's eyes met
the picture hanging on the wall. He averted his gaze from
the two bodies while in his ears could suddenly be heard
Mazal Bengtson's confession to Vahaba in the interrogation room, that he heard through the glass window.

Bengtson wore the uniform for the first time here.

It was as if all the sights that Avraham saw and the testimony that he heard crowded into this room: Leah Yeger's
body was sprawled out next to the white dog and next to
her kneeled her son who had collapsed on her grave, and
Mazal Bengtson was lying in the bed and recovering from
the rape, and her husband, who took care of her with de-
votion, entered the room dressed in a policeman's uniform
and asked her to tell him exactly what happened.

Every detail. From the beginning.

Avraham took a step into the room in order to convince himself that none of this was there and because he
needed to search the drawers next to the bed as well, and
the white dog again stretched its head and looked at him

while his knees buckled as if all on their own and he had to leave.

He called Marianka from his office and told her that he'd return tomorrow morning. She asked him if the killer had been arrested, and Avraham only said, "Yes," and didn't elaborate. The station was opened to the public, and behind the reception desk stood a different policeman, not David Ezra. Policemen approached Avraham and asked him how he was doing, and no one blamed him for anything. Lital Levy checked if he had eaten and asked that a sandwich be brought up to him from the cafeteria, and before he took a bite of it he washed his hands in the bathroom.

Were Mazal Bengtson not at the hospital with Vahaba perhaps he would have gone there, but he had a report to write, and when Saban called to remind him that the district commander was waiting, Avraham promised that he'd get started on it. Vahaba told him that the girls were with Mazal Bengtson's parents and still didn't know a thing about what had happened, and that Bengtson wasn't there alone but rather with her twin sister.

When Ma'alul entered his office after five, Avraham still hadn't started writing the report. On the computer screen the video of Mazal Bengtson's interrogation was frozen but he hadn't dared to watch it. In the file that he had opened only two lines were written, which were cut off: *In my role as head of Leah Yeger's murder investigation staff, this morning I received Mazal Bengtson, the wife of the murder suspect, Yaakov Bengtson, who*

arrived at the station voluntarily and without advance
notice in order to deliver

"You okay?" Ma'alul asked, and Avraham nodded.

"You sure?"

"Yeah."

"I spoke with Saban, and it looks to me that every-thing will work out, Avi. They think that we should have assumed that Bengtson had a gun, but assuming that he's the murderer, no one's going to come to us with too many complaints."

When Ma'alul asked him, "What else do you need to do, Chief? Can I help you with something or should I go home?" Avraham was filled with a desire for him to stay so they could together watch the video of Mazal Bengt-son's interrogation and the video of the security camera at the station's entrance, in which Yaakov Bengtson is seen shooting his neck and then he himself bending over him and David Ezra and stopping up his wound. And so they could together write the report for the district commander. He said to Ma'alul, "Sure, you can go," and Ma'alul's dark eyes smiled at him when he said to him, "You sure?"

The gun was in Bengtson's hand when he opened the station door, but it was impossible to know that he wasn't a cop. As Ezra testified, he didn't speak but instead pointed the barrel at his neck and pulled the trigger even before the door had closed. Avraham was in the puddle of blood and massaged his chest. The shout that he remembered shout-ing wasn't recorded by the camera's video.

They notated the exact times according to the camera's video and then switched to watching Mazal Bengtson's interrogation video, and when Ma'alul asked why they were watching it, Avraham explained that he had to detail in the report how Bengtson voluntarily offered to bring her husband to the station. But after they started they were soon watching it for other reasons. Ma'alul looked at the video as if hypnotized, even when Avraham was seen in it drawing near to Bengtson and raising his voice, when he himself couldn't watch. He wouldn't question either of them nor would he get answers to the questions he had composed. Everything that was possible to know was seen and spoken in the video being screened before them.

The continuation of the conversation between Vahaba and Mazal Bengtson, which Avraham watched that morning through the glass window, did not resemble the interrogation. Vahaba remained in the room without him, placed her hand on Mazal Bengtson's hair and stroked it while she spoke. Vahaba asked her, "Mazal, do you want to tell me what he did to you?" And when Bengtson answered it was in a whisper, and on the tape it was hard to hear everything she said.

"It can't be that he hurt her. You don't know Kobi. He couldn't bear it anymore."

"So what did he do?"

"You have to know him to understand. I simply didn't want to go back to it. I didn't want to tell him. I just wanted to forget it all."

"And he insisted?"

"Yes."

"How did he insist? Was he violent with you?"

"He repeated it. Tell me what happened."

"Did he threaten you?"

"No."

"Did he beat you, Mali? You can tell me the truth."

"No, you don't know Kobi. He's not a violent person."

"So why did he want to know?"

. . .

"Why did he want to know, Mali?"

"I don't know."

"You didn't ask him?"

"It was hard for him not to have a job, and he couldn't find anything. He was ashamed that he wasn't supporting the family and that only I was working."

"But how are they connected to each other?"

"They're connected. He couldn't stand himself anymore."

"But why did he want you to tell him about what happened in Eilat? Did he want to prove to the police that he could find whoever assaulted you?"

"No. He didn't try to find him."

"So what then?"

"He returned with the uniform. I asked him why he was wearing it, and he told me that he questioned a woman who was raped."

"Do you remember what her name was?"

"No."

"Did he tell you what her name was?"

"I didn't ask him."

"And when was this?"

"A few weeks after Eilat."

"And what did he tell you? What did he do to this woman?"

"Like I told you. He was at her place and questioned her."

"How did he obtain her information?"

"I didn't ask him. I think from the page I got of the support group."

"And did he record her? Did he let you hear the recording?"

"Record with what?"

"What did you say to him about this?"

"You don't understand how he was. He cried all the time. He didn't want . . . you don't know Kobi; he wasn't supposed to be like that. Something happened to him. I don't understand what, but he had no choice. He wanted to be other things. And I think he wanted you to catch him. Maybe because of that he went back to it now."

"Why do you think he wanted us to catch him?"

"Because he was suffering."

"Suffering from what?"

"From himself. From everything that happened."

"And then did you tell him yourself? So that he wouldn't do it another time?"

"Yes."

"What?"

"Everything. What happened in Eilat. My rape."

"What?"

"Everything. How I went back to the room and he came in while I was asleep or was already on the balcony. How he put his hand on my neck, and the knife."

"And Kobi didn't return to it anymore? Did that stop him?"

"He saw that it was hard for me, so he let me stop, but after a few days he put on the uniform again and asked."

"For the same story?"

"Yes. But with all the details about how he did it and how long it lasted."

"And how many times did it happen? Once?"

"No, maybe a month. Afterwards he saw that I couldn't anymore so he stopped."

"And why did you agree to tell him?"

Silence.

"Did you agree because you didn't want him to do the same thing to other women?"

"Yes. What could I do?"

"You could have complained about him to the police, Mali. You didn't have to agree to that."

"But I didn't want anything to happen to Kobi; I didn't want there . . ."

"What?"

"You don't know him, he wouldn't have been able to stand it. He's not strong and he was . . ."

Avraham and Ma'alul watched the video in silence and didn't say a thing about it that day. And when Ma'alul left Avraham's office in the evening hours, the report still wasn't complete. He finished it alone at night and sent it to Saban after four in the morning. He walked Ma'alul out of the station and thanked him for staying with him, and when Eliyahu walked away in the direction of the bus station, Avraham asked for a cigarette from a man who was standing in front of the station and smoked. Its taste was potent and scorched his throat, and when he put it out he walked to a kiosk nearby and bought two packs of Time, like he used to.

The rain had stopped completely, but the streets still glistened with water.

In the report that he wrote at night he noted that *Yaakov (Kobi) Bengtson murdered Leah Yeger on Monday, February 23, at approximately 2:00 p.m.*, because that is what needed to be written, but he already understood that the murder began a long time before then, in a different room and in a different apartment, without anyone sensing that it had begun.

A few hours after this, Vahaba called and informed him that Bengtson died in the hospital.

16

Yaakov Bengtson's cell phone was found in his pants' pocket, and Esty Vahaba brought it from the hospital the next morning. It was registered as evidence and transferred to the computing unit, and a short time after this the voice file in which Bengtson recorded the moments preceding the murder was sent to them by e-mail. Avraham listened to the recording for the first time in Benny Saban's office, in the company of Eliyahu Ma'alul and Esty Vahaba. He didn't sleep at night and hadn't showered since the shooting, and throughout that whole morning he barely said a word. In the pocket of his pants were a lighter and a pack of Time cigarettes, and once an hour he again went out to smoke on the stairs leading to the station.

And it was exactly as he thought.

Bengtson turned on the recording app on the device only when they sat down at the kitchen table in Leah Yeger's apartment, so Avraham couldn't hear the knocks on the door that he imagined from the moment he entered the scene, nor the first sentences they said to each other, but the exchange that led to the struggle and murder were heard clearly. Bengtson asked Leah Yeger to say her full name and her identity card number, and then said, "Tell me, please, about the rape," and she said, "What do I need to tell?"

Bengtson's accent was more noticeable in the recording than Avraham had expected. Avraham now knew that it was an Australian accent, and that this was also the source of his strange last name. Bengtson was born in Perth to an Israeli mother and an Australian father, and arrived in Israel at age fifteen.

There was hoarseness in Leah Yeger's low voice, perhaps traces of the flu. And what especially surprised Avraham was her confidence and courage.

Saban was glad the recording was found, because it confirmed beyond any doubt, and prior even to lab tests, that Bengtson was the killer. Vahaba, who like Avraham hadn't slept all night, rested her elbows on the table and covered her mouth with her hands. Ma'alul looked at Avraham when Bengtson said on the recording, "Tell me everything you remember. From the beginning. Where did it happen? How did it begin? When did you sense that the rapist was there?"

The same questions that Diana Goldin had been asked.

Only Leah Yeger said to him, "What do you mean 'there'? I invited him to my home. He was my husband's partner." And Bengtson said, "Right, I mean when did you feel that you were in danger."

Leah Yeger was silent. Avraham wanted her to continue speaking, because when her voice was heard in the room it was as if he had succeeded in bringing her back to life. She said to Bengtson, "But what do you need this for, actually? You know this." The words in Bengtson's mouth shook when he said to her, "For the needs of our inquiry it's important that you tell everything from the beginning."

When Esty Vahaba's name was mentioned suddenly in the recorded conversation, Saban and Ma'alul looked at her. Leah Yeger said to Bengtson that she would like to speak with the policewoman who took her testimony, and he explained to her that he didn't have her phone number. "I think I have it," Yeger said. "Her name is Esty." Based on the creak of the chair she got up, and Bengtson said, "If you prefer to do this with the policewoman then we can postpone it to another day," and Yeger's response was not recorded by the device. The creaking of another chair indicated that perhaps Bengtson, too, got up from his seat. A few seconds after this, the recording was stopped, and the rest Avraham had to complete by himself on the basis of what he knew. And imagined.

Her fear. And his.

The quickening heartbeats of the two of them once they understood.

They didn't know each other, but nevertheless they were imprisoned there together with no way to escape. Everything could have happened differently but the two of them had no such luck.

Saban asked, "Can you explain how he didn't even

erase this from his phone?" and Avraham remembered that Mazal Bengtson said in her interrogation that her husband wanted to be caught. Had he therefore forgotten the umbrella in Diana Goldin's apartment on purpose? And despite this took a risk and carried out the same offense a few days later? And did Leah Yeger lock the door with the key so that Bengtson wouldn't flee? According to the confidence in her voice this was possible. Maybe she didn't lock the door and only walked quickly to the study to look there for Esty Vahaba's phone number, maybe in the datebook that Avraham discovered in the room, but didn't find it because in the end she didn't call Vahaba but the police instead. When she went to the study, Bengtson presumably tried to escape, but if Yeger did indeed lock the door, as Avraham imagined she had, so that he wouldn't flee, he discovered that he couldn't leave. So he followed her to the study. In Avraham's imagination Leah Yeger held the phone receiver and put it down when she saw Bengtson approaching. Did she hide the datebook under the papers on the desk because she understood what was about to happen and wanted to leave a sign for him?

2.23; 2:00.

Bengtson pulled on the chord and tore it from the outlet on the wall because he understood who she was calling, and then she knew.

But even then everything could have ended otherwise. He could have admitted that he wasn't a policeman and asked her to let him leave. And she could have opened the door for him.

"Can you give me the key? I'd like to leave here."

"Tell me who you are."

These sentences weren't recorded and only Avraham could hear them in his mind.

Saban called the district commander in order to let him know he could breathe easy.

"Please give me the key so that I may leave. I am a police detective."

"What are you doing here? What do you want from me?"

This was the beginning of the struggle that the neighbor from the second floor heard above him.

Buses passed by him, and at the construction site workers carried metal beams in an elevator up to the top floor, when Avraham went out to smoke. The gunshot echoed in his head and drowned out everything, and it was also impossible to erase the images. Mazal Bengtson's distorted face in the interrogation room when she broke. The empty apartment that he wandered around in without looking for a thing. The sight of the street from the roof and the sense that Bengtson had stood there before him and noticed the police car and the trap they had set for him. And David Ezra crouched down on his knees in the widening puddle of blood.

When Vahaba returned to the station from the hospital before morning, Avraham saw in her face not just the exhaustion but the sadness as well. When he returned to Saban's office he found them watching the video of the suicide and of the interrogation that preceded it. Vahaba stroked Mazal Bengtson's head on the screen as she said,

You have to know him to understand. I simply didn't want to go back to it. I didn't want to tell him. I just wanted to forget it all.

And he insisted?

Avraham was unable to watch it. Ma'alul suggested that they stop the video, but Saban insisted that they continue watching.

Why did he want to know, Mali?

I don't know.

You didn't ask him?

It was hard for him not to have a job, and he couldn't find anything. He was ashamed that he wasn't supporting the family and that only I was working.

But how are they connected to each other?

Avraham got up from his seat, but before he left he heard Saban asking Vahaba if she understood what Bengtson was explaining to her, and Vahaba answered that she thought so.

"Because I don't understand," Saban said, "Do you think that it turned him on? That that's what it was about? That it turned him on sexually to talk to these women?" And Vahaba said no. She spent the night with Mazal Bengtson outside the operating room where the doctors fought for her husband's life, and Mazal Bengtson insisted that if Kobi had found work he wouldn't have done what he did. When her husband died she just repeated, "I murdered him," and Vahaba tried to convince her that she had no way of knowing or preventing what had happened. Other than Vahaba there was only Bengtson's twin sister who had arrived at the hospital in the evening and remained.

When Avraham left the room, he heard Saban saying, "Her explanation seems like nonsense to me, Esty. I'm sure it was also a matter of sexual stimulation," and his words blended with Mazal Bengtson's voice when she said to Esty Vahaba, *You don't know Kobi; he wasn't supposed to be like that. He wanted to be other things.*

He remained in the station until the afternoon, even though he had nothing to do there and despite the exhaustion. Leah Yeger's picture lay on his desk before him, as if the case weren't closed, and next to it materials from the investigation arranged in order and the paper with the questions he wrote by hand and planned to ask Bengtson. *Can you tell me what happened when you arrived at Leah Yeger's apartment last Monday?* He had to move on to other cases, one of those that he had neglected since his first murder investigation was opened. After all, the killer had been caught and shot himself, and there were no more questions to ask. In the late morning hours an article was even published on the news sites about the fact that the criminal who shot himself the day before at the Holon police station was Leah Yeger's killer. There were no names in the article because the court had only partially removed the gag order. And for some reason it was written that the killer's cell phone was found in a search that the detective team conducted in the apartment where he resided, and that the voice file in which Yeger was recorded minutes before her death was successfully restored by the Advanced Computing Unit of the Israeli police, even though the killer had erased it from the device.

When Avraham went to Jaffa he discovered that most of the streets in Holon's city center were blocked off because of the Purim carnival and remembered the costume he saw on the couch in the living room of the empty apartment. He sat in a traffic jam for more than a quarter of an hour while the open trucks with clowns and princesses and soldiers passed by him on the main street. A boy, age five or six, wearing a black Batman outfit and a mask, stood by Avraham's car window with his mother and little sister and didn't stop crying. And when he reached Abu Kabir detention center they told him that Shrapstein had already released Leah Yeger's son from custody, so there was no point in him coming.

On the way home, from the car, he called Erez Yeger. He apologized for the fact that he had been arrested during the investigation but he actually wanted to say something else to him, perhaps that his mother was a brave woman, and that he, too, would carry these days inside himself for a long time, like a fracture that sometimes, with the passing of the seasons, aches faintly. He spoke with almost no one that day, until everything burst from him in the evening with Marianka, but the conversation with Erez Yeger he actually tried to prolong, even though the son, too, like him, mainly kept quiet. Before they hung up Avraham asked him, without planning to, "Are you still not ready to tell me why you hid from us that you were adopted and the call with your mother?

That could have spared you the days in custody." Erez Yeger didn't answer.

There was no reason to continue asking, because the investigation was over. Yeger was in his car on the way to the north and Avraham, too, needed to return to his apartment, to take off the clothes he hadn't removed since yesterday and shower, and then sink into sleep and not think anymore.

"You're also not ready to explain why you weren't in touch with her ever since she was assaulted?" he nevertheless asked and wasn't hoping for an answer, and then of all times he heard Erez Yeger say, "Because she had relations with him before."

"With whom?"

"With David Danon, the so-called rapist."

Avraham stopped his car on the side of the road because he was stunned by the answer. He turned off the engine.

"He didn't rape her. They had an affair even before my father died."

But this wasn't true! And the police investigation proved it. This was the rapist and his relatives' line of the defense, and her son believed them and not her. And even if it were true, on the day he came to her to talk about the taxi, David Danon raped Leah Yeger.

Avraham was silent and Yeger was as well, and only then Avraham understood. He felt the beating of his heart quicken and removed the pack of cigarettes from his pants pocket and lit a cigarette in the car and added, "She called in order to ask you to come to her, right?" This is what Yeger hid and wasn't ready to say in the interrogation room even at the price of being arrested. He didn't hide from them that he was in her apartment on the day when the murder occurred, as Shrapstein had thought, but rather that *he could have been there because his mother asked him to come and he didn't*. Had she wanted her son to be present at the meeting she set up with the policeman so he'd believe her? He asked him again, "She asked you to come to her, Erez?" And Yeger immediately said, "That's not correct," and then added, "She didn't say anything to me about a meeting with a policeman, I swear to you," but Avraham didn't believe him. And he didn't say to Yeger the things he planned to tell him about his mother's bravery.

Only in the evening, in a conversation with Marianka, everything that he hadn't yet said to anyone and that had seethed in him since the shot was heard, burst forth.

Marianka wasn't in the apartment when he returned, and this relieved him. He took off his pants and blue sweater and put them in the full laundry basket. He stood a long time under the flow of hot water. When he woke up from his sleep, there was darkness in the window and Marianka was home, but she didn't ask him a thing, and when Avraham suggested that they go eat out, she got dressed and waited in the living room until he finished drinking coffee. They went to Tel Aviv, but there were girls and boys dressed up in the streets, and the restaurants were decorated with colorful lights for Purim dinners, and since they hadn't reserved a place, there wasn't an available table for them anywhere and that was just as well. So they returned to Holon and sat in a café in Weitzman Square. The pasta with cream sauce was the first thing Avraham had put in his mouth since yesterday, and he ate it quickly.

"Can you tell me what happened finally?" Marianka asked him when he finished, and he answered, "Tell you what?"

"Why you feel so bad. So guilty. You caught the killer, no?"

He looked at her, surprised, because he hadn't told her he felt that. From time to time the explosions of firecrackers could be heard in the square, and revelers in costume on their way to parties passed by the window. And he told her everything. How he behaved harshly with Mazal Bengtson in the interrogation room and how he hid the real news about her husband from her. He didn't say a word to her even when she offered to phone and invite him to the station, and in fact used her in order to lay a trap for her husband. And even though he tried since to blur his guilt in his thinking, it deepened like the stain on the blue sweater. He reminded himself over and over that Mazal Bengtson told Vahaba in her questioning that her husband wanted to be caught because he couldn't suffer anymore and that he didn't even erase the incriminating file from his cell phone. Yaakov Bengtson watched the squad car parked in front of his building from the roof of his apartment, of this Avraham was almost certain, and nevertheless he decided to go to the police station. And since he watched Mazal Bengtson's interrogation another time this morning, Avraham hadn't stopped thinking about something else: the fact that the man who raped Mazal Bengtson put his hand on her neck and then placed the knife up against it and cut her—and that Yaakov Bengtson had shot his neck as well.

Marianka interrupted him. "So what are you guilty of, Avi?" she asked. "He alone decided to shoot himself, no? Apparently because he preferred not to deal with the consequences of what he did. And you just did your job. You're a cop."

Did she not understand that it wasn't supposed to end like this?

This was his first murder investigation, and it ended with a man shooting himself in the entrance to the station and dying in the hospital while his wife was certain that it's her fault he died. He only wanted to sit across from Bengtson in the interrogation room on the second floor of the station and try to understand.

Marianka didn't touch the salad that the waitress set down before her. And didn't drink the wine.

"But you're taking responsibility for things that you didn't do," she said. "You caught him, you didn't—" But Avraham didn't allow her to finish the sentence, because the things she said were so wrong. Other than them there was only an older couple and two waitresses in the café, one of whom looked at Avraham when he raised his voice. "If I had revealed to her that her husband was suspected of murder, she wouldn't have turned him in, Marianka," he said. "Or she wouldn't have brought him to the station. Don't you understand? Do you not understand why he shot himself? He was sure that his wife turned him in, that he was betrayed by her, that he was left with nobody else in the world to trust, but *she didn't turn him in* because she didn't know what he was suspected of. And even if he had committed suicide regardless, when he understood he was caught, at least it wouldn't have been *because of her*. Do you know what she said? That she killed him. That it was her fault he died."

This was the thing that hadn't let go of Avraham since yesterday and that bothered no one other than him. Not the district commander and not Benny Saban and not even Eliyahu Ma'alul. And Marianka wasn't convinced, either. She asked, "Why are you certain that she didn't know what her husband really did?" And Avraham looked at her without understanding and said, "What do you mean why? Because we didn't reveal it to her. Because *I* didn't reveal to her that he was suspected of murder."

"And it can't be that she understood this, even though you didn't reveal it to her? And that she turned him in precisely because of this?"

Avraham shook his head, and Marianka insisted, and only afterward he understood why. She was actually talking about herself and about him. And only when she told him this explicitly, did he think that perhaps she was right and feel that he had to question Mazal Bengtson immediately and try to clarify what she truly understood about what her husband had done when she entered the station to turn him in. But he didn't do this. In the weeks to come, after he heard from Vahaba that Mazal Bengtson left her parents' home and returned to her apartment, he traveled to her street a few times and waited in front of the building in his car, with the window closed. Maybe if she had noticed him and approached, maybe he would have asked her, even though Marianka and Esty Vahaba pleaded with him not to.

Marianka said, "You really think that you, who didn't know him, who never once spoke to him, you knew that he's a murderer, and that his wife, who lived with him and who definitely saw him on the day he carried out the murder and the next day, and who went through with him what she told you she went through, it didn't even occur to her? She didn't see what he was going through and didn't see his gun or know that he would kill himself?" It was as if that gunshot could be heard again in his office. Marianka's eyes burned as she spoke, and Avraham was no longer convinced, even though he said, "I'm sure you're wrong. Why would she bring him to the station for us, if it was like that? If she knew that she was pinning a murder on him. She thought he carried out a misdemeanor and that he would be questioned and released within a few hours. And that they'd return home together. She told us this explicitly."

"You're truly asking why?" Marianka asked.

"Yes. Why would she do this?"

"Maybe because she wanted it to be over. For the nightmare of their lives together to be over."

When they returned home Avraham called Esty Vahaba and it seemed to him that he woke her from her sleep. He asked her if she knows where Mazal Bengtson is, and she said to him that she's with her parents. He still wasn't sure that Marianka was right and understood that her words appealed to him, since if they were right it would be easier for him to clean the stain that clung to the blue sweater, but this wasn't the only reason he believed that perhaps Marianka wasn't wrong.

The man who assaulted Mazal Bengtson wasn't caught, he thought, and perhaps she couldn't bear the possibility that another assailant would escape without punishment. That another woman would be, like her, a victim of an assailant who would never be found. For a moment he thought to himself that the case wasn't closed and that he had more to understand, and later that week he wanted to go to the shiva held at Mazal Bengtson's parents' home or to the funeral that took place at the civil cemetery in Herzliya, because Bengtson refused to have her husband buried in the plot reserved for people who had killed themselves. Vahaba told him that at the funeral there were no more than twenty people, and that Bengtson's father didn't come from Australia because of his health condition. The girls Avraham saw in the apartment weren't brought to the cemetery, either, and Vahaba didn't know what Mazal Bengtson had told them.

When the waitress approached their table and informed them that the café was closing, Avraham took out his wallet, but Marianka asked, "Can you sit for another moment?" and he set it down on the table.

"I want to tell you something about us," she said and he listened, even though at the beginning of what she said he thought only about Bengtson. "I know that you were busy and that you were stressed and that my parents' visit was hard for you, but you're doing exactly the same thing with me. Exactly the same thing."

He didn't understand what she meant and waited.

"Like what you're doing with the woman you questioned, Avi. You take responsibility for my decisions as if I'm a girl, and blame yourself and don't believe that I understand very well what I'm doing and that I'm making decisions for myself."

He looked at her as if he hadn't seen her for a long time. And tried to place his hand on her hand but she wouldn't let him.

"From the moment I came here you feel guilty that I'm here, as if I didn't decide to come to you. And then you close yourself off and withdraw and hide from me everything tied to your work, because you're guilty of the fact that I left everything and came to you and you have a job and I don't yet know what to do with myself."

He said that wasn't right, and Marianka continued anyway.

"But I'm here because I want to be here for now. This was my decision. This is a chapter in *my life*, Avi, not just in yours. And you didn't force me to do anything. I know how to decide for myself what's good for me, do you understand?"

The things that Ilana Lis said to him at their meeting rose up in his memory, and he tried to forget them.

"I brought myself here, Avi, and if it won't be good for me, I won't stay. And maybe that's what's hard for you to accept and that's what you try to cover up when it seems to you that everything is your fault and your responsibility."

When he asked, "So it's not hard for you here?" he felt how much he had wanted to ask her this before then, on each day that had passed since she came, not only since the investigation opened. She said to him, "Yes it's hard for me. Clearly it's hard for me. It's hard because I'm a stranger here and don't know the language and because I miss things, but it's mainly hard with you. It's hard for me that you're quiet and hide what you're going through from me. And that you need to close the door and hide from me in order to eat. And that you started smoking again and didn't tell me. I didn't come here in order to live alone, but instead in order to try to live together with you."

Her two hands were on the table, and when he placed his hands on them this time she didn't pull them away. He didn't understand how she knew that he started smoking again, and Marianka said, "You don't need to be a detective for that, Avi. There wasn't just a bloodstain on your sweater."

Avraham asked her, "So if it gets too hard for you, will you really leave?" and she said, "Probably. Even though I don't know to where."

"Can I join you?"

"If you're not in the middle of an investigation."

Outside the café the chairs were already stacked up in a pile, but Avraham wasn't yet ready to leave. Marianka suggested that they smoke a cigarette in the square.

"It's true that I don't want to think that I'm a chapter

in your life," he said to her when they sat on a bench, and Marianka asked him, "Why? What's so bad about that?"

"Because I want to be the whole book. Until the happy ending. Or until the bitter end."

"And you might be. But that's what's beautiful about books, no? That you can't know in advance how they'll end."

"In a detective novel you actually always know," he said.

The guilty one is caught. The innocent continue on with their lives.

"But our lives aren't a detective novel, Avi," she told him. "And besides, you explained to me that it's always possible to prove that the detective is wrong, so maybe even a detective novel doesn't really end. Do you remember you told me that the day we met? On our first walk together in Brussels? Would you have believed it if I said to you that a year later we'd be living together?"

He recalled this conversation at the café the last time that he waited in front of the building where Mazal and Yaakov Bengtson lived, a few weeks later, on the last day of March.

He saw Mazal Bengtson a few times before then, mainly when she went out alone to run in the evening, but he didn't dare approach and didn't know exactly what to ask. That same day Esty Vahaba told him that Bengtson returned to work and asked her father to vacate the apartment and leave her alone with the girls, and Avraham thought that this would be a chance to go up to her and knock on the door without any advance notice. He parked his car and remained in front of the building almost half an hour, and as he had done a few times in the weeks that had passed, he took advantage of the time in order to call Ilana Lis, and this time someone actually answered. But it was her husband who answered the phone instead of her and informed him that Ilana wouldn't be able to talk soon, and when he asked Avraham if he wanted to leave a message, he said it wasn't necessary.

The time was six o'clock and evening hadn't yet fallen because the days were getting longer.

And it was only when he turned on the car and intended to drive off that he saw her. Mazal Bengtson exited the stairwell with the two girls and crossed the street with them, not very far from him. One of the girls held the leash of the white dog that he saw back then in the apartment. Did they notice him? And was he wrong when it seemed to him that her stomach curved out under the short shirt that she wore? He turned off the car and then remembered the things that Marianka said to him in the café, and waited for them to walk away before turning it on and leaving.

His thoughts and imagination were occupied by cases that he neglected during the murder investigation and cases that had been opened since then, but the picture of Leah Yeger was still on his desk, among them, for a few more days in April, and the heavy blue coat that he wore on the day when the investigation opened and on the morning when he greeted Mazal Bengtson at the station remained on the door, unused, because the storm was a receding memory, and spring flooded his office with light.

Epilogue

After he fell asleep she left the bedroom and went to the study to call her parents. She hoped that her mother would answer, but when she heard her father's voice she was glad. For a few seconds they were silent, and then Marianka said to him, "I called in order to apologize. That we said good-bye like that." And he said, "That's okay. We forgive you. And we tried calling you a few times since then." When she asked him if she woke him up and he said no, she suddenly felt how much she missed listening to herself speak their language, her language, and how life in English draws strange words out of her mouth.

"I'm sorry if we were——" he said, and she cut him off and said to him, "Yes. I know. You were."

There was in her a flood of love and anger and longing that had been stopped up in the last days that passed wordlessly, and the conversation with Avi in the café freed her up all at once. She didn't know what her father was able to hear of all this in her voice, because he was never able to hear anything. He said, "But I truly don't understand what's keeping you there, Marianka. He—" and Marianka again interrupted his words and said, "Nothing's keeping me here. And if something's keeping me it's not him. And what do you know about him? Did you try to get to know him when you were here? From the first moment that you heard about him you were frightened that he would take me from you, like you were always afraid when I met someone."

She spoke much too loudly, but Avi was sound asleep. He fell asleep immediately after getting into bed, and she could still hear his deep breaths that as the night progressed would turn into snoring. Her father was silent and this made her happy because it meant he was listening, but also saddened her because she hoped they would talk some more. She apologized for interrupting, and he said that they're thinking about what's best for her, and he didn't even once say that he simply misses her. When he asked if the murder investigation had ended and she said yes, her father said, "So perhaps now you two will come to visit us?" And when she went out to the street afterward she thought about the two of them in Brussels, walking in the snow that perhaps would fall, because there the winter wasn't over. She sat for a moment or two opposite the computer in the study, considered writing an e-mail, or something else, a letter to Avi perhaps, or even a detective story, why not, but she was too worked up to write, and for the first time since arriving she went out alone at night as she had done when she was a girl in Koper and afterward in Brussels.

The blast of cold that she was expecting when she

went out to the street didn't come. The dry, dusty air cast a strange foreignness upon her. The streets of Holon were empty and most of the buildings dark, and Marianka didn't in fact know where she was going. Nor if all this wasn't a mistake—or the start of an adventure.

ABOUT THE AUTHOR

D. A. Mishani is an Israeli crime writer, translator, and literary scholar who specializes in the history of detective fiction. His detective series featuring police inspector Avraham Avraham was first published in Hebrew in 2011 and has been translated into fifteen languages. The first novel in the series, *The Missing File*, was short-listed for the 2013 CWA International Dagger Award, and won the Martin Beck Award for the best-translated crime novel and the Grand Prix de Littérature Policière. His second novel, *A Possibility of Violence*, won the prestigious Bernstein Award for best Hebrew novel.

He lives with his wife and two children in Tel Aviv.

BOOKS BY D. A. MISHANI

THE MISSING FILE
A Novel

Available in Paperback and E-book

In the first volume in D. A. Mishani's literary crime series, Israeli detective Avraham Avraham must find a teenage boy gone missing from the suburbs of Tel Aviv.

"Combines the procedural and the puzzle with artful misdirection." —*Publishers Weekly* (starred review)

A POSSIBILITY OF VIOLENCE
A Novel

Available in Paperback and E-book

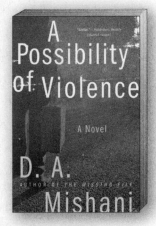

Haunted by the past and his own limitations, Detective Avraham Avraham must stop a ruthless crimingal in this evocative and gripping tale.

"The freshness of Mr. Mishani's novel comes from its striking locale, and the way the story is told through alternating points of view." —*Wall Street Journal*

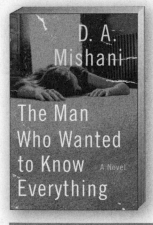

THE MAN WHO WANTED TO KNOW EVERYTHING
A Novel

Available in Paperback and E-book

Inspector Avraham Avraham is back in this chilling investigation of the secrets, family, and what happens when the people you love may not be who you think.

"Mishani writes with profound originality."
—Henning Mankell, author of the Wallander series

HARPER